# Whiskey Jug Genie

Sultonna Nadine

Published by Mellie Miller, 2023.

This is a work of fiction. Similarities to real people, places, or events are entirely coincidental.

WHISKEY JUG GENIE

**First edition. November 30, 2023.**

Copyright © 2023 Sultonna Nadine.

ISBN: 979-8223931225

Written by Sultonna Nadine.

# Also by Sultonna Nadine

Moonlight and Shadows
Whiskey Jug Genie

Watch for more at https://sultonnanadine.com.

# Table of Contents

A special thanks to my husband, Steve, for the original idea of a genie in a whiskey jug. This story has been so very much fun to write.

Also a big thanks to our daughter, Dawn, who helps keep me sane, as well as helping with proofreading.

And as always, a big thanks to my readers, who make all of this worthwhile.

Enjoy!

# Whiskey Jug Genie

# Chapter 1

Martin Pritchard settled back into the business class seat, champagne in hand, as the flight out of Atlanta got ready to take off for London. It had been a pleasant holiday trip, but he would be glad to get back home. He had never been to the Southeast part of the United States before, so he'd indulged in a three week autumn holiday to tour Georgia and the Carolinas.

The scenic drive across Georgia brought him to the sultry city of Savannah. The idyllic islands of St. Simon's and Jekyll Islands were a nice rest before he turned north toward Myrtle Beach in South Carolina and on up to historic Kitty Hawk.

Taking secondary roads inland, he stopped here and there at second-hand shops, looking for something unique for his herbalist shop back home. All he'd found were a few souvenirs, until he came to an old junk shop in a little country town on his way back to Atlanta. According to what he'd read, pottery had been quite the thing around this part of the state decades ago, and was still fired today in the area. In a dark corner, along the back wall, under a dusty display of old crockery, he found the perfect item.

A little over a foot tall, the jug was a dark cocoa brown, with one handle, and stopped with a rag-wrapped corn cob. Covered with who knew how many years of dust and grime, once cleaned it would be a perfect addition to his eclectic collection of old bottles and equipment.

"No, sir," the proprietor answered when he asked about it. "I have no idea exactly how old it is. It was here when I bought the shop twenty years ago. Nobody ever showed any particular interest in it, so I never bothered to check it out."

It didn't matter. Martin was determined to buy the jug and the man was only too happy to let it go for little more than a song. Back at his hotel, with an almost drinkable beer in hand, Martin set about identifying the piece of crockery which had caught his eye.

The dark brown, salt glazed pottery had been around in the USA from the 18th century through the early 20th century. The jugs had been famous for holding moonshine liquor, in an assortment of sizes. The one he'd purchased was one of the larger ones and worth much more than he'd paid for it. The shop owner must simply have been glad to free up the space the thing occupied.

Rather than risk breaking it on the flight home, a local shipping firm, packaged it for him for it's journey to England. With any luck, it should arrive a few days after he did. He'd gladly paid the extra for some insurance. Not that he expected to need it, but why take the chance?

After a nice meal and an after dinner drink, Martin dozed until the flight attendant woke him before touch down. Relieved to be home once again, and excited about his new purchase, he got through customs as quickly as possible, claimed his car from the car park, and made his way through the countryside to his shop and apartment.

His little apothecary shop wasn't on the high street, but it wasn't horribly situated. With the trend toward natural remedies, he had a growing clientele. After four years of study, plus the time to get his masters degree, and two more years of residency with an established herbalist, he wanted to get ahead enough to buy a separate dwelling, rather than live above his shop.

Yes, it was convenient, but somehow he never felt like he'd left work. And it was inconvenient for people coming to him for his other services, having to push through the shop and up the stairs to consult with him. While consulting psychics were becoming more accepted, he didn't want to scare away his apothecary clients when the others came in asking for a psychic.

Along with his psychic abilities, he had a few other talents he kept under wraps. Almost no one understood about remote-viewing, but it did help him when trying to locate a missing person. A little white magic helped also, and let him set up wards to keep his premises safe from intruders. What they didn't know wouldn't hurt them, or him either. As long as his clients were happy with the results, did it matter how he got there in the end?

Ah, well. Home and safe at last, he retrieved his cat, Joker, from the neighbor who'd seen after him during his absence, and went up to his apartment to see if there was anything he could fix for dinner.

Tomorrow he would definitely need to go grocery shopping, but he was fed, as was Joker, now curled up on his chest and purring loudly. Martin had rescued the creature from a downpour a few years ago, when he'd still been a kitten. Hunched up on his doorstep, yowling, he'd been a pitiful sight. Someone must have adopted him from a shelter, as he'd been altered when he'd found him. Though Martin asked around so he could return him to his owner, no one had come forward, so he'd accepted him as part of his household.

Now weighing in at over two stone, the huge feline had become a fixture around the place. With shaggy tabby fur and white feet and belly, there was no fat on Joker. The vet said he was probably a Maine Coon mix. Mostly good tempered, he tolerated the attention he drew from Martin's customers as they waited for their remedies. Perched on top of the counter like a furry gargoyle, amidst Martin's antique bottles and pharmacy equipment, he watched over his domain when he wasn't napping.

While the shop was like a vignette from the past, furnished in dark wood, with old glass bottles, scales with individual weights for measuring medicines, and old tweezers and tongs decorating the shelves, Martin's apartment was quite modern, nearly minimalist. Shining glass and chrome tables sat on cream carpet next to black leather furniture.

Somehow, Joker had not been inclined to shred the furniture, only the tall post Martin had bought for him. They'd reached an understanding early on about claws and furnishings. While Joker occasionally looked longingly at the soft leather, he would turn away and tear a small mound of sawdust off the pole before curling up on his cushion.

What would he make of the new jug? Fortunately, Martin thought it was too heavy for him to push over easily. Maybe he should fill it with something before he put it on display so it would be more difficult to shift. He could hardly wait for it to arrive. There was something about it that called to him, as if it needed him as much as he wanted it.

Ridiculous. It was just a jug. A unique one in this day and age, but just a jug. Perhaps it would make a nice conversation piece. He would print up a card with information about it for people to read while he counted out capsules, or added drops of tincture to a bottle of purified water.

Though it would be several days before the jug arrived in London, he was anxious to have it in his possession. Perhaps it was the mystery of it. Who had crafted it? What had been stored in it? How did it come to be in the little shop where he'd found it? He doubted he'd ever have the answers to any of those questions, but he could speculate.

Finally, five days after he'd returned, the jug was delivered. Hauling the box into the back of the shop, he opened it up and checked the contents. Nestled there in all the packaging, the old jug was in perfect condition, and still covered in decades of dust.

With a sigh of relief, and half the afternoon ahead of him, he gave the jug a reassuring pat and went back around to serve a customer at the sales counter.

"Hello, Diane," he greeted the young blond with wide blue eyes. "How are you this fine day?"

They'd dated a few times, and he hoped a stronger relationship developed.

"Not bad at all, Martin," she answered, batting her long lashes at him.

"How can I help you?"

"I need some more of those sore throat lozenges. They work fantastically, but I've run out."

"Have you seen your doctor? If you keep having the same problem, you should have it checked out."

"I think a lot of it has to do with cleaning in the attic. I went up there to look for an old book and decided it was time to get organized. All the dust makes me cough and sneeze. And then I get a sore throat."

"All the same, it could be something more serious. Have you considered wearing a dust mask?"

"No, I hadn't. I suppose it's worth a try."

"If it doesn't stop once you've finished cleaning, make that appointment."

Reaching into the cabinet beneath the counter, he brought out the lozenges she'd asked for. After accepting her payment, he asked if she would be free Friday evening.

"I am, as a matter of fact. What did you have in mind?"

"I have a nice bottle of wine and some nibbles. Perhaps we could have an evening in."

"Sounds lovely. Can I bring anything?" she asked.

"If there's anything in particular you'd like, feel free."

"Did your jug ever get here?" she asked.

"This afternoon. I'll get it cleaned up and put it out for display in a day or two."

Finally, Martin locked the door, pulled down the blinds, and went back to get the jug from the store room. Hauling it up the stairs, he set it in the tub, grabbed a cleaning rag, and set to work scrubbing it. Not wanting to get water down into it, he left the cob and rag in the neck. Later he would see if he could get it out for a look inside.

It took a while to get the thing clean, with who knew how many decades of dust and grime on it. Satisfied with his work, he hauled it out onto the bathroom rug to dry it off before taking it into the living room. With a glass of wine in hand, and the jug on the coffee table, he sat back and admired his purchase.

"What all have you seen?" he mused, sipping his wine.

Hearing his stomach growl, Martin left his latest souvenir on the table and fixed some pasta for dinner. Musing over the jug kept his mind engaged while he ate. He would have to do a little more research on it to display it properly. Surely there would be enough information online to do the job.

With a glass of after dinner Scotch in hand, he moved back to the couch and stretched out.

No, this would never do. He had to take a peek inside. Setting the Scotch on the end table, he perched on the edge of his seat, got a firm grip on the handle of the jug, and began to twist the homemade stopper in an attempt to remove it from the neck.

Just about the time he was ready to admit defeat, the corn cob popped out as if it had been pushed from underneath. And as it did, a plume of purplish-gray smoke, or fog, began to boil from the interior. Hurriedly reaching for the corn cob to re-plug the jug, he knocked it onto the floor, where it rolled to the far side of the coffee table, and out of reach. Joker bolted out of the room all fluffed out and hissing.

Diving onto the floor, Martin managed to grab the stopper and regain his seat, but the damage was already done. The smoke had finished pouring out of the jug and hovered in the air near the ceiling, But as he watched it coalesced into a figure, which settled onto the floor across the room, before becoming a solid individual a few seconds before the smell reached him, nearly knocking him over.

What the hell was going on?

# Chapter 2

E yes watering and trying to hold his breath, Martin finally got the front windows and the back door opened to let the stench out of his dwelling.

"Whew-wee!" he heard from the figure before him. "That was a good one. Been holding it for a long time."

"What the hell are you?" he demanded.

The figure looked him over for a moment and then answered him with the strongest southern accent he'd ever heard.

"You can call me Bubba," it said.

"I didn't ask *who* you were. I asked *what* you were," Martin demanded again.

The figure was about as tall as he was, around six feet, with dark curly hair, dark eyes, and a crooked smile.

"Don't get your panties in a wad. I am a djinn."

"Gin? I'm a Scotch man myself."

"No, djinn."

"Yeah, gin. I've got it."

"Were you born slow, son? D-j-i-n-n. Djinn."

"A genie? I thought you guys lived in bottles. Not whiskey jugs."

"I prefer djinn. Not genie. No, we usually live peacefully in dwellings around an oasis, places like that. But we sometimes get trapped in things like bottles or jugs. And I'll be tellin' ya, it ain't pleasant."

"Why are you here?" Martin asked, reaching for his Scotch.

"You bought my jug."

"But if you're free of the jug, why are you still here?"

All he needed was a magical roommate. Now how did he get rid of this guy—Bubba? What sort of name was Bubba?

"That's where the curse comes in. Unless you can take off the curse, I'm bound to this dad-blamed thing forever. I don't suppose you're a wizard?"

"I dabble in white magic, but curses? Don't know a thing about reversing them."

"It figures. Somebody finally comes along, buys the damned jug, but can't help a fella out. Story of my life. What have you got to eat around here?"

"What have you been eating?" Martin asked, since he seemed to have been eating more than well enough.

"Anything I could manage to conjure into the damned jug."

"How about a bath first?" Martin asked.

His nose had stopped up shortly after the smoke had come out of the jug. And the man's—djinn's—clothes were something else. Bib overalls, over a hairy chest, and bare feet. No shirt at all. Just the overalls. He didn't even want to know if he had anything else on under them.

"You some kind of clean freak?" Bubba demanded.

"You could say that. And I'll get you something else to put on. Those things are ready for the bin."

"My overalls? No, siree. I ain't partin' with those."

"You are until they've been laundered, at least. Look, I run a shop downstairs. You can't go around looking like that. We've got to get you cleaned up."

"All right, all right. You got a wash tub somewhere?"

Getting him into the tub, and telling him to take his time, Martin called a shop down the street which stayed open a little later and asked if they had any large jogging pants and some T-shirts. Making a quick trip, he got there and back before Bubba had finished bathing and laid the clothing out for him.

"Bubba," he called through the bathroom door. "I've put some clothes out in the spare room for you. They should work for tonight."

"Thank you kindly," he answered. "I'll be done in a minute or three."

"I'll find something for you to eat in the meantime."

What did one do with a genie? Martin had heard of them here and there, but mainly in jest. He'd had no idea they actually existed. Was he now the master of this creature, since he owned the jug to which it was bound?

8

For now, they needed some ground rules. While he warmed up some frozen pizza, he tried to decide on where to start. One thing he knew for sure. The jug wasn't going out front just yet, not until he had a little more information on djinn and their bottles.

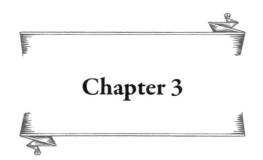

# Chapter 3

**B**ubba came out wearing the new clothes and breathed in the aroma of the pizza.

"Whatever that is, I'll have some of it."

"It's called pizza, and you can have all of it. I've already eaten," Martin told the genie—djinn—standing in front of him.

"You wouldn't kid a fella would you?"

"Not right now. Go on. Dig in."

Watching Bubba eat the pizza was educational. As he'd apparently never eaten pizza before, he was at first hesitant. But one taste cured that. The rest of the medium pizza disappeared as if by magic, except for the leftover sauce around his mouth.

"How about something to drink?" Martin asked.

"Now that would hit the spot, for sure."

Thinking before he grabbed anything alcoholic, he poured a large glass of filtered water from the pitcher and handed it to his new roommate. He could almost see the spiral swirl in the glass as Bubba drained the liquid.

"Got anything a little stronger?"

"Are you sure you're ready for it?" Martin asked.

"I've been stuck in that damned jar for a couple centuries. I am definitely ready."

"Ever had single malt scotch?"

"Can't say I have."

"You're in for a treat," Martin told him, mentally making a note to buy something a little cheaper the next day.

Bringing the drinks into the living room, he handed one small glass to Bubba.

"Now it can have a bite, so take it easy at first."

Tipping up his glass, Martin sipped at the smokey tasting liquid and watched Bubba. Cautiously sniffing the liquid in the glass first, Bubba carefully took a sip of the whiskey. A violent coughing fit ensued, but no Scotch was spilled.

"Boy howdy! That is a little stronger than I expected. Of course, it has been a while."

"What did you drink, before you were trapped in the jug?" Martin asked.

"Mostly moonshine. We didn't have anything fancy where I was at the time."

"Moonshine. Is that like home-made liquor?"

"Yeah, son. Where have you been all your life?"

"In England. Where else?"

"What were you doin' over there?"

"Bubba, maybe you should take a breath and have a little more Scotch."

Bubba sat uneasily in an armchair across from him, held his glass up for more Scotch, and took a good sized drink.

"Ready, son."

"The fact is, Bubba, we're in England."

"What?"

"We're—you're—in England, not far from London. We're in my homeland now."

"Well, son of a gun. What am I supposed to do in England?"

"That is something we'll have to figure out. Tomorrow. I had no idea there was anything, or anyone, in this jug when I bought it, so this is all rather sudden. I need a good night's sleep before I try to get this sorted. And we need some ground rules if you're going to stay here."

"What kind of rules? I'd rather not go back in the jug for a bit," Bubba said, eyeing him suspiciously.

"I can understand your concern there. No, not back into the jug. For tonight, I have a guest room you can use. Tomorrow, after work, we'll see what we can do. Fair enough?"

"Fair enough, for now," Bubba agreed.

# Chapter 4

M artin got Bubba settled into the guest room, with instructions to stay upstairs until they had their talk. All he needed was this hick from the southern states of America wandering around his shop spouting nonsense.

Sleep was rather hit and miss during the night, with his dreams invaded by magical beings playing pranks on him. So when he got up, he made coffee instead of his usual morning tea. It was going to be one of those days.

"Morning, son," he heard before he spewed coffee all over his kitchen.

"Whoa! Hold on there. Didn't mean to startle you," Bubba told him, slapping him on the back.

"Right. I should have been expecting you. Help yourself to some coffee, if you drink it. Or I have tea," Martin finally managed.

"Thanks. I'll just grab a cup."

The genie strolled across the kitchen, snagged a cup off the cup holder and poured a cup of the dark brew.

"Do you have anything for breakfast?" Bubba asked him.

"Yeah, in a minute. I've got to wake up first."

"I slept great last night. First time I've had room to stretch out in a long time," the genie told him, stretching his arms overhead.

"While we have coffee, maybe we could get acquainted a little."

"Whatever you say, boss."

"I run a little apothecary downstairs, and my clientele is rather, shall we say, up market. I'm not sure how they would react to you and your ways just now."

"So you want me to keep out of the shop. I can do that."

"Once you kind of get settled in and we get you a few sets of clothes, maybe you can learn to help me out down there or something."

"I guess my other clothes are pretty ragged. I've been wearin' em for a while now."

"And as long as you've been in that jug, you probably need to catch up on life in the world these days. Maybe you could watch some news on the telly today and sort of get up to speed."

"Telly? Is that some newfangled kind of machine or something?"

"Something like that. But it will give you a little information about where we live, what's been going on since you were trapped in your jug, and that sort of thing. And it'll give you something to do while I work."

"Maybe I can get some ideas on what you want me to wear."

"I'm sure you can. I think I can manage breakfast now. Eggs, muffins, and juice all right?" Martin asked.

"Anything will be fine for now."

Bubba sat on a kitchen stool and watched as Martin fried some eggs, warmed the muffins, and got the juice out of the refrigerator.

"Is that some sort of ice box?" Bubba asked.

"It's called a refrigerator, or fridge for short," Martin explained.

"Where do you put the ice in?"

"It doesn't actually use ice," Martin answered patiently. After all, the guy must have been in a jug for a long time. He had a lot to take in.

"How does it stay cold? Is it some sort of spell?"

"No spell, but the explanation would take longer than we have this morning. You'll get used to it."

His guest nearly inhaled his breakfast, while Martin took his time. He had a lot to take in, too. What exactly were the rules regarding genies?

After rinsing the dishes and drinking more coffee, he got Bubba settled in the living room and showed him how to work the telly.

"Has a demon captured all these people and locked them in this box?" Bubba asked skeptically.

"No, but again, the explanation would take longer than I have time for. I would have to explain electronics to you, and I don't have the time. I'm not sure I have the knowledge, either. Just trust me. No demons or magic involved."

"All right, son. If you insist."

"I'll check on you in a bit, see how you're doing. And I'll get something for lunch later."

"I'll be fine. Don't worry yourself over me. As long as I spent in that jug, I'll be enjoying the freedom."

With one last look at the genie watching television, Martin made his way down the stairs to the shop, with Joker bounding down ahead of him. The cat hadn't forgiven Bubba for scaring him half to death yet. With only a quarter of an hour before opening, Martin ran a duster over the counter, dusted the shelves, and got everything ready for his customers.

At least the morning wasn't too busy, and there was nothing out of the ordinary. Just the usual coughs and sore throats from the change in weather, and from the pollen. Autumn had arrived in England and brought with it the usual ills. He'd gone to check on Bubba—that name had to change—several times and found him glued to the telly. At least he wasn't causing any trouble.

Lunch time came and he turned the Open sign to Closed, told Bubba he'd be back in a few minutes, and hurried down the street to an Indian place. What would Bubba like? He had no idea if he could manage the spicy curries Martin preferred, or whether he should try something a little milder.

After dithering about it, he chose a spicy curry for himself and ordered chicken masala for Bubba. Tomorrow they could try Chinese. His stomach protested the wait as he strolled back toward the shop. Juggling the bag of food and his keys, he got the door opened and jogged upstairs to see what awaited him.

Bubba was still watching the telly, which was good. He had hoped his new room mate would stick to the news, but a murder mystery had him fascinated.

"Foods up, Bubba. I hope you like chicken."

"Chicken is fine. Smells kinda spicy."

"I got you something that isn't too hot. Tomorrow we'll try something else, but I eat at this place several times a week."

Bubba dug right in, and while the first couple bites seemed to take him by surprise, he seemed to relish the blend of flavors.

"What do you think?" Martin asked him, polishing off his curry.

"I've never had chicken like that, but it's good. What is that you're eating?"

"Curry. It's pretty spicy and it's not for everyone. I thought I'd start you off on something milder."

"I like a bit of spice. Maybe I'll try that next time."

"I'll keep it in mind. What have you been watching?" Martin asked him.

"I don't rightly know. Some of it seems real, but a lot of it must be pure bull shit," Bubba answered.

"Language! This is an upscale establishment. What seems like nonsense to you?"

"That thing I was watching a minute ago. Unless there is a lot more mischief in the world now, there can't be that many murders in one town."

"You're right. That's just a story told to entertain people. It isn't real. The program I had on when I left was the news. Most of that is real, though I doubt some of that, too. If you have any questions, just ask."

"I have some ideas on clothes I'd like to try out for you. Make sure they'd be suitable for your shop and all."

And suddenly Bubba stood in front of him in casual trousers, a long-sleeved shirt open at the neck and smart leather shoes.

"How did you do that?" Martin asked.

"I am Djinn. I conjured it."

"Isn't that like stealing?"

"Naw. Conjurin' ain't stealin'. You said I needed something else to wear, so I conjured up something like what they had on this magic box of yours."

"The telly isn't magic," Martin explained patiently. "I'll see if one of my friends can explain it to you soon."

"Whatever it is, I used it as a guide. What do you think?"

"Much better," Martin agreed. "Once you get used to things and tone down that accent a little, you might be ready for polite company."

"All right, now. You're pullin' my leg. Polite company? I know how to behave in polite company."

"Maybe, but let me be the judge. Look, I've got to go back to work. Make yourself comfortable, watch the telly, or if you know how to read, I have books around you could look at. And I'll bring up the morning paper," Martin told him.

15

"I can read all right. The newspaper might be a good idea."

Dashing quickly down and returning with the paper, Martin got Bubba settled again and re-opened the shop. How was he going to cope with this being now living in his spare room?

# Chapter 5

What kind of world had he entered? Bubba watched Martin go back down to his shop and dropped onto the sofa to read the newspaper. Honestly, he wasn't sure most of it wasn't bull shit, too. How did people ever sort out the wheat from the chaff? Like that magic box—telly. It all looked so real, how did you know which was which? Even the news seemed suspicious to him.

Martin claimed there was no magic involved anywhere, but Bubba was sure he was fibbing. All the stuff in here, the way it worked? It had to be magic. There was no other explanation.

Not that he could sense any magic around any of it. Of course, there were the protection sigils over Martin's doors, but he'd said he dabbled in white magic. The sigils would make sense for him. Why someone who ran an apothecary would need protective sigils he couldn't fathom, but at least Bubba understood magic.

He didn't understand much else in this world. So much had changed since he went into the jug the last time. Trapped and forgotten, all he'd thought about for years was getting free and having his revenge.

But how could he get revenge on someone so long dead and buried? And as far as he knew, she'd never had any offspring, so he couldn't seek revenge there either. That bitch of a witch had escaped him again. Now, what could he do about this new jug owner? The man seemed all right, but it just didn't set well, being at the beck and call of someone else. Especially someone with such limited powers.

Oh, well. Time to sort that out after he got a handle on what the world was like in this day and time. Back to the news.

When Martin came back upstairs, Bubba was still as confused as ever. People talking to each other over mobile phones. What was a phone? Mobile he understood, but phone? He was still trying to figure out how they got all those people in the telly. And an ice box that took no ice.

And as for the lights... It had to be some form of magic, no matter what Martin said.

"How did you get on today?" Martin asked.

"All right, I guess, but I don't understand this world you live in. Is it this way everywhere, or just in England?"

Bubba explained some of his confusion and Martin simply shook his head.

"No, most of the world is the same as it is here, with telephones, televisions, refrigerators, cars, and a whole host of other things you've never seen. Maybe this weekend we can take a short trip so you can see a little bit of what you've missed."

This brought up another problem. The jug.

"I can't get too far from the jug," he explained.

"Why not?"

"I'm bound to the thing, is why not," Bubba answered tersely.

"Oh. So how far can you go without it?"

"Just about across the street from here," Bubba told him, looking out the window and wishing he'd found a way to deal with the witch before she bound him to the damned jug.

"How about if we took the jug with us? You know, put it in the boot of the car, so it was close enough for you to come with me?"

"What's a car? And why does it wear boots?

"A car is a motorized vehicle we use to go from one place to another. You must have seen them on the telly. And the boot is a storage compartment in the vehicle."

"So that's what those things were," Bubba said, suddenly understanding at least one thing he'd seen.

"Yes. Automobiles or cars. There are all kinds of motorized vehicles to get us around, but I have a small car."

"Yeah, I reckon if we take the jug, I should be all right."

Martin sat and thought for a minute and then asked, "So what is the deal with the jug? Can't you break the thing and be released from it? Surely the witch who bound you to it is dead by now."

That was the thing, wasn't it?

"The curse bound me to the jug for life, or until the curse was lifted. And since I'm still alive, I'm still bound. Even if the jug is broken, I'm bound to the pieces of it, wherever it is. As a djinn, if it breaks, I can always repair it, and I have—several times in fact. It's better than being homeless, or bound to some scrap heap somewhere."

"Now, can you move the jug?" Martin asked.

"As long as I'm not in it I can move it around. So if it gets broken and thrown over a ship's rail, I can bring all the pieces back and fix it. But either way, I'm stuck with the thing."

Again, Martin sat in thought, while Bubba wondered what the man was thinking so hard about.

"Does it have to be the whole jug?"

"Does what have to be the whole jug?" Bubba asked, mystified.

"Let's say we took the stopper out of the top, such as it is, and I put it in my pocket. Would that be enough of the jug to let you come out with me, instead of bringing the whole thing?"

Bubba sat back and looked at Martin for a moment and then shook his head.

"I don't rightly know. It's never been tried. But since you own the jug, and I am now beholden to you, it might work."

"Let's give it a try this weekend and see if it works. If not, we'll find a way to drag the jug around with us. How about some dinner?"

If nothing else, the world had developed some good food over the years. Tonight's fair was shepherd's pie, which was just a fancy name for mashed potatoes and gravy, as far as Bubba could tell. But it was a good hearty meal and tasty to boot.

Martin hadn't mentioned rules again, yet. Maybe he'd forgotten about them. Bubba supposed they should come to some sort of understanding, but the man didn't seem to know anything about the djinn. Had the world forgotten about his kind since he'd arrived in America?

19

As crazy as the world was, did they really need magic now? Or had they somehow tamed magic, chained it, and bent it to their will so anyone could use it? Digging into the shepherd's pie again, he shook his head and wondered what he'd gotten into this time.

# Chapter 6

Friday had finally arrived and Martin looked forward to an evening of conversation over wine and cheese with Diane. Joker normally put in an appearance and tried to steal all the attention, but it made Diane laugh, so Martin didn't object.

But what about Bubba? He had moved him into a room of his own downstairs, behind his shop storefront, so they could both have some privacy. He had a couple rooms and a workshop where he could compound his herbs, which weren't accessible to the public. And Martin didn't want to introduce Bubba to anyone yet, as rough around the edges as he was. Could he convince him to stay in his room and just relax for the evening? It wasn't like he'd neglected the man—or djinn—since he'd arrived. Maybe everything would work out.

He hoped to take a drive Saturday and show Bubba a little bit of the country nearby and see if he could explain anything about the modern world to him. At the moment, he assumed everything was either supernatural or magic, or maybe a combination of the two.

But how could he explain mobile phones, televisions, computers, and all the other things people today took for granted? How far back would he have to go to reach common ground? Somewhere there would be a starting point, but he wasn't sure he had enough expertise to answer all the questions Bubba would have.

They really should sit down and have a talk about where Bubba came from, how he'd wound up in America, and what he remembered of the world before he was trapped. Some of that information should point Martin in the right direction when he began his explanations.

And what was the genie's name? It couldn't possibly be Bubba. From what he remembered, most genies were from the middle east, not America. And the name Bubba wasn't even vaguely Arabic in origin. Honestly, he couldn't introduce him as Bubba to anyone he knew. If nothing else, they could pick a name the two of them agreed on and go with it. Nearly anything was better than Bubba.

What he should do, when he had a little time, was do some research on genies, or the djinn. What was the real story there? There were all kinds of legends and rumors about them, but how much of it was true?

He'd never actually believed genies were real, so he hadn't paid any attention to most of the stories anyway. And now he was saddled with one because he'd fallen in love with a jug.

Or was the reason he was drawn to the jug because it contained the genie? He had some small magical ability himself. Was this awareness of energies what made him search in the back corner of the little store to find the jug?

It was rather a moot point now. Unless he sold the thing, he was stuck with Bubba. But he adored the jug, and once he had everything sorted, it would look wonderful on his countertop.

Finally finished for the day, he dashed up the stairs to fix dinner for the two of them before Diane came over for wine and snacks. He'd put chicken in the oven during a slack time in the shop, and the aroma wafting through the air brought his stomach to attention.

Bubba was standing in the kitchen staring at the cooker.

"Something wrong?" he asked.

"I smell food cooking, but there isn't any fire. This thing is hot to the touch, but I don't see anything burning. I suppose you'll claim there's no magic here either."

"No, there is no magic involved. It's an electric oven. Electricity runs through the heating elements, making them very hot. The heat is trapped inside the oven and heats the food."

"Electricity? Is that some fancy word for magic?"

With a sigh, Martin shook his head.

"We've got a lot to talk about. Why don't we eat?"

The chicken was tasty, and the fried potatoes he fixed to go with them were a hit with Bubba. He still couldn't figure out why the cooker worked, but was satisfied with the outcome.

With the kitchen tidied, he joined Bubba in the living room.

"Now, Bubba, could I ask you a favor?" Martin asked.

"Ask? I suppose."

"I have a lady friend coming over for the evening, and I would appreciate it if we had the time alone. I have some wine and snacks for us. If you'd like, I can get some for you to enjoy in your room."

With a deep laugh, Bubba shook his head.

"I got you. Hopin' to get lucky, huh?"

"Hoping to have some time to win the lady over."

"I'll be fine, especially if you plan to bribe me with food and drink. Don't worry. I won't interrupt anything."

"Thanks, man. We need to get you up to speed before you meet too many people around here. Don't worry. We'll get there."

Bubba kept him company while he put cheese cubes and crackers out on a plate and opened the wine. He put out a separate plate with cheese and crackers for Bubba and opened another bottle of wine.

"Now, don't get drunk," he warned. "You haven't had anything to drink in a long time. There is no telling how it will affect you."

"A little wine like this? Back in the day, before the jug, I was into moonshine whiskey. As a matter of fact, that contributed to me being in the jug, which is a moonshine jug."

"I'm just saying."

Martin checked his candles and replaced the ones which had burned down, so they could have a little candlelight.

"Gettin' fancy," Bubba commented.

"Trying to make a good impression is all," he answered, making sure of the placement before he began lighting the wicks.

Martin heard Bubba snap his fingers, and suddenly all the candles were glowing, the gentle flames casting soft shadows around the room.

"How did you do that?" he demanded.

"I am one of the djinn. We have magical abilities. Don't you know anything?"

"We need to talk," Martin answered bluntly. "Maybe on our drive tomorrow we can have a chat and figure out some of this. But for now, why don't you head to your room before Diane gets here."

"Sure thing, boss," the genie said with a smile. He then picked up his snacks and wine, grinned widely, and disappeared, just as the doorbell rang.

They had to have that talk real soon.

# Chapter 7

Diane was dressed nicely, in soft brown trousers and a knit cardigan over a lacy blouse.

"Come on through," he said as he held the door.

"I hope I'm not too early," she answered.

"Not at all. Everything is ready to bring out, the candles are lit, and I can turn on some music if you like."

"Some nice background music would be wonderful," she told him, fluttering her eyelashes.

Martin had been going to have the music cued up before she arrived, but she was a few minutes early. Between that and Bubba, he was a little off balance. Choosing some new age guitar, he turned the volume down to an acceptable level before bringing the snacks in from the kitchen.

With the wine poured and nibbles at hand, the two of them relaxed back into the sofa to talk about what was going on in their lives. Of course, there was no mention of Bubba.

"Did you ever get that old jug cleaned up," Diane asked, spearing a cheese cube with a pick.

"I did, yes," Martin answered, wondering how he could get the jug without dealing with Bubba.

"You promised I could see it when it was clean," she chided.

"Yes, I did. Let me go get it for you."

Leaving her to sip wine, he hurried down the stairs to the back room. Poking his head into Bubba's room, he saw the genie reading a newspaper.

"I'm just going to show Diane the jug. Won't be a minute."

"That's fine, as long as she doesn't leave with it," Bubba joked.

"No, I told her I'd show it to her, before I understood about you being in it. Need anything?"

"I'm good. You go romance your girl."

Hauling the jug up the stairs, he set it on the coffee table for Diane to see.

"Oh, that is so lovely and rustic! Wherever did you find it?"

Martin told her about the quaint little shop, the dark, dusty corner, and finding the jug.

"I haven't been able to trace this particular jug, but it could be from the late 19th century. They were used mainly for homemade liquor in the southern states of America."

"I'll bet it has seen a lot of things in its history," Diane mused.

"Depending on how long it sat in that shop. The owner didn't even know how long it had been in the corner."

"When are you going to put it on display?" she asked, as Joker put in his appearance.

"No! Stay out of the cheese," Martin scolded the cat. "I'm trying to decide where I want it, but it should be out for display this coming week sometime."

"I love the way it feels," Diane told him, running her hand over the surface. "It's not perfectly smooth, but I wouldn't say it's rough. Primitive, maybe."

Sitting back with Joker in her lap, the jug held her attention for several minutes before she spoke again.

"Heaven only knows what's been in the thing," she said, moving a little closer to him.

"I wouldn't know," Martin answered, thinking about Bubba downstairs.

As things became a little more cozy, he poured more wine and sat back with his arm around the charming lady beside him. Joker had curled up next to Diane and was contentedly purring. Life was good, he thought as he brought the goblet up to his lips.

"Hey, boss," he suddenly heard.

The spray from the wine went everywhere as he leapt to his feet. Diane slipped off the sofa onto the floor and peered up at Bubba, her eyes barely above the seat cushions. Joker had simply disappeared.

"Who is that?" she whispered.

"What are you doing?" Martin demanded. "I thought we had an agreement."

He helped Diane back up to the sofa, wondering what to do about his house mate.

"Boy howdy! Ain't you a looker?" Bubba exclaimed, sweeping his eyes over Diane's figure.

"What do you want? Why are you here?" Martin demanded.

"Well, I thought you might want to know someone is trying to get into the shop downstairs. Rattling doorknobs, testing the windows, and peering in. Want me to do something about it?"

"No! Let me. Oh, Diane, this is Bubba, a guy I met in America. He's come over for a little while to see England. Bubba, meet Diane Sinclair."

Downstairs with Bubba, Martin checked the alarms and the protective spells he had around the place, but everything seemed fine. The windows were all locked, as was the door.

"Are you sure you heard someone?" he asked the genie.

"Yup. Sure as I know you're standing here. They started at the front door and worked their way around. I know you have protective spells around, but if they come back I could take care of them for you."

"I don't know," Martin said. "What would that mean?"

"What do you want done? I could immobilize them until you got here, or disappear them for good, if you know what I mean."

"No, we won't do that. If you could hold them for me until I can contact the authorities, that would be fine."

"You got it, boss. Should I let them get into the shop first?"

"That might be a good idea. That way they would actually be trespassing."

"All right. Go on back up to the lady. I'll watch out for intruders."

The rest of the evening was a little strained, which was not quite the atmosphere Martin had hoped for at the outset. He and Diane went back to the wine and cheese, but the mood was ruined.

"Why don't we try it another night?" Diane suggested as she got ready to leave. "Maybe you should call the police and let them know someone was trying to break it."

"What can they do? Nothing was broken, nobody came in, no one was hurt. All they can tell me is to make sure and lock up, ask if I have an alarm, and suggest caution."

"I suppose you're right. How long is Bubba going to be with you?" she asked.

That was a good question. How long would he have Bubba underfoot, ruining his social life.

"We're still sorting that out," he told her.

With a quick kiss goodnight, Diane headed back to her apartment, leaving Martin to wonder about the evenings events. He'd been at this location for several years and never had a problem. The shop was in a low crime area, and though he had an alarm and had put magical protective sigils around the place, he'd never expected to have to use them. The main reason he'd done any of that was for the insurance in case of a break-in, and because he sold herbal remedies, some of which were expensive and dangerous.

Not dangerous as in addictive, but in the sense that they had to be carefully measured and prescribed or they could be lethal. He had studied hard to make the grade and obtain his license to practice. No point losing the privilege due to negligence.

"Bubba," he called and then started violently when the genie suddenly appeared in front of him.

"Yeah, boss?"

"Stop doing that! Can't you just walk up the stairs?"

"Seems like a waste of time and energy, but I suppose I could."

"Have you heard anything else lately?"

"Naw, once you came downstairs and took a look around, everything's been quiet. How often do you have the problem?"

"I've never had a problem before, so I'm wondering why now."

"Can I ask a couple questions?" Bubba asked.

"I guess."

"You say you practice a little magic. Have you ever trained?"

"Only a little, as a sideline. I'm an herbalist with a little psychic ability for finding lost objects and the like. I mainly use the magic to amplify the ability and put protection around the shop. Why?"

"Can you sense me with your abilities?"

"What do you mean?"

"Someone with moderate to strong abilities, or someone who is a wizard or sorcerer, should be able to sense my presence. I was wondering if you could is all."

"Would I need to do anything, or would I simply sense something odd?"

"I don't rightly know. Depends on how sensitive you are."

Martin thought for a moment and then reached out with his sixth sense to see what he could find. And sure enough, if he tried, he could sense an aura with a strong magical signature."

""What difference does it make whether I can sense you or not?" Martin asked.

"Well, son, the problem isn't whether you can, but whether others can."

"Others?"

"Yeah. Others with magical tendencies. Some of them might not even need to try. They could feel a difference just by walking by."

"Do you think it was someone like that who tried to break-in tonight?" Martin asked, concerned.

"I don't know, but it would make sense. If a body can sense a magical being, he might be inclined to investigate."

"So what do we do?" Martin asked. "I have an alarm system and protective spells in place. I could call the police and have them patrol more frequently for a while and see if they find anything unusual."

"I can't think of anything, unless you know some stronger protective spells. What are alarm systems? Some other modern magic?" Bubba asked, scratching his head.

"Once they're set, unless you have the code to turn them off, they make a very loud sound if someone comes through the doors or windows. They also notify the alarm company, who then calls the police."

"How strong are your protective spells?"

"Not very strong. I've never had a problem. They were mainly a backup, and sort of for the hell of it. I never thought I'd actually need them for anything."

"You might oughta check on them. I have no idea who or what might be interested."

"Do you have a lot of enemies?" Martin asked. That's all he needed. A magical being with enemies after him.

"Not personal ones, but a captive djinn is always a prize."

"We need to talk. Tomorrow. Maybe we'll go ahead and take that drive to someplace quiet and you can answer a few questions I have."

"And you can answer some of mine."

# Chapter 8

Martin slept in a little on Saturday. After dreams of demons chasing Bubba around London and the English countryside, he hadn't rested well. Bubba seemed in a good mood, though, and dug right into breakfast.

"One of these mornings we'll go out and you can order a full English breakfast," he told the genie.

"Full English? What's that?"

"Don't worry. I'm sure you'll enjoy it. But for now, let's see if we can take a drive out of the city for a while."

The problem was the bottle. It was too big to be unobtrusive, and even cleaned up with a change of clothes, Bubba stood out among the crowd.

"Bubba, if I put the stopper of the jug in my pocket, would that be enough for you to leave the apartment with me? Or does the whole jug have to go?"

"I don't rightly know. As far as I know nobody ever tried it."

"What happens if you get too far from the jug?"

"I feel a strong pull drawing me back to the jug. If I ignore it, the curse yanks me back into the thing."

"Should we try with just the stopper? Or do you want to get into the jug and let me carry you and it out to the car? Me carrying the jug wouldn't be too note worthy, but adding you into the equation might spark some interest."

"I'd rather not get in the jug."

"Even if I left out the stopper?"

"Well, now, you see, I've been tricked before. You say you'll leave the stopper out, but can I trust you? Granted, the last time I was drunk off my ass, but still, I don't know."

"Let's try it with just the stopper then. If you feel the pull, just turn around and come back. I'll follow you and we can figure out something else."

Grabbing up the rag-wrapped corn cob, Martin headed for the door. Once the two of them were out, he locked the door, checked all the protective devices, and strolled toward his car. All seemed fine until they were nearly to the car.

"Hey, boss. I've gotta go back," he heard Bubba say, as the genie turned around and hurried back to the house.

Damn! Was he going to have to haul that blasted jug around everywhere he went? Unlocking the door again, they went back upstairs.

There was nothing else on the jug to take off. It was made from potter's clay and salt glazed all as one big jug. If it had originally had a proper stopper or lid, it was long gone.

"Is there anything in the jug that's been with it long enough to represent the whole jug?" Martin asked.

"I don't think so, and I've been in the thing for a long while."

"Is there anything inside there we could remove, like a little flaw in the pottery we could chip off? Maybe as long as it was a piece of the jug it would work."

"But I would have to go inside to look, and I don't want to go back inside."

Martin looked over the jug, top to bottom and all the way around. Outside of a few scratches in the glazing, there was nothing much to find.

"I guess we'll have to take the thing with us today," he finally said. "I've got a couple ideas, but they'll take a little doing."

So off they trudged one more time, jug in hand. Bracing it firmly in the boot of the car, so it wouldn't roll around and break, Martin turned toward the main northeast road, with Bubba taking in all the sights of the city.

The day was lovely, and Bubba seemed to enjoy the fresh air and sunshine for a change, after who knew how long locked away in a jug. Finally reaching an open area, he found a place to park his car and sit under a tree to have a talk with his new friend from America.

"Okay, Bubba, I think it's time for that talk. And I want a real name I can call you. Bubba is not a name."

"Yeah, I guess a little history might be an idea. But you don't get my full name. There will be no conjuring with it. Understood?"

"I don't intend to use it for anything other than something to call you. Just your christian name would be fine. Or pick a name out of thin air."

"I suppose you should call me Ali. It is one of my names, at least, from quite a while back."

And Ali began to spin him the story of how he came to be trapped in a bottle in Arabia, was forced to find a way for his master to get to America, and how he and his bottle were lost on a game of chance.

"So this Arabian master of yours lost you to someone else. Did they know you were in the bottle?"

"Oh, yeah. They knew. They were all magi of some sort."

"But that doesn't explain the jug. What happened to the bottle?"

Since he wasn't cursed at the time, when the bottle was broken, he was freed. And he could have stayed free if he hadn't developed a taste for moonshine whiskey.

"Yeah, I was out partying one night, and someone slipped me some bad whiskey.

"Bad whiskey?" Martin asked.

"Yeah. If it ain't distilled properly it can produce something that gives a fella the worst hangover ever. And once in a while, something will go way off in the process and make something that can kill a guy."

"I take it you got a hangover?"

"Well, yeah. And then I woke up in the jug. I was still pretty drunk."

"Do you remember what happened?" Martin asked. He'd never been that drunk.

"It sort of come back to me, gradually. I'd been to see this swamp witch down in Louisiana. She usually made some good stuff. I don't know. Maybe she drugged me intentional like. But we had a couple drinks there on her porch. I'd seen the jug settin' there, but didn't think anything of it. There were others just like it anywhere there was moonshine. I figured it had whiskey in it."

"But how could she put you in the jug? Don't you have to do that yourself?" Marin asked, his curiosity getting the better of him.

"Best I can remember, I'd run out of whiskey. She said there was some in the jug, but I'd have to go get it, as kind of a joke. She knew what I was. Had known for a long time. So drunk as I was, it sounded like a good idea."

"What about the curse?"

"After I was in the jug, she put that stopper in there and then cast a spell so I couldn't get it out. When I came to and discovered where I was, I got pretty riled up. That's when she cursed me to be bound to the damned thing."

"I take it you were hoping she'd eventually lift the curse and you could go free."

"Yeah, a guy can hope, ya know. But it didn't work out that way. The jug got stolen, but the guys were caught before they could open it up. Then it sat around for a long while with the sheriff where the witch couldn't get at it. After that, it kept traveling around, for people to look at, just for the jug."

"Which is why I bought it," Martin added.

"Yeah. At some point, it wound up someplace and got forgotten until you come along."

"Couldn't you have called out to somebody, got their attention, and have them let you out?"

"Do you think I didn't try?" Bubba—Ali—asked. "Must have been part of the curse or somethin'. I couldn't get anybody to pay me any mind. After a while, I gave up tryin'."

"So what do we do now? I don't need a genie. You don't want to be in the jug. As long as I have the jug, we're stuck with each other, unless we find a way to lift the curse."

"I can be useful, ya know," Bubba told him.

"Useful?"

"It's not just clothes I can conjure. Or I can help in the shop. I can tidy up, keep it clean, help out in your apartment. You know, bring you your favorite foods. That kind of thing."

"Scare off my girlfriend?"

"Now you know I didn't mean anything the other night. I just thought you ought to know someone was tryin' to get in. That's all. Hey, I could fix things up with her if you like."

"No. Leave Diane out of this. I don't know how to explain that you're going to be around most of the time now. She's a little put off by the visitor from America thing."

"Gourmet meals. What does she like to eat?"

"I don't think that's a good idea, Bubba."

The guy was going to be Bubba forever. He had to remember to use his name, if he could get his brain around the idea.

"Another thing, Bubba—Ali," Martin began. "What about these other sensitives who are trying to get at you? I don't want my home under attack constantly from people trying to bag a genie of their very own."

"I don't know. I don't understand the magic around here. I know what I can do, could do anyways, but how it might affect the magic here is another thing. And these police of yours. What if I get you in trouble with them without even knowing it?"

"I've told you, Bub—Ali. We don't use magic. It's all logical. Scientific. I just don't have the knowledge to explain it to you properly. We're so used to it, we don't even think about it any more."

"All I know is that right now, as long as you own the jug, I am at your beck and call."

"I don't need a servant."

"Well, I don't want to be a servant, but I got no choice."

"Maybe we could be more like partners, or you could work for me in a different capacity."

"How, when I've got to stick by that jug?"

"I'm working on it."

# Chapter 9

This Martin guy seemed all right, but he didn't strike me as too smart. Why couldn't he get it through his head that he had a genie bound to him by the jug? And that this put him in danger from some pretty powerful people? Some of them were people at least.

But until Ali understood how things worked in this day and age, he would bide his time and learn all he could. Then, when he figured the time was right, he could get someone else to steal the jug and let him get on with being the djinn he was, instead of piddling around cleaning the shop.

Yeah, all right. He would still be bound to the jug, most likely. Nobody with any sense at all was going to set him free. Not with the powers he had, if he could still access them. Hell, he wouldn't even let him free, if positions were reversed. And if things worked out, it wouldn't be too bad.

He'd have to get Martin thinking in the right direction. If he could get the girl interested, at least the guy would have one thing off his mind. She was a looker. No doubt about it, with silky blond hair and blue eyes a guy could fall into. Yup. Martin was a lucky guy there, if he didn't blow his chances.

Martin had talked about him helping in the shop. He supposed he could do that for now. At least he could meet a few people, figure out how things worked in this new place, and do something to earn his keep. He owed the guy that much for letting him out of the jug.

He'd got some new clothes—more than the one set—so he could be seen and not stand out too much. It seemed important to his new master. And he was working on his speech. He thought Martin was overreacting, but he absolutely wouldn't have him around his clients until he learned to speak "proper English." So he helped tidy the shop in the morning, dispelling dust from shelves and the things which sat on them before going back upstairs to watch the "telly" and try to learn how to speak properly.

Since the night of the attempted break-in, he had been vigilant in watching out for intruders. No point switching horses right now. Not until he go his feet solidly under him.

"Hey, Ali, could you give me a hand for a minute?" he heard from downstairs.

"Sure, boss," he called back with a sigh. The guy would never understand they were not friends. Martin owned his jug. He owned Ali. And things and beings that were owned didn't have the option of saying no.

ALI HAD BEEN QUIET since they'd taken their drive. And Martin understood a little more of what was going on with the djinn. If he could free him, he would, but he had no knowledge of black magic, curses, and the like. And he didn't know anyone who did. He'd tended to avoid those sorts of things. Black magic had a way of taking over.

Bubba had begun to help out around the shop and apartment with minor things. Martin had ordered some new furniture for Bubba's—Ali's—room and, when it came, Martin wondered how he was going to move it.

With Ali around there was no problem. With a flick of his wrist, the boxes disappeared from the doorway and reappeared in the room. Another gesture saw the room rearranged, the new bed put together and made up, and everything tidied.

"That is amazing," he'd commented.

"It's not much, but it can come in handy," Ali had answered.

"Thanks for your help. I'd better get back to the shop."

Ali had promised him a special meal one day, and tonight the aromas coming down the stairway nearly convinced him to close early. Similar in some ways to the Indian food he liked, yet different, he couldn't wait to take his first bite.

"Ali, that was fantastic," Martin said, after finishing the delightful Um Ali had for dessert. The lamb kabobs he'd had before that, along with the fresh flat bread had been amazing. He'd had Arabic food before, but it was nothing compared to this.

"I'm glad you liked it," Ali answered sitting back in his chair, obviously as full as Martin was.

"Now we have to clean up," Martin told him, contemplating getting to his feet.

"No problem," Ali told him.

With a few waves of his and a snap of his fingers, everything was magically cleaned and put away. The leftovers were in the fridge ready for tomorrow's lunch, unless Martin got up for a midnight snack. This was a distinct possibility. As much as he'd eaten, and as full as his stomach was, he could still find room for one more bite.

"Do you think we'll have any more trouble with our window rattler?" Martin asked. They hadn't heard so much as a peep since the first time.

"I don't know," Ali told him. "I would have thought we'd have heard something by now, and I'm a little worried about it."

"Why worried?"

"What if their first trip was just recon to get an idea of your defenses? They could be planning for their return trip."

"Hm... What sort of plans would you expect?"

"Since you have more than just regular locks and things, I would guess something magical to get around your alarms and sigils."

"Are we looking for a witch or warlock?"

"Could be. Or a wizard or sorcerer. I doubt a truly magical being would be taking so long."

"By magical being, you're talking about someone like you. Right?"

"Not exactly like me, but yes. Some sort of demon perhaps or another genie under orders to find out what you have here."

"Any suggestions?"

"No. You've already improved your protective spells and locks on the doors. You have your alarms, which I still think are magic. Until something happens, there isn't much I can tell you."

"Will you be all right here on your own if I take Diane out to dinner one evening?" Martin asked.

"I would guess so. As good as I'd be with you here, except if anything happened you wouldn't know about it until later."

"I have the alarm linked to my mobile, so I would know if the alarm goes off."

"I'll be fine. You go work some magic on that pretty girl of yours."

"We're not going out until Friday evening, so we have a couple days yet," Martin told him.

"Special day?"

"What? Friday? Nothing in particular. I just thought dinner would be nice."

The rest of the week passed quickly. Ali was beginning to get into the routine around the shop and had made dinner several times. Martin wasn't sure where he got the ingredients for his fabulous meals, but he enjoyed them. Maybe he could ask Ali to fix dinner one evening when Diane came over.

Friday morning Diane came by the shop, excited about dinner later in the evening.

"We said seven tonight, right?" she asked.

"Seven it is."

"Dressy casual all right?"

"That would be perfect."

Martin wasn't a formal type of guy, but one evening he would take her out to someplace upscale. The seasons were moving from autumn into winter soon. Perhaps something nearer to the holidays...

"How is Bubba working out?" she asked, breaking into his thoughts.

"Ali. I finally got a name from him. He's doing well at helping keep the shop tidy and he's a fantastic cook. I thought I'd ask him to do dinner for us one night, if you'd like. His Arabic food is something else."

"That might be fun, as long as I know he's there."

"Sorry about the other night."

"Have you had any more trouble?" Diane asked.

"Not so much as the wind rattling the windows. I think it was probably just kids trying to be funny."

"Probably so. Did you have your alarm checked to make sure it's working?"

"Yeah. They came out and said everything was fine."
"I'll see you tonight then."

# Chapter 10

"Are you sure you'll be all right?" Martin asked Ali one more time.

"Boss, just get out of here and have dinner with your girl. If anything happens, I'll let you know."

"And how will you do that?"

"Let's just say I have my ways."

"Well, stay out of sight. I have the jug hidden from casual view. A person would have to search pretty thoroughly to find it. Hopefully that would at least slow them down."

"You worry too much. You're going to be late."

"All right. See you later."

With a sigh and an slight uncomfortable feeling, Martin took off to pick up Diane for dinner. She didn't live too far away from his apartment, and the restaurant was only a mile or so away from her place. With any luck, they could finish their meal, go back to her place for a drink, and he wouldn't be too late getting home.

Dressed smartly in charcoal grey trousers and a soft blue jumper over a white blouse, Diane was a sight after his hectic week. After a short drive to the restaurant, they were seated next to the fireplace, while they looked over the menu.

Mostly home cooked meals, the menu wasn't extensive, but the choices were difficult. Martin had never had anything here that wasn't fantastic and they had everything from roast beef and chicken to shepherd's pie.

Choosing the roast beef, mixed vegetables, and potatoes, he sipped at his ale as he enjoyed the warmth of the fire. Diane finally decided on baked chicken with vegetables and a salad. Sipping at a nice white wine, she looked lovely in the firelight.

"What is Ali doing this evening?" she asked.

"He's just hanging out at the apartment. Knowing him, he'll be watching a murder mystery on the telly, or something on the history channel. He'll be fine."

I hope, he thought. What would he do if someone broke in and stole the jug, with Ali inside? How would they get Ali inside? If Martin owned the jug, could someone else force him into it?

Of course, if someone stole the jug, they would then own it, sort of.

"Martin? Are you in there somewhere?" Diane asked, breaking into his thoughts.

"Sorry. Long week."

"Are you worried about something? You haven't been yourself lately."

"I guess having someone rattle door knobs last time you came over has me worried about security."

"Well, you have a good alarm system. Surely, if anyone tries to break-in, you'll be fine."

"I suppose. But I would have locks to fix, windows to replace, insurance forms to fill out, police reports. All the stuff that would go with it. Plus anything that actually got damaged or stolen in the shop or my apartment."

"Isn't Ali there? Certainly he could do something. He's a pretty big guy."

"He may be big, but I have no idea how he would be in a fight. Or whether he would feel comfortable trying to do anything, not knowing how things work over here."

"I can see that, sort of. But surely he would do something, like call 999."

Martin had never thought of that. He'd never shown Ali how to call the emergency number. Telephones weren't something Ali understood, let alone know how to use. Add that to the list of things they needed to go over.

"Yeah, he could do that. I'm probably worrying over nothing."

They enjoyed dinner and ordered coffee and lemon tart for dessert, before Martin paid the check and they got ready to leave. As they were walking toward the door his mobile sounded. It wasn't the usual ring, but the one alerting him to the alarm system.

"Damn!" he said as he hurried Diane out the door.

"What is it?" she asked.

"My alarm just went off," he told her, punching in 999 for the police.

"What is it with you and Friday night?"

"I wish I knew," he answered as the call connected and he explained what was happening.

"They had already been alerted by the alarm company and officers have been dispatched. Do you mind coming back with me?"

"Not at all. You need to get home as soon as you can and find out what has happened."

Two police cars blocked his parking area, so Martin pulled up across the street. As he rushed over to his shop, he saw they had someone in handcuffs.

Ali.

"What are you doing?" he asked.

"We found this man in your apartment brandishing a chef's knife. He says he's staying with you."

"Yes. He is a friend from out of town who's helping me out in the shop. Did you find anything else?"

"One window is broken in the back and it looks like someone tried to force the door. This guy...," the officer began.

"Ali"

"Yeah, Ali, says he heard someone at the door and went into the kitchen to get something to defend himself. As he got to the kitchen, he heard the window break and ran to see what was happening. It appears, as it wasn't him breaking in, that he scared the other person away."

"I would think seeing Ali with a chef's knife would do that. Yes."

"Yes sir, Mr.Pritchard. We will need a statement from you and from your friend, but you can come down tomorrow. We'll leave you to clean up and get Ali calmed down."

Once Martin had assured the officers that Ali had permission to be in his apartment, they had taken off the cuffs, but Ali was still fuming.

"Come on, Diane, Ali. Let's all go in and have a drink. I know I could use one," Martin said as he watched the police cars pull away.

He moved his car first, before a traffic cop came by and ticketed it, and then went in to join his friends.

"What will you have, Diane?" he asked.

"A little brandy would be nice. Otherwise, whiskey and soda."

"Ali? How about you?"

"I think I'll have whiskey straight up."

Martin poured some brandy for Diane and joined Ali for a whiskey, the burn of the strong drink bringing a little sense to the confusion.

"Ali, what happened?" he finally asked.

"I was in here reading when I heard someone rattling the door handle, same as the other time. So I went in to find something to use as a weapon, found that big knife, and I was going down the stairs to the shop. Then I heard the glass break and ran in to see if I could keep whoever it was from getting in."

"Did you see the person?"

"No. I think they heard me running down the stairs and left. Sorry boss."

"No. That's fine. At least nobody got hurt and all I have to do is fix one window. I should go down and see what it will take, so I can call a shop tomorrow. Which window is it?"

"One of the smaller ones next to the back door."

Along the back there were four windows with four panes of glass each. Whoever tried to break-in had broken the lower pane on the window closest to the door. Martin assumed they were trying to reach through and unlock the door."

"Wouldn't they figure you had an alarm system?" Diane asked, the excitement and brandy beginning to show their effects.

"I would, but I couldn't speak for someone else. I need to get you home."

"Just call me a cab. I don't think you should be driving."

"Probably not, and I don't want to leave the shop with the window broken out like that. Give me a minute."

Pulling out his mobile, he located a cab company, rang them up, and soon had Diane on her way.

"Now, Ali, is there anything else you can tell me that you couldn't talk about with the others here?" Martin asked.

"Whoever this was, they had no magical abilities I could sense. They could be working for someone who does, but they had no talents in that area."

"So we are still at a loss as to who is behind this."

"Yeah. Looks like.

"Is there anyway to mask your presence here? You know, make it look like you've gone somewhere else?"

"Maybe for an hour or so, but not over any length of time. Unless you know a cloaking spell of some sort you could use."

"No. Nothing like that. I'll have to think about it later. I'm too tired, I've had too much to drink, and I'm keyed up over this nonsense. It isn't a good time to try using reason or logic."

"Do you want me to stay up and keep watch?"

"Don't you need to sleep?"

"Not really."

"If you wouldn't mind..."

"You go get some rest. We'll worry about this tomorrow," Ali told him.

# Chapter 11

After a fitful night, Martin got Ali and his jug into the car and drove to the local police station so they could give statements. There wasn't much he could tell them that he hadn't told them before, but this made it official somehow.

Ali had pulled a surname out of the blue for them—Badawi. Martin had no idea where it had come from, or even if it was really one of his names. Not that it mattered. As long as the police accepted it as his legitimate name, he was good with it.

Where he had come up with an ID card was another thing, though. But he presented it to the sergeant taking down their information, complete with photo and everything, listing his address as somewhere in Manchester.

Back in the car and on the way home, Martin asked him about it.

"Well, after I heard them talking to everyone ahead of us, I decided I should have something, so I put together something that would work and conjured it up. Looks pretty good, don't it?"

"It looks real, but I hope you never have to prove anything on that ID card. Could get a bit tricky."

The sergeant had been a little irritated Martin hadn't called in about the other break-in attempt, but he explained that nothing had been damaged or taken. Nobody had broken into the shop, so what could they have done?

"It would have provided background, given us a heads up that there was something going on in your area. If we'd known, we might have been able to keep the second attempt from happening."

Neither Martin nor Ali shared his opinion. If Ali was correct, and whoever was behind this had magical abilities, nothing the police could have done would have made any difference. Even if they were dealing with bored teenagers, Martin doubted the police would have done anything.

"Now that we're finished with them, why don't we get something to eat?" Martin suggested.

"Now I like that idea," Ali told him. "Maybe find someplace where a guy can get a beer."

"How about ale? I know a place that has a good ploughman's lunch and a good house ale to go with it."

"As long as there's plenty of it, I'm game."

Martin took him to one of his favorite pubs and ordered him one of their lunches. As always, the sandwiches were thick, the cheese tasty, and the ale the perfect compliment.

"I could get used to this," Ali told him around a mouthful of roast beef. "And this beer ain't half bad."

"See what you've missed not coming to England before?" Martin chided.

"It ain't like I had a choice, ya know what I mean?"

"I do. I'm just glad we didn't have to park too far away," he answered, figuring Ali would understand.

"Yeah. We've got to do something about that. I just don't know what."

"It is rather inconvenient," Martin agreed. "But I've had a couple ideas. Let's talk when we get home."

Finishing the last of their ale, they drove in comfortable silence back to the shop. Everything still seemed fine. The board he'd nailed up over the broken window was still in place and nothing new was broken.

"Let me call a glass shop and see about getting the window replaced," he called to Ali.

"Good idea. I think I'm gonna stretch out for a bit. I might be getting too old for all this excitement, followed by too much good food."

Martin chuckled and then thought about how old Ali must be. Did Ali even know?

The glass shop was open for half a day on Saturday, but they could come out on Monday and replace the pane.

"I guess that will have to be fine. Just try to make it as early as possible."

Now that he had the window sorted, as much as he could anyway, it was time to think about Ali. He couldn't, well, he didn't want to leave him alone here at the shop and apartment all the time. If he was going to be here, Martin wanted to be able to take him places, show him a little bit of his world, without having to haul the jug around at the same time.

And it wasn't just taking it in the car. Anything over about a hundred meters was out, so even going out to eat could be tricky. And taking him to someplace like the coast was impractical. How could they walk along the shoreline hauling the jug all the way?

He supposed if he broke the jug into pieces, he could carry it in a satchel, but he'd bought it so he could display it in the shop. And he hadn't been able to do that for fear of someone stealing it to get Ali. So now he had a jug he couldn't display, along with a genie he hadn't reckoned on, both of which put a serious crimp in his life.

He'd thought of trying to find someone who could lift the curse, but who could he trust? If Ali were correct, anyone with those sorts of abilities would be a threat to Ali. So instead of freeing him, they could simply transfer control of him by stealing the jug and binding him to them instead of Martin.

For now, he needed for Ali to be able to move around freely with him, instead of having to stay within sight of the jug. And he'd had a few thoughts along those lines. Later today, after he'd had a nap, he would ask Ali's opinion and they'd see what they could do.

# Chapter 12

The meal had been good, and getting out of the house had been a wonderful break. Ali wished there was a way to do it more often, but being bound to the damned jug made it impossible. All in all, his new master wasn't a bad guy. Undemanding, considerate of his feelings, Ali couldn't fault the guy, especially since he hadn't known what he was getting into when he bought the jug.

Ah, well, a nap after a great meal would be nice. And then he could see what Martin had in mind. Drifting off to sleep, Ali dreamt of hot sunny days, seas of sand, and of palms around an oasis. It had been a long time since he'd left his home land. Maybe one day he could return.

When he woke, Martin was making tea in the kitchen. Ali was developing a taste for the stuff. He'd never liked the tea in America, but the English stuff wasn't bad.

"So, are you ready to toss around a few ideas?" Martin asked him.

"Ready when you are. I haven't come up with anything practical."

"On examining the jug again, I saw a little nick in the glaze around the neck of the jug," Martin began.

"Yeah, I've seen it."

"If we think about the Law of Contagion, where the part of the thing is the whole of the thing, wouldn't having a bit of the jug with us be the same as having the whole jug? If we add to that with the Law of Sympathy—like attracts like or the image is the thing—I think we could combine the two and have a solution."

"Combine them how?" Ali asked, not sure what Martin was getting at.

"What if we take a file and remove a little dust from the nick in the jug. Not a lot, but enough to work with, then mix it with some clay. Then we form the clay into a replica of your jug and fire it so it will keep its shape. Shouldn't that work?"

Ali thought about it for a moment. In theory, either should work on its own. Combining the two should make it even better. He could think of nothing wrong with the idea.

"I don't see why it wouldn't," he answered. "If the laws of magic are right, the image of the jug, with dust from the jug contained in it, should be as good as the jug itself."

"Tomorrow I'll go see a friend of mine who does pottery and get some clay from him. He'll probably let me add our little jug to his kiln the next time he's firing. And then we'll give it a try. It can't hurt. Right?"

Ali couldn't think of any drawback to it. The worst it could do was nothing at all.

"I'm game. Let's give it a try and see what happens."

SUNDAY THERE WASN'T much going on. The shop wasn't open, and neither was much of anything else. So Martin decided to do a little research online to check on his theories of magic. While he was at it, he might check on the subject of curses. Maybe he could find a way to lift the curse for Ali. Then the jug wouldn't be an issue at all.

"What is that thing?" he heard.

Ali still hadn't gotten his head around technology and insisted it was all magic. But what was magic anyway, except something you couldn't explain? Even as much as two hundred years ago, most of today's technology would be considered magic. So why did it irritate him that Ali couldn't understand?

"It's called a computer. It lets me research things, like I would in a library, only it's a lot faster."

"More magic?"

"From your point of view, I suppose it is," Martin agreed.

"As long as it works."

"The main problem is making sure the sources are reliable. Anybody with a computer can upload information to the internet, but it might not be valid.

Sort of like the difference between fiction and non-fiction at the library, only the sites aren't marked that way."

"How do you know what to believe?" Ali asked.

"That can be the trick," Martin admitted. "It helps if you have a little knowledge of the subject before you go online, or if you know somebody who knows a little about what you're researching."

"I'm not sure I like all this magical stuff you guys have these days. It sounds kind of dangerous."

"It can be, if you don't know what you're doing. And a lot of it doesn't work if the power goes out."

"Power?"

"Yes, the electrical power that makes it all work. Like the lights, the computer, the kettle. Without electricity, or power, none of it works."

"So it all has to have a magical power source?"

"Well, we don't consider it magical, but yes. Without power none of it works. A lot of the things that need power today replace things which worked without power in earlier days, so a lot of people don't have any sort of back up in case of a power failure."

"Why would you do that?" Ali asked, confused. "Why would you make yourself dependent on a particular magic which can fail and leave you stranded?"

"It all happened gradually, a little here, a little there. Plugging a kettle into the power plug is a lot easier than building a fire and waiting for the water to heat. Turning on the electric heater is easier than building a fire for radiators or fireplaces. It's all about convenience."

"Until you're freezing and have no way to stay warm," Ali added.

"Well, yes. But it doesn't happen often, and seldom lasts for too long."

Martin had never thought about it too much. He'd grown up in town and with the convenience of modern life. Seriously, how many people in this day and age actually had a wood fired cooker in the kitchen or a fireplace sufficient to heat their house? And who had a well with a bucket to draw water instead of an electric pump or the city water company?

It was worth thinking about, though. What would happen to society if a major breakdown occurred? Maybe it was best not to dwell on it.

"Anyway, I'm looking up information regarding our experiment this week, for you and your jug. So far, I haven't come up with any negatives. As far as lifting curses, that's a little trickier."

"Yeah, and that witch was pretty powerful."

"Can you remember the spell she used or do you know what type of magic she was into?"

"I remember a good bit of the spell, and she was a swamp witch. I know she used to read the future using water from the swamp. Some of her spells were cast using swamp water and crayfish. Stuff like that."

"Hm..." Martin thought for a minute. Swamp magic must be similar to elemental magic, especially if she used water in her spells.

"I'll see what I can find. If we can lift the curse, the rest of it will be irrelevant. I can have my jug for display, you can do whatever you'd like. Travel the world, go back home to wherever you came from, stay here in England and help me in the shop."

The last was said in jest. Why would a powerful being, such as a genie, stay here to work in his shop? The idea was absurd.

"I might take you up on that," Ali said. "I've got a lot to catch up on. And I'm not sure if I can go home. Home might not be a place anymore."

Martin hadn't thought of that. The world had changed considerably even in his lifetime.

"How long have you been around. Ali? You never did say," he asked.

"Let's just say I remember when Rome tried to conquer Britain and leave it at that."

"And when was the last time you were out of the jug?"

"Around the same time the Americans fought y'all in 1812."

That long ago? No wonder everything in the world was magic to him.

"I guess you do have some catching up to do."

# Chapter 13

Monday morning was busy. With the weather changing, allergies and colds were a nuisance, so quite a few of his regular customers came in for herbal remedies. He hadn't had any call for his psychic investigations lately, which was probably a good thing. What with having to deal with a genie and break-ins, things had been a little busy.

He hoped the afternoon slowed down. He wanted to go over to Peter's house and see about getting some potter's clay from him and ask about firing the little jug. He and Ali had talked it over and neither of them could see a problem with at least trying it.

One thing that worried him was someone stealing the big jug and leaving him with the small one. Would possession of the original jug supersede his claim on Ali with the dust and small jug in his possession?

Not that it mattered. They still needed to see if it would work.

"Hey, boss," he heard. "Want to go ahead and get something for lunch?"

It was getting on toward that time, so he closed up shop to go grab something. Since Ali now had a little money from working in the shop, he offered to pay for the meal today. It would be so much simpler if he could send Ali out rather than having to go himself.

"Are you sure you want to buy lunch today?" he asked Ali.

"I should have enough," Ali told him. "What do I have to spend it on?"

Point taken. He could conjure up any clothing he needed. For that matter, he could conjure up lunch if he chose, but Martin had something specific in mind.

Of course, the men from the glass company came by just as he was getting ready to close for lunch, so he let them in, gave them instructions and left Ali to keep an eye on things, while he ran to pick up their food. He had called ahead to the Indian place, which was becoming Ali's favorite, so all he had to do was zip in, get the take away, and dash back to the shop.

As he hurried back, his thoughts turned to the shop. With the one window broken, he would also have to get the guys from the alarm company out to make sure everything was working. Who would have dreamed buying an old jug would cause so much trouble and confusion?

"Why the long face, boss?" Ali asked.

"Just trying to sort out everything I need to get done. The window should be fixed before we open the shop again. Then there is the alarm company to call, Peter to see about some clay and kiln, and I want to check on Diane. I haven't heard from here in a couple days."

"You don't want to let her get away," Ali told him with a wide grin.

"You're right. I don't. But here lately it seems every time we try to get together, something comes up."

"It's probably my fault. Sorry," Ali said. "I suppose you might have had a break-in even if I wasn't here, but I'm not sure. I don't want to bring bad luck to you. After all, you let me out of the jug."

"I didn't know you were in the jug," Martin countered. "Of course, if I'd known, I would have let you out anyway. Maybe even sooner. I can't say I agree with keeping someone locked up like that."

"I'm definitely not in favor of it," Ali agreed.

A voice from downstairs called out that they were finished and needed him to sign the paperwork. He would need that for the insurance claim. Martin doubted it would help, since he had a deductible to meet, but if anything else happened at least it would be filed.

Finished with lunch and the glass company, Martin told Ali to take it easy for the afternoon. There wasn't much to be done in the shop and the apartment was tidy. He suggested he look at some things on the history channel. Maybe it would help him get up to speed.

First things first. He called Peter, who told him to come on over after work. He would have some things to fire in a couple days, so the small project he was working on would be no problem to include in the kiln.

The alarm company could come out the next day to check the system and make sure everything was working properly after the repairs. Of course, they suggested an upgrade for an additional fee. How this would have helped,

Martin couldn't figure. The window would still have been broken, the police would still have been called, and there would still have been no sign of who was to blame.

Now for Diane.

"Hi, Diane. Martin here. I hadn't heard from you in a couple days. Throat feeling better?"

"Oh, Martin! I've just been a little busy at work. And yes, my throat is feeling better. I don't think I'll go to my doctor, unless it starts getting worse again. I've finished in the attic, so it should be fine."

"I wanted to make sure you were all right after all the excitement the other night."

"I'm fine. How are you and Ali? Did you get your window fixed?"

He told her all the particulars and they agreed to meet Thursday evening to try dinner again. Since both break-ins had occurred on Friday evenings, maybe a change of schedules would give them a chance for a leisurely meal.

The afternoon started off slowly, but about halfway to closing time a whole crowd of people came in. At this rate he was going to have to make up some more sore throat remedy. Of course, it was like this every year about this time. Something with the change in season brought it on.

Finally locking the door and flipping the sign to Closed, he went upstairs to talk to Ali, who had fallen asleep watching the telly.

"Hey, Ali," he called.

"Wha... Oh! Boss. Sorry. What can I do for you?"

"I'm headed over to get some of that clay from Peter. Is there anything in particular you'd like for dinner? I could pick something up on the way back."

Ali had developed a taste for Indian food, so they agreed to Indian take-away for the evening.

"And tomorrow or the next day, I'll fix some more Arabic food for you," Ali promised.

"Sounds good. I'll see you in a little while. Watch the store and apartment for me, and don't answer any doors. I have no idea what's been going on, but I want you safe."

"You've got it, boss."

He spent a little more time with Peter than he'd planned, but the guy did such fabulous work it was always a treat to see what he'd been creating.

Once he had the clay and a few bits of advice, he called the Indian restaurant nearest his apartment, put in his order, and was assured it would be ready when he arrived.

For some reason, he'd been a little uneasy leaving Ali by himself, and if the genie understood about phones, he would have called him. One of these days he had to explain some of the basics of modern life to the guy.

With the aroma of the chicken biryani filling his car, he hurried back to the apartment. Going around to the back door of the shop, he stopped short at the sight before him, dinner forgotten for the moment.

"Ali!" he shouted through the open door. "What's happened?"

"Well, about that. I heard noises around back here and I knew the door was locked, so I left it alone like you said. But then I heard a noise like wood breaking and came around. This guy had just stepped through the door and was looking around.

"Did you call the police?" he asked, knowing even as he spoke the genie had no clue how to do that.

"Naw, but I did freeze him until you could figure out what to do with him. I reckoned you wouldn't be long."

"When did this happen?"

"Just a minute or two ago. I was still trying to figure what to do with the guy."

As the sirens came closer to the shop, Martin decided the alarm system must have worked. But what could they do before they police came around back?

"Let him loose once I put the food down," Martin said, "and then grab him so he doesn't get away. Actually, let me grab him first, then let him go."

Martin was able to move the man's arm into an arm bar, so apparently whatever Ali did only affected him moving by himself. He was awfully red in the face, though, from fighting the magical spell, or whatever it was.

"Let me go!" the man shouted as soon as he was able.

Hearing the ruckus, the police came around back and put the man in handcuffs until they could question everyone. Martin reminded them of the two break-in attempts previously and gave his bit of the story.

Ali filled in the details of what had happened before Martin got home, omitting the magical bit.

"You'll probably need to get your alarm company out," the officer told him. "I see you got your window fixed."

"Yes, sir. They came by today and the alarm people were already scheduled for tomorrow. Now I need someone to fix the door and lock. Any suggestions?"

They weren't allowed to make recommendations, so there was another task for the next day. With the man in custody and their dinner now cold, Martin and Ali went into the back of the shop and tried to block the door so no one else could come through.

With their dinner warming in the oven, Martin poured them both a drink.

"That hits the spot," Ali said. "I needed that."

"Now that we're alone, did you sense any magic around this guy? Anything at all?"

"No. Not a thing. Only thing I can figure is somebody with magical ability is hiring these guys to do his dirty work."

"I got the clay," Martin said, pulling it from his jacket pocket. "Tomorrow, barring any more excitement, we'll see about getting some dust from your jug and fashioning an image with it."

"Might as well. And then we can find a secure place for the jug."

# Chapter 14

After work the next day, Martin and Ali had a bite to eat and then got the jug out of the closet. Martin had found a small file to use on the rim to obtain a little bit of the old pottery.

"Are you sure this will work?" he asked Ali.

"Sure? No. But it should. I think."

"Any idea how much of this we need to mix with the clay?"

"You're the witch, not me."

"Seriously? This isn't the sort of thing I normally do, so any advice would be welcomed."

"It shouldn't take too much, if what they say is right. The voodoo guys only need a little bit of hair or some such to make their magic work."

"This is not voodoo," Martin argued.

"Didn't say it was, but the principle should be the same."

Locating the chip along the inside of the rim, Martin stuck a small portion of the clay to the jug underneath it to catch any filings that fell. With a deep breath, hoping it would work and not do too much damage to the jug, he took the file and gently rasped it across the exposed pottery.

Dust almost too fine to see trickled from the file onto the clay beneath. It was like catching early morning mist. Three or four strokes of the file later, he had a tiny pinch of dust on the clay.

Now to remove it without losing it anywhere. Holding his breath, lest he blow the dust all over the apartment, he unstuck the clay from the jug and carefully folded the clay inside it.

"All right. So far, so good," he muttered.

"Anything you need me to do?" Ali asked.

"Not yet, but hang around."

After talking with Peter about his project, he'd learned that too much foreign material in the clay would make it crack when fired, but he thought it would be fine. There was less than an eight of a teaspoon of the dust and a chunk of clay the size of his fist. What he didn't know about pottery would fill tomes though.

Kneading the small bit of clay into the larger piece, he tried to work it all in so the dust from the jug was evenly distributed. It was sort of like kneading bread dough. Not that he made bread himself, but he'd watched his mum as he was growing up. Baking bread was one of her specialties.

After a few minutes, he stopped and examined the lump of clay on the table.

"Do you think that's mixed up well enough?"

"You're askin' me?" Bubba answered. "I know less about this than you do."

"Fine. Now to make an image of the jug from it."

He didn't intend to make it hollow, but a single solid item more like a sculpture than a jug. Hopefully the fact that the shape would be similar, along with the intent behind it, would let it work. Looking at the original, he got to work.

After twenty minutes and several starts, he still wasn't happy. The thing was lopsided, lumpy, and the handle was pathetic.

"I don't think you should change jobs anytime soon," Bubba told him, looking at the miserable attempt.

"Can you do any better?" Martin snapped, his hands tired, his neck stiff, and a headache threatening to become a problem.

"I don't know. I might could," Ali said.

"Well, then, have at it."

Ali gave the original jug a good hard look, looked at the misshapen lump of clay on the table and snapped his fingers, with a definite smirk on his face.

Sitting there in front of him was a nearly perfect replica of the jug in green clay. Like they'd discussed before, it wasn't hollow, so it would never hold water or anything else, but it was a work of art.

"If you could do that, why did you sit here and watch me mangle this stuff?" Martin demanded.

"You seemed to want to make a go of it, so I figured you were havin' fun."

"Did it look like I was having fun?"

"Not so much, but you never know."

"Fine. Let's put the original back in the closet and set this somewhere to dry. I'll take it over to Peter in a few days."

Snapping a picture of it with his phone, along with the dimensions of it, he sent it to Peter to see about how long it would be before they could fire it.

"He said he'll be heating the kiln on Friday, so if we take it over to him Thursday after work, he'll put it in with his stuff."

"All right, boss. Let's hope this works. Do you need to say a spell over it or anything?"

"Maybe. I don't know. Like I said, this isn't the sort of thing I usually do."

Thinking about it for a few minutes, Martin got up, got a small notebook and tore out a sheet of paper. With a pencil, he wrote down few rhyming lines indicating the smaller image should be considered the same as the larger jug. Going over to a cupboard, he pulled out a small candle, chose some oil to rub onto it, and repeated the lines quietly to himself as he did so.

The two jugs were still sitting side by side on the table, so he chose a holder for the candle, placed it between the two jugs, and lit it, chanting as he did so. Once the candle was burning steadily, he took the piece of paper, held it in the candle flame until it caught up, and let it burn. When it had burned to ash, he powdered the ash with his fingers and lightly sprinkled it over the two jugs.

"Is that it?" Ali asked.

"As far as I know. The candle should only burn for a couple hours. Why don't we find something to drink and have a few snacks. We could watch a movie while it burns."

"All right. After the stuff going on around this place, I need a drink."

"I'm with you."

The evening passed quietly, at least on the outside. Martin thought a comedy would be good for the two of them, so he dug out some old Pink Panther DVD's and had Ali practically rolling in the floor. It's hard to beat the Pink Panther. And without all the modern technology, it was easier for Ali to understand.

The contractor who was going to fix the door would be along in the morning, so before they went to bed, they blocked the door up as best they could one more time. Ali offered to stay up and keep watch, but Martin told him to go on to bed. If they managed to break through all the stuff they had in front of the door, both of them should hear the commotion.

Maybe he should get a dog. He'd never considered it before, but then he'd never had any trouble until recently. Maybe something like a mastiff. Anything that size would scare any burglar away, or give him a heart attack. Either way, it would keep his property safe.

Now, what to do about the jug? He wanted to display it in the shop, but with all the kerfuffle, he wasn't sure it wouldn't invite even more trouble. When he'd bought the thing, he had never imagined all this. Who had ever heard of a genie in a whiskey jug, after all?

If he could find a way to reverse the curse, Ali would be free of the jug, he could display it without inviting any more trouble, get back to life as usual, and Ali could decide what he was going to do with his newly found freedom.

How did one go about lifting a curse? According to the law of reversal, whatever magic does, magic can undo. Did you have to use the same form of magic? Or could any type of magic work? He had only dabbled a little here and there. Even his protective spells he'd got out of a book. He assumed they would work, but he didn't know for sure.

It wasn't even as serious as a hobby, but more of a phase he'd gone through a few years back. He'd been interested in herbal remedies and chose to make it his occupation. Somewhere along the line he'd discovered his psychic ability to find things, which led to his interest in magic. After a few months of reading about it and trying out a few things, his interest had tapered off and only the protective spells remained.

It looked like he had some research to do and he should get to it soon, before anything more serious happened. Was there anyone he knew who could help him? He'd met with a group who practiced white magic, who were mainly a group of beginners. There had been one woman who seemed to have a bit more knowledge than the others. Now what was her name?

Crawling into bed, he spent a fitful night, between worrying about another break-in during the night and dreams about magical beings and powerful wizards. He was definitely not ready to open the shop when his alarm rang the next morning.

# Chapter 15

Ali hadn't had a good laugh in so long, he'd about forgotten how it was done. Even though he didn't understand everything about the movie, he got enough of it to appreciate the humour. He was a light sleeper, so he wasn't particularly worried about someone coming in during the night. He'd heard Martin tossing and turning, though.

Staggering into the kitchen from his bedroom, Martin looked like he'd risen from the dead instead of the bed.

"Son, you look like hell this morning. Are you sure you want to open the shop?"

"No, I don't want to, but I like having money to spend.. Besides, the contractor is coming over later to fix the door and frame, as well as replace the locks. That all takes money."

"You really don't understand about the djinn, do you?" he asked.

"What?"

"I could take care of the door, and probably the lock. The alarm system is beyond my understanding, but I could return everything to the way it was before the break-in."

"I suppose I'm used to doing everything the hard way. Besides, what would your price be for that? I've heard you guys are tricksters. After everything else going on around here, I don't need any more stress in my life."

"Well, yeah. We are tricksters, or we can be. But if we like someone, we can be a lot of help, too. And after all you've done for me, without being a selfish son of a bitch and wanting the whole world on a platter, I would be inclined to help out. Besides, there is a lot I need to learn about how things work these days."

"I've already got the guys coming over. Next time—I hope there is no next time—remind me before I call and I'll think about it. Okay?"

"If that's what you want. Are you sure you want breakfast this morning? You don't look too good."

Martin decided he wasn't hungry and just had a glass of juice. Ali wasn't sure that was enough to get by on, and he definitely wasn't sure Martin needed to be out of bed. But before they were ready to open the shop, the contractor knocked on what was left of the door and Martin got them started to work on it.

MARTIN FELT TERRIBLE. All the stress lately probably wasn't doing him any good. He tried to eat healthy foods and stay in shape, which usually worked out pretty well. But with all the surprises during the past couple weeks, it was all beginning to gang up on him.

What he needed was another holiday. Not an extended one like his tour of the American Southeast. Just a weekend, or a long weekend to relax in a cabin up by a lake. Anything to give him a break from all the goings on here at the shop.

But what could he do with Ali? Unless their trick with the small jug worked, taking him anywhere meant hauling that jug around, too. It was too big to go unnoticed anywhere. If there was someway to make it invisible or something, that would be great. But he wasn't a wizard.

Maybe Ali could do something, though if he could why hadn't he done it before now? Once he got these next few customers out of the shop, he'd ask him and see what his thoughts were. And he still needed to research curses or find someone else who could lift it for him.

But who could he trust? If Ali was right, anyone with magical talents could develop selfish ideas about owning the jug, with Ali still bound to it. So when he started asking around about lifting curses, he might open up another problem.

He hadn't seen Diane since their last fiasco. She was probably about finished with him after all the interruptions they'd had lately. Why couldn't he simply take a lady, who he was hoping would become his girlfriend, out for a nice evening without worrying about what disaster would await him when he returned? Was it seriously asking too much?

And how could he blame her if she decided to back off and refuse to go out with him again? He wouldn't go out with him either. Maybe he'd call her and at least find out how her day had gone.

By lunchtime he was feeling a little better. He had taken some of his cold remedy and drunk enough tea to float a battleship. Maybe something had helped. The contractors had finished replacing his door and the lock on it, given him the new keys and the bill, which he would submit to the insurance company. With a little luck, they would have a day or two of peace and quiet.

Ali had offered to make soup for lunch, which smelled wonderful. Hearing his stomach growl, Martin decided to close a few minutes early, as there were no customers in the shop. Turning the sign on the door, he climbed the stairs to give it a taste.

"This is wonderful, Ali," he said, taking another bite of the broth. "Do I want to know what it's called?"

"Now don't be like that, boss. It's chicken soup. It's supposed to be good for what ails ya."

The left over flat bread they had from a couple nights ago, which Ali had warmed up in the oven, went well with the soup. The guy was beginning to get the hang of a few things around the house, the oven being one of them. He still didn't understand how it worked, but he'd learned to use it.

"You look like you're feeling a bit better," Ali said. "Are you going back to work this afternoon?"

"Yeah, I need to. I've got bills to pay, same as anyone else. They sure won't pay themselves."

"Is there any way I could help? I can conjure up about anything," Ali offered.

"What? Have you conjure up money for my bank account? While it might be tempting, it wouldn't be right. For now, you're helping me out around the place here, and that's fine. Unless you had some sort of crafting skills?"

"What sort of crafting skills?"

"I don't know. Wood carving, glass blowing. No idea. I was thinking about something we could sell in the shop. But I don't need for you to do anything. It's not your fault you're here, and the troubles we've had recently aren't your fault either."

"If you had an idea of what you would like, I could probably conjure up some little trinkets of some kind."

"Really? Like what?"

"This is an apothecary shop, right? How about tiny apothecary jars or bottles filled with something sparkly for the ladies?" Al asked, snapping his fingers and extending a small bottle toward him.

The little bottle was clear glass with a cork-type stopper in it. There was a little ribbon around the neck, with a card bearing the name of the shop and the address. Inside the bottle, a shimmering liquid, like light mineral oil filled with fine glitter, moved and sparkled as he turned the bottle around.

"This is nice," he said. "but we would have to put a warning label on it so people would know not to drink it or anything. And maybe put the phone number and website address on the card as well."

"Do you think they would sell?" Ali asked.

"It's about that holiday time of year, with winter almost here and Christmas coming up. I can see using these as decorations, with all the pretty glitter in them."

"How many do you want?" Ali asked.

"I don't even know. Not too many for now, until we see how they sell. What are you asking in return?"

"From you, right now? Nothing. Only a place to stay and your help to learn about things in your world."

"You have that already. And I see no reason to change. I enjoy having you around, barring the break-ins of course."

"Sorry about that."

"I had an idea earlier, about the jug. Can you do anything to make it more portable, or make it invisible? It would make things a little easier."

"I can't change the size or shape of that particular jug. It's part of the curse. If I could change its size, I could pick it up, conceal it in a pocket or something, and disappear. Now, she couldn't have that, so she included something about it in the curse. Make it invisible? I might could do that, at least make it invisible to sight. Not necessarily to magic."

"Unless they send out someone who can sense magic next time, sight should be enough, shouldn't it?"

"At least for now, I reckon. You still can't display it in your shop, though. And if it's invisible nobody could see it anyway."

"Yeah, but if they couldn't see it, they couldn't steal it either."

"We could give it a try later, see what happens."

"And it's time to get back to work. See you after a while. I may close up a bit early if business is light."

"You do that. No point in being sick."

# Chapter 16

After work, Martin was supposed to take the small jug over to Peter's so he could fire it for him. Even Ali didn't know if it would work. Martin supposed that if it didn't work for some reason, they could try casting another spell on it. It could be that the firing would counteract the spell. Why hadn't he paid more attention when he was dabbling?

Finally finished for the day, he told Ali he would be back soon and would pick up something for dinner on the way, and then headed to Peter's with the little jug in his pocket. It looked dried to him, so hopefully it wouldn't shatter in the kiln.

"Martin," Peter called out to him from his workshop. "I was wondering when you would be here. Do you have your item with you?"

Pulling the little jug out of his pocket, he showed it to Peter. About five inches tall, in the same proportions as the original, it was kind of cute.

"I didn't know you did any sculpting," Peter told him.

"I don't, really. A friend helped me with it. Do you think it's ready for the kiln?" he asked.

Turning it around and examining it, Peter nodded.

"Looks fine. Feels cured. I'll put it in tomorrow morning with these other small things I have and we'll see what happens."

"When will it be finished?"

"Come around Saturday morning. By then everything will have finished firing and cooling down, and I'll have it out of the kiln. Are you going to want to glaze it?"

Glaze it? He hadn't even thought about glazing. The original was done in what they called a salt glaze, whatever that was.

"I don't know. This is a small replica of a jug I saw on my trip to America. It was a dark brown, about two hundred years old or so, and about eighteen inches tall."

"Salt glazed. I can't do a replica salt glaze on it. It's not allowed any more. But I have a glaze that's about the same color I could put on it. It wouldn't look quite like the salt glaze, but it would be close."

"Let me think about it. When would you be doing the glazing?"

"Come over Saturday and let's see if it survived firing. Then, if you want to glaze it, leave it here. I'll be glazing my things anyway and they'll probably be ready for the next fire on Monday, if I get busy. So around Tuesday next week?"

"All right. I'll come by Saturday morning and see what we've got and decide. Glazing would keep it nicer looking, wouldn't it?"

"Yeah, it would. The clay, even after firing is porous. The glaze would seal it."

"Okay. I've gotta go and grab something for dinner. I'll talk to you Saturday."

Martin had been having thoughts of fish and chips lately, so he ran by the shop and got enough for the two of them and hurried home. He worried anytime he wasn't there these days, wondering what disaster would strike next.

But this time he was relieved to find nothing wrong when he went through the back door and into the shop. Calling for Ali, he started up the stairs, looking forward to fish and chips.

"Everything all right, Ali?" he asked.

"Well, I think so," Ali told him, scratching his head.

"You think so? What happened?"

"Your phone thing in there has been ringing off and on for a while now. I didn't want to answer it, because I don't know what to do once I have. I heard someone talking."

Martin went to check on the answering machine and found it was from the contractor. Someone had mislaid his keys. Could they come by and see if they'd dropped them at his place?

Ringing them back, he said he'd take a look around, but they could come over. If he found them, he'd put them aside.

"Ali, have you seen a ring of keys around here anyplace? he asked.

"No, but I haven't looked either. What sort of keys?"

"The man said it was a small key ring with about 5 keys on it. The key ring logo was for Ford cars."

"What does that look like?" Ali asked.

"I would have to show you. Let's just look and see if there are any keys anywhere around back."

They started in the back entry, looking on the table by the door, under the table and all the way into the shop with no luck. Next would be outside.

"I'm not sure I want you outside, Ali," Martin said. "What if our intruder is still looking for you or the jug? Wouldn't you be safer inside?"

"We both would, most likely, but if it will make you happier, I'll stay in here and see if I can do anything to help."

Closing the door behind him, Martin went out through the back. There had been two men working on the door replacement, and most of the time they had been around in the back garden area. Not that the garden was very big. Mostly it was the sidewalk and a tiny strip of grass alongside it.

He checked the grassy area all the way to the corner of the building with no luck. Moving on, he trudged around front to where they had parked. They'd managed to find a spot not too far from the entrance to the back, so he checked all around the curb, the sidewalk, and the whole length of the little alleyway.

With the flashlight app on his mobile, he even looked down the street drain outside the building, but he didn't see anything which resembled keys of any sort. Lots of trash, but no keys.

About the time he had given up looking, a vehicle pulled up in front of the shops and parked.

"Hello! Martin?"

It was the man who had lost his keys along with the other guy who had helped with the job earlier.

"That's right. I think I've looked everywhere you might have been, but I haven't found anything yet. Feel free to have a look for yourself."

"Yeah, we got back to the shop late, and when I went to get in my truck to drive home, I discovered my keys missing. My house key is on that ring, too, so if I don't find them I'll have to break into my own house."

"You have a locksmith on the payroll. Why not just ask him to let you into your house?" Martin asked.

"That would work for tonight, I suppose. I have a spare key in the house, so I could get another key made tomorrow. But all my other keys are on that ring, too. I would much rather find them."

They searched all around the front of the building before asking if they could come around and look in the back.

"Sure. I've already looked, before it started getting so dark, but if you have a torch, you could have another look."

Leading the way back around the building, Martin suddenly felt a hint of something not being right. Speeding up a little, he tried to hurry to his back door, only to find the other two catching up with him.

"What's going on?" he demanded.

"You have something our boss wants. If you'll just hand it over, nobody gets hurt," the larger of the two men told him. The smaller of the two showed him a knife.

"So there are no keys. Right?"

"Right. Now where is the jug?"

"What jug are you talking about?" he asked trying to stall for time. "I have all sorts of jugs in my shop. It is an apothecary after all."

"You know which jug it is. Let's just go inside and you can get it for us."

"So who is your boss? I'm thinking it's probably not the guy who owns the contractor business."

"We work for him, too. This is a side job for someone else," the other man told him.

"Was it one of you who broke into my shop before?"

"Don't know nothin' about that," the first man said. "We're just here for the jug."

Martin opened the back door. He'd stalled about as much as he could. Perhaps Ali would see what was going on and lend a hand. Once they were inside, he looked around, but didn't see Ali anywhere. Maybe he could stall a little longer.

"Now, what does this jug you're after look like?" he asked. "Like I said, I've got all sorts of jugs around. Should we start in the shop?"

Turning down the corridor toward the shop, he heard a quick conference between the two ruffians behind him. Pretending nothing was wrong, he kept on walking, hoping Ali would do something.

As he passed through the doorway into the shop, he caught a slight motion to one side. A glance sideways told him Ali was there, and waiting for them. Hoping to give him a clue, he said, "So what's so important about this jug that you want? What were you going to do with it?"

"That isn't your concern," the first man said as he came into the shop and stopped dead in his tracks. The other one soon joined him, still as a statue, knife held out in front of him.

"Ali! I hoped you would get the hint. Now what do we do with them? I need to call the police, but how do I explain this to them?"

"I couldn't rightly say. All that legal stuff is your department. Are you allowed to defend yourself if someone breaks in?"

"But they didn't break in. Of course, they did threaten me with a weapon. How about this..."

A few minutes later, sirens blaring, the local officers came to the front of the shop and Martin let them in.

"Now, how did this happen?" the detective asked.

Martin explained about the phone call and let them listen to the message. He told them everything right up to the point where they stepped into the shop.

"My friend here, Ali, heard what was happening and when they stepped through the door, he hit the one guy over the head with one of the larger books behind the counter. This distracted the other guy and gave me time for an uppercut before he could do anything with that knife."

"And then you tied them up. Is that it?" the officer asked.

"We didn't want them to get away, after several break-in attempts.

"That must have been some uppercut. You don't look that big," the officer told Martin.

"Well, it mainly took him by surprise and he stumbled and fell. It didn't knock him out, just gave Ali the chance to give me a hand and get him restrained."

After the officers took the two would be burglars away, Martin and Ali tidied up the shop once again. The fish and chips were stone cold, so he wrapped them in foil and put them in the oven to reheat. Not that they would taste nearly as good as they would have earlier, but by this time he was definitely hungry.

"Any idea who their boss is?" Martin asked Ali.

"No, I couldn't get anything out of them."

They had attempted to get a name from them before the police arrived, but had no luck. Ali thought he might be able to get a face telepathically or something, but it seemed they had never actually met the person involved. Everything was done by phone.

"Maybe they can get something out of them at the station. I think I'll take a shower while the food heats. Can you just keep an eye on the door for me?"

"Yeah, and I think we should do something more to secure it again tonight. Maybe have the locks changed tomorrow."

Ali had a point. These were the same two men who had installed the new door and lock. One more claim with the insurance. At this rate, they were either going to drop him or start charging more. After all the years he had been with this company, with no claims, he was certainly making up for it lately.

The shower felt wonderful. Something about the altercation with those two just made him feel grubby. But as the bathroom door opened and the smell of fish and chips drifted through, his stomach made him forget all about it.

"Let's see if this is still edible," he told Ali.

Toasting his fingers slightly on the foil while trying to unwrap their dinner, he stuck his finger in his mouth and got a quick taste of the fish.

"Ah... This hits the spot," Ali said as he dug in.

If he'd known they would be eating so late, Martin would have brought more food. As it was, he was tempted to go back to the shop and splurge on another serving. If only he didn't have to leave Ali here alone. Maybe...

"Ali, could you eat a little more if we had it?" he asked.

"I could."

"Do you want me to go back out, or can you conjure us up some?" he asked, not sure what to expect.

"I would be delighted to help you out, boss. And with no charge or deals of any kind necessary. I like you and so far my being here has caused you quite a bit of trouble. It's on me."

Within seconds more fish and chips appeared on the table, much fresher than the first round.. Dividing it between them, he and Ali tore into the food like they were starving.

"It must be all the stress," Martin told the genie. "I can't remember the last time I had such an appetite."

"I ain't never had fish and chips before. Fish? Yeah. But this way of fixin' taters is a new one on me."

"Really? People have been fixing chips for a long time."

Thinking back, he decided they probably hadn't been around before Ali went int his jug that last time.

"They're fried in a special way so they cook quickly and crisp up nicely," he explained. "Haven't you ever had fried potatoes?"

"Yeah, but they never tasted like this. A guy could get used to these things," Ali told him finishing off the last of his chips.

"Yes, and a guy could gain too much weight if he ate too m any of them, too."

"I reckon so. What do you want to do with the door for the night?"

They blocked the door once again and Martin made a note to call a different locksmith the next day. With any luck, they could come change the lock the same day, so he wouldn't have to worry so much.

And he had to get back over to Peter's to check on the little jug he was firing for them. He had hoped to call Diane afterwards and see if they could get together for dinner or something, but with everything else going on he just wasn't sure he'd have time.

Martin went to bed a little later than normal. He couldn't have gone to sleep any earlier anyway, as keyed up as he was. And every little noise woke him during the night. So when the alarm sounded the next morning, he was seriously tempted to turn it off, roll over, and go back to sleep.

But there was too much to do. First things first. Breakfast.

Ali must have been up early, too. The smell of coffee reached him as he stepped into the corridor on his way to the kitchen. Coffee and bacon.

On the table he found coffee already poured, a carafe filled with more, and bacon, eggs, and scones nearly finished.

"Where did all this come from?" he asked.

"Well, I figured you'd been having a rough time, and I knew today was going to be busy and you would need a good meal. So I worked a little magic and made sure you would have enough to get you through until lunch," Ali told him, sitting across from him and helping himself to breakfast.

"I certainly appreciate it, man," he said, digging right in. "It is going to be busy. As soon as I eat, I'll see about a locksmith and go from there."

The locksmith he managed to reach said he would be out in the afternoon, around two, so Martin arranged to meet Peter around eleven to take a look at the jug.

"Did it survive firing?" he asked him over the phone.

"Yes, it did. For some reason, it slumped a little bit to one side, but it's kind of cute that way. I think it would look fantastic if you decided to glaze it."

Rather than leave Ali on his own, he wrestled the original jug into the boot of his car and took him along. He certainly hoped this worked. Dragging the big jug around was a nuisance.

"Is there no countryside left anymore?" Ali asked.

"Of course there is. But I live here in London, and it's pretty crowded around here. Everyone wants to live in the city."

"Why? Don't they get tired of it all after a while?"

"People like it for the convenience and because anything you want is here in town. All the shopping you might ever want to do, entertainment, restaurants. It's all here."

"Couldn't they just come in when they needed something? I've only been here a short time, and most of that in your place, but it feels like I can't breathe. So many people and vehicles. How do they make them go so fast?"

"That's another thing I can't explain very well. You'd have to understand about engines and the like."

"More magic," Ali mumbled.

"Not magic. Technology."

"Well, I don't think much of it," Ali replied. "The whole world rushes around without even taking time to breathe, seems like."

74

"I can't disagree with you there," he said as they pulled into Peter's drive.

After the introductions, Peter led the way to his shop. He had all manner of things displayed, some ready to sell, some waiting for the glaze, and other things waiting for their first firing.

"You must keep busy," Ali told the man. "People buy all these things?"

"Yes, they do," Peter told him. "I sell just about everything I craft. And here is your little jug."

It was just a little wonky. It looked like the jug was bowing slightly at the waist, directly away from the handle. Or like it was getting ready to pour itself.

"It's kind of cute that way," Martin said, examining the jug. "I think it'll be just fine. Ali," he said as he turned toward the genie, "what do you think? Should we go ahead and glaze it, too?"

"HOW LONG WOULD THAT take?" Ali asked.

He was hoping the idea worked, and he didn't want to wait much longer to find out. At the moment, he was bound to the original jug, so he couldn't go out for a walk, even with Martin. And he would love to see a little bit of the world he now lived in. But who wants to walk around toting a jug that size?

"I'll be done with my other things today, they'll finish drying over the weekend, and I'll plan to fire Monday afternoon. So you could come around Tuesday after work and take a look."

Thinking it over, Ali had to agree it would be a better idea to have it glazed. Otherwise it would pick up every bit of dirt and grease in the world and soon it would look horrible.

"I guess we can wait that long," he told Martin and Peter. "What color is it going to be?"

Martin had told him they couldn't glaze it in the same manner as the original, but he hoped it would be close to the same color, if for no other reason than to keep it as close as possible for the sake of the magic.

Turning toward some of his finished items, Peter picked up something and held it up for them to see. It was a small plate with a country scene on it.

The dirt road running between the fields was a rich brown color, very much like the color of his jug.

"That should be fine," he told Martin. "I think it will look great when it's finished."

Thanking Peter for his time, Martin offered to pay him for his trouble, but he refused.

"You never know. I might need your services at some point in the future."

"Call me anytime," Martin answered, as they made their way back toward the car.

Once inside and on their way back to the shop, asked, "What do you think?"

"I could feel a bit of magic still there, something kind of like I get with the real jug. Maybe it'll work out."

"Great! If it will work for now, we'll have some time to work on lifting the curse, without having you stuck in the apartment for the duration."

"I mean, your place is fine and all, but it does get a little tight after a while," Ali admitted.

"Yeah, it can. With a little bit of luck, you'll soon be able to get out of the shop every now and again."

"With a little luck and a bit of magic."

# Chapter 17

After a bite of lunch at a little Chinese place on the way, Martin and Ali made it back in time to get the jug tucked away inside again before the locksmith arrived .

"Now, what do we have on for the rest of the day?" Ali asked.

"Aside from the locksmith, not much," Martin answered. "I'd thought I'd call Diane and see if she'd like to come over for a little while this evening. Maybe order some take-away for the three of us, before we had some wine and she and I spent a little time together."

"Don't worry, boss. If she comes over, I'll disappear—unless trouble comes looking for us again."

"Don't even joke about it," Martin warned. "I've had about enough trouble. I almost wish I'd never seen that damned jug."

"I understand, but I'm just as glad you did. It's the first time in recent history I've had the possibility of chucking the thing for good."

"I would say I understand, but I really don't. I can't even imagine living as long as you must have, let alone spending so much time in the jug."

"It's all right. No harm done, particularly. And if you can lift the curse, you'll soon be free of me."

"I don't need to be free of you, Ali," Martin explained. "Unless you're ready to take off and see the world, you're welcome to stay here and make this your home base. I'm not trying to get rid of you, but your jug is a little inconvenient."

"I appreciate it, boss, and I may take you up on it once we're all settled. But at least I would have the option."

The locksmith was an older gentleman who must have been working with locks his whole life. He fussed at the installation the other company had done and then set about fixing their problem.

Martin had chosen to go with a whole new lock set instead of simply re-keying the lock. He wanted no way for the other bunch to get back into his shop and into his flat. A new lock set from a different company seemed a better idea. And he upgraded to a better quality set, too. His insurance company should appreciate it, after all the recent claims.

While the locksmith did his work under Ali's watchful eye, he called Diane to ask her about dinner.

"I have nothing else on tonight," she told him. "If you could pick up some Indian food, I'll bring drinks and snacks for the three of us. How is Ali working out in the shop?"

"He's doing well. I have to say I'm impressed. But don't worry. Once dinner is finished, he has something else to do for the evening. It'll just be the two of us."

"Sounds good. Around seven?" Diane asked.

"Seven is great."

After they saw the locksmith on his way, Martin shuddered at the bill, and got the paperwork all sorted for the insurance company.

"What do you think, boss? Should I go ahead and conjure up some of those little bottles you liked?"

Shaped like little Arabic styled perfume bottles, they were enchanting filled with the glittery oil.

"Sure, if you feel like giving it a go," Martin answered. "Not too many for now, until we see if they sell, but it would be nice to have some for Monday morning."

"Where do you want them for now?" Ali asked.

That was a good question. He didn't want them in the shop yet. Maybe in the storage room behind the shop.

"Let's go look in the junk room."

After clearing some space on one of the shelves, Ali got ready to conjure up some trinkets. Martin left him to it, preferring not to know how it was going to happen. As far as he was concerned, the less he knew, the better.

About an hour later, Ali asked him to come back and have a look, and there on the shelf stood around twenty-five little bottles standing about three inches tall, with tall slender necks, and sparkling with glittery oil inside. The bottles were slightly different, depending on the color of the glitter, which went from deep reds and oranges to mysterious blues and violets, and every color in between.

"Wow! These are amazing," Martin said, holding one up to the light.

Giving the bottle a little shake, he was taken with the swirl of colored glitter inside. Around the neck of each bottle was a silk ribbon the same color as the glitter.

"It took a little longer than I'd expected," Ali explained. "I thought it would be easier if I did each kind separately until I got the hang of it. Do you like them?"

"These a marvelous," Martin said. "They should sell well in the shop. Now all I have to do is decide how much to charge for them. Could we give one to Diane tonight and see what she thinks about them?"

"They're your bottles. Do what you like with them," Ali said.

"They may be mine, but you're the one who made them. If you don't want to give one to Diane, then we won't."

"Oh, no! It's fine and it would be a good test. Does she have a favorite color?"

What was her favorite color? Blue? Green?

"I don't know," he admitted. "She wears blue a lot. We could try one of the blue ones."

"DIANE! RIGHT ON TIME," Ali heard Martin say as he opened the door.

"I hope this wine is all right," she answered. "I knew you were picking up Indian food, so I thought something a little more robust in a white wine would work."

"This looks great," the man said, taking her parcels upstairs and into the kitchen.

He had just returned with their food about ten minutes before and had it in the oven to keep warm. Ali had helped set the table and was now putting the snacks into bowls for them. There were some of the regular sort of crisps along with some poppadoms Diane had picked up. They looked tasty and Ali was looking forward to dinner. As the food came out of the oven, the scent of chicken biryani filled the kitchen. There was a heaping portion of rice alongside. Ali was hoping they could sit down soon.

"Shall we?" he heard as Martin finished pouring the wine.

"Absolutely. It smells fantastic," Diane told him. "Which place did you order it from?"

They discussed different restaurant locations, which told Ali nothing at all, but the food was tasty and filling. He had always loved to eat and living so long in the jug had done nothing to change that.

They had a leisurely meal before they cleaned up the table and returned to the living room.

"What about some dessert?" Ali asked.

"Did we have something for dessert?" Martin asked him, unaware that Ali planned to conjure up something in the kitchen.

"I thought earlier that something sweet would be nice after dinner. What do you think?"

"By all means."

Back in the kitchen, Ali focused his mind on some of the Jordanian filled cookies he had always loved. A butter pastry filled with nuts and honey, they were delightful with coffee. They went even better with Turkish coffee, but he wasn't sure how either of his two friends felt about Turkish. It could be an acquired taste. Better stick with the kind Martin normally made.

Coffee and pastries in hand, Ali returned to the living room.

"Oh! These are scrumptious," Diane proclaimed after biting into one of the delicate cookies. "Where did you get them?"

"They're something my mother used to make," Ali explained, hoping she would drop the subject. Technically this was true. His mother had actually made them quite often a long, long time ago.

"I do wish I had the recipe. Is it difficult to make?"

"Only if you make the pastry by hand."

"I'm rubbish with pastry. I suppose I'll just have to come over and wheedle some out of you every now and again."

"Before I forget," Martin said, pushing off the sofa onto his feet, "I had something to give you. Ali and I are thinking of selling them before the holidays."

Quickly skipping down the stairs, he soon returned with one of the little bottles filled with blue glitter. Diane's face lit up in surprise and delight.

"These are so adorable," she declared. "Where did you get them?"

"Ali made them up. We were thinking they would look good as ornaments or holiday decorations."

"They would for sure," the woman agreed. "Do they come in different colors?"

"We have several different colors in this first batch. I thought you would like the blue," Martin told her.

"I do. It is my favorite color, you know. What other colors do you have?"

They took her down to look at the assortment and watched as she nodded her head.

"These are great, but you should do some in a shimmery white or silver, for people who like to do an all white Christmas. And maybe some in gold,"

"Why didn't we think of that?" Martin asked her. "Those would look great."

"I'll do some of those with the next batch," Ali agreed. He didn't quite understand the whole Christmas tradition, but was happy to benefit from it.

"When will you start selling these?" Diane asked.

"I thought we'd put a few out on Monday and see what sort of interest there was. We're just past Halloween, so we have around six or seven weeks before Christmas. What do you think?"

"I think you should go ahead and give them a try. Then, if people like them, you could do up some more in time for the holiday."

"Sounds good," Martin said. "What do you think, Ali?"

"I could take some time and get some of the silver and gold ones done. Any other colors you'd like to see?"

"Make sure you have lots of red and green. With the silver and gold, I think that should be wonderful."

"If you'll excuse me, I'll head up to my room and turn in," Ali said, glancing up at Martin. There was no point spoiling their evening. Again.

"All right, Ali," Diane called out as he turned toward the corridor. "And let me see those other ones when you're done. These are marvelous."

MARTIN HAD THOUGHT Diane would like the little bottles, but she seemed mesmerized by the blue one he'd given her. Ali wouldn't have done anything sneaky, would he?

If everyone was as taken with them as Diane seemed to be, they should sell quickly. Pouring a little more wine for the two of them, Martin sat back to relax, but he was having a little trouble. The last two times he and Diane had tried to get together, something had happened, so tonight he felt like he was waiting for the other shoe to drop.

"Martin, what is it," Diane asked.

"I suppose it's all the break-ins we've had, and the supposed contractors who tried to come back and steal from me after hanging the new door. I just feel on edge."

"Should I go?" she asked.

"No, not at all," he quickly answered. "I'll be fine, unless something else comes up."

"It has been a little exciting lately, hasn't it?" she said with a smile.

After another glass of wine, things got a little more exciting in the living room, but went no further. Before they took their friendship that extra step, they called a halt to the proceedings. But maybe there was hope.

"I had a wonderful time," Diane told him as he helped her with her coat. "And nothing strange happened this evening."

"I know. I worried for nothing."

He'd called a taxi for her and it came as she adjusted her scarf and found her purse. After another kiss, he walked her around to the front of the building to catch her taxi. He could get used to this. Not the taxi bit, but the snuggling in front of the fire after a glass of wine.

There was still a little wine left in the bottle, and it would be a shame to let it go to waste. Right? Pouring it into his glass, Martin dropped down onto the sofa to enjoy it before he turned in.

"Hey, boss," he heard behind him.

Nearly spitting the wine all over the coffee table, he spun around and glared at Ali.

"Sorry. I heard you come back in and thought I'd ask you something real quick."

"What is it?" he asked in a slightly irritated tone.

"How many more of those bottles do we want to make and how soon do you want them?"

"I don't know. Let's talk about it in the morning."

Thinking back to the way Diane had reacted to the one he'd given her, he asked, "Did you do something to make them more attractive than they would normally be? Some sort of magic to draw people in?"

"Not intentionally, but a little something might have got added to the mix. Why?"

"Just wondering. I would rather not trick people into buying them," Martin told him.

"No, but if you'd like I could add a little something next time."

"No, let's see how they sell first. I don't think we'll need to add anything."

"You're the boss.

# Chapter 18

The rest of the weekend was relaxed for a change. He called Diane Saturday morning to make sure she got home all right, then he and Ali took another drive in the country. His uninvited guest was a little frayed around the edges from all the people and the traffic noise of the city.

Martin could kind of understand his problem. He would prefer something quieter, in a village perhaps, but with his line of work, the larger population worked out better for him. Of course, he could take a drive anytime he liked, unlike Ali, who was tied to his jug.

"I have a question, Ali," he began as they neared the outskirts of the city.

"What's that?"

"If this little jug thing doesn't work out, do you have any other ideas?"

"I sure don't."

"Question two. Let's say it does work. What happens if someone steals the original jug, assuming I retain possession of the smaller one?"

"Well, now. Let me think. Whoever stole it wouldn't be the rightful owner, but they would have possession. Even with the little image, they would have more in their possession than you would. Still, you would be the owner of the thing and in possession of an image of it. I couldn't say for sure."

Martin had given some thought to the matter previously and come to about the same conclusion. They did say possession was nine tenths of the law. But if he was still alive and still possessed part of it, enough of it for the laws of magic to work with...

"Hopefully it won't come to that," he said with a sigh. "I hope we can get you some freedom while I find a way to undo the curse. I'm working on that, too. But I seriously don't want to mess it up."

"Yeah. Nothing quite like magic gone wrong to ruin a guy's day," Ali agreed. "So how did it go with Diane last night?"

Keeping the more intimate details to himself, he told Ali he had enjoyed the evening and hoped they could do it again soon.

"I don't know much about this holiday you have coming up, but it seems like a good time to celebrate. Maybe the two of you can step it up a little bit."

"I don't know, Ali. I'm not sure I'm ready for all that yet," he admitted. "Yes, I would like to get married someday, and Diane is a someone I care for very much. But I'm not sure now is the right time. And while I enjoy Diane's company, I'm not sure she's the right woman."

"Well, if you need a little boost, let me know."

"Thanks, but no. Any magic between us needs to be the real thing."

"All right, boss. But if you change your mind..."

Sunday was his day to tidy up around the house, catch up on any projects in his flat or in the shop, or catch up on his reading. He normally liked to read mysteries or intrigue, but after the past couple weeks, he was right off the subject.

What about the holidays?

His family lived farther north, up toward Bedford. He usually went home for Christmas, but if he didn't have the whole genie thing sorted out by then, what should he do? Explain him away as an old college friend come visiting?

No, that wouldn't work. He could never pull that off and Ali wouldn't have a clue. There was no way he could even pass as being from this century.

Diane said she usually went to visit family, also. Her folks were out toward Oxford. If they got together during this next year, they would have to sort out the holidays as well. Of course, working with Diane was a little easier than working with Ali. She could at least hold her own in a conversation.

Should he tell Diane about Ali? And what would she do if he told her Ali was a genie? Think he was mental, most likely. Until recently he would have thought the same thing.

Diane was a level-headed woman. She had a shop a little further toward the outskirts of the city where she did therapeutic massage and energy healing. But did she believe in magic? That was the thing. How could he explain what had been going on without delving into the subject of magic?

He'd finished all his chores, tidied up everything, dusted all the shelves—even though Ali kept them spotless—and had finally run out of things to take his mind off his dilemma. Maybe a walk would help clear his head.

"Ali," he called. "I'm going for a walk. I shouldn't be long."

"All right, boss. You go ahead. I'll hold the fort here, in case anything comes up."

Right. They'd had several days of quiet. Maybe it was all over. Changing clothes and slipping on his trainers, Martin headed out the back and around the building. He set a timer on his phone in case he got distracted and headed out down the pavement.

After a few minutes, he picked up the pace to a jog. He needed to get out for more exercise. Since Ali had been here, he'd neglected his fitness plan dreadfully. Before long, and far too soon, he was breathing hard and ready to turn back. Checking the time, he saw he had overshot the halfway point by a few minutes. Apparently he'd failed to make sure the timer had started before he headed off.

Break over. Time to pick it up and get back to the flat.

About a block before he reached his building, he slowed down and did some stretching. There was no point being sore the next day and it would only take a few minutes. The jog had given him a spark of energy he'd been missing. Hopefully it would also help him sleep tonight.

Rounding the back corner of his building, he saw the back door was open. Rushing to investigate, he heard Ali talking to someone in the shop. Trying to be quiet so he could hear what was being said, he crept in through the back and tiptoed down the corridor.

"Now look, son," he heard Ali say, "tell whoever you work for that we can't have any more of this nonsense. Me and Martin are about tired of people breaking into his shop and trying to snitch stuff. Who do you work for anyway?"

"I can't say," a voice said. It sounded like a younger male.

"Of course you can," Ali argued.

"No. You don't understand. If I tell who he is, he'll kill me. I can't say."

Maybe it was time to intervene. Martin strode down the hall and into the back room of the shop. Standing stock still in the middle of the room was a young man in about his mid-twenties. It looked like he was struggling to free himself, but couldn't move except to blink his eyes, breathe, and answer questions.

"Hi, boss," Ali said. "We had another visitor while you were out."

"So I see."

Walking around to face the man, Martin asked, "What is your boss so interested in?"

"Some old jug," the fellow finally admitted. "I don't know why, only that he wants it real bad."

"I have a lot of old jugs," Martin told him. "I collect old bottles and jugs to display in my shop."

"Yeah, but this one is special," the thief told him. "It's supposed to be a bigger jug, dark brown, and he said there was a genie in it."

"Do you believe in genies?" Martin asked, amused at the guy's tone.

"Not me, but he was paying good if I could snag it for him. I figured it was just an old jug you'd found somewhere and wouldn't really miss."

"Have you found it yet?" Martin asked.

"No. Your friend here did something weird to me almost as soon as I got in. Must be some sort of taser or something. Nobody said anything about you havin' a flat mate."

Martin told Ali to keep an eye on the guy while he called the police. Again. This was getting to be a bit redundant.

Half an hour later, the police had come and gone, he and Ali had fixed the door. Well, Ali had fixed it. Martin was about out of money for contractors and locksmiths.

"How did he get in?" Martin asked.

"He tried to pick the lock. When that didn't work, he gave it a whoppin' great kick," Ali explained. "I'd been waiting in the back room here, hopin' he'd give it up. When he got in, I did what I could until you got here."

"Thanks again," Martin told him. "And thanks for fixing the door. I'm tired of talking to the insurance company. What do you feel like having for dinner?"

Ali had never had pizza before he met Martin, so Martin phoned in an order. Leaving Ali to watch the place once again, he dashed off to pick it up. He was only gone fifteen minutes, but was worried the whole time he. After he'd thought they were done with all this, to have another break-in rattled him.

Ali dug right into the pizza. Martin had ordered one with a lot of meats on it, and one that was chicken and veggies. By the time they were finished eating, there was just enough left over to snack on for breakfast.

"Trust me. There's nothing like cold pizza for breakfast."

"Cold pizza? Don't you warm it up first?" Ali asked.

"I suppose you could, but I like it cold in the morning. I'm not sure why, but I think it's better that way."

After a glass of wine, he called Diane to let her in on the happenings at the shop.

"What is everyone after?" she asked. "You've never had any trouble before."

"The only thing I know is what this guy said before the police got here. He said he was supposed to steal a jug. It sounded like the jug I brought back from America."

"But why would anyone want that?" she asked. "It's just an old, empty jug. Kind of cute in its own way, but just a jug."

"Yes. Next time you're over you can have another look and help me see if there's something we're missing," he told her, suddenly worried about anyone else seeing it. But surely it would be safe to show it to Diane. Wouldn't it?

Once he'd finished the call, he called to Ali.

"I told Diane she could have another look at the jug, and see if there was something she could find out about it. Can you think of any reason Diane shouldn't see the jug?" he asked.

"Not unless she's a wizard or something, but I didn't feel anything like that around her. There's a little more energy than around most people, but not wizard-like."

"She works with energy for healing," Martin explained, "but nothing else as far as I know."

"I don't think I'd tell her about me being in it, but just showing it to her should be fine."

"Is there anything you can do to help with the break-ins? Maybe do something to keep the door from opening from the outside? Make it kick proof? I'm running out of options."

"Let me think a mite on it," Ali told him. "I might could come up with something."

# Chapter 19

Monday was the start of the average week, except that they had put out the little glass trinkets for sale. Martin had put together a small display in the front window to attract people into the shop, and it seemed to have worked. By lunchtime, they had sold all of the bottles Ali had previously made.

"I guess I'll have to get busy tonight and get some more ready," Ali told him.

"Yes. If they keep selling this well, we could make a pretty good profit on them," Martin told him.

"Maybe you can use it to buy something special for your girl," Ali suggested.

"Maybe I can. And here she comes now," he said as Diane strolled down the walk toward his door.

"Hi, Martin! How are your little bottles selling? Do you have any more?" she asked.

"We're sold out, as a matter of fact," he told her, giving her a little hug.

With a pout she said, "I guess I'll have to wait for another shipment to buy some for my mother. I sent her a picture of mine and she adored it."

"We should have some more in a couple days. Do you want to go somewhere for lunch?" he asked.

"Well, that might be nice," she said looking up at him with those blue eyes sparkling.

"Ali, will you be all right for lunch?" he asked. "I'll lock up for an hour and be back around two o'clock."

"I'll be fine. I'm sure I can come up with something."

There was a little family owned place just down the street, so they walked arm in arm, almost without a care in the world. Once they were seated, Diane looked at him with a serious look on her face.

"Now, tell me about this jug," she said. "Why do so many people want it? Who have you told about it?"

"You're the only person I've told about buying the jug. I haven't even told my family. I got it cleaned up and stuck it in the back room until I could figure out where I wanted to put it. Since then, everyone in the world has been trying to get their hands on it."

"What makes it so special?" she asked.

"I don't know. I did some research on it when I first got it. It's old, but not exceedingly old. It was probably made in the USA around two hundred years ago. This particular type of jug was used quite often for storing home-made whiskey. It's dark brown and salt glazed. They were pretty common at one time."

"So why would anyone want this one?" Diane persisted.

"You tell me."

"Hm... Maybe I can take a look at it when we get back from lunch."

"Of course. I had intended to ask for your help in placing it out front, but with all this trouble lately..."

"That's all right. You can make it up to me with dinner later in the week."

Now this was different. Maybe she was beginning to think seriously about their dating.

"I'll give it some thought and come up with something nice."

"I'll hold you to it," she said with a big smile.

They took a leisurely walk back to the shop, Diane's arm through his. Wouldn't it be nice to close up for the rest of the day and go do something fun with her? Sadly, bills got in the way of his leisure time, especially after fixing and replacing so many things at the shop.

Opening the door, he called for Ali and let him know they'd returned. Hanging his coat up in the back, he motioned for Diane to follow him into the back room to see the jug. It was still sitting where it had been since he'd cleaned it, right there on the work bench. He'd left the stopper out, but it was lying there as well, next to the jug.

"So this is what everybody has to have, is it?" Diane asked.

"It would seem so. Nobody showed any interest in breaking in until this was delivered after my trip. Since then it has been a circus around here."

"May I?" Diane asked as she reached out toward the jug.

"Of course."

As Martin watched, she stroked her fingers down the side of the jug, caressing the curve of the pottery. Sliding her hand back up the jug, she ran her fingers around the outside of the handle before slipping them through the opening, as if to pick it up.

"It's a bit heavy," he cautioned her.

"Oh, I wasn't going to pick it up. I just wanted to see what the handle felt like."

Next, she ran a finger around the very rim of the jug's opening. Standing on her tiptoes, she peered inside.

"What do you see?" Martin asked. Who knew she would be so taken with this old jug.

"Nothing inside," she told him, "but there is so much energy in and around it, it simply calls to me. I can't figure out where all the energy comes from."

"Maybe that's why I had to have it once I saw it in that old shop," Martin said.

"It could be. You're not extremely energy sensitive, but with any inclination at all it would have drawn you in."

"Is that why everyone wants it?" he asked.

"Hm. I'm sure it has something to do with it. But there must be more to it than that. Was there anything in the jug? Like gems, old papers, coins?"

"Nothing like that, no," he told her. Which was mostly true. Ali wouldn't fit into any of those categories.

"I'm wondering if it held something valuable, something the owner cherished so much that his love for whatever it was left this energy behind."

"But how long would something like that hang around?" Martin asked. "The guy I bought it from said it had been in the shop before he even bought it from the previous owner. And he'd been there for twenty years."

"That does seem like an awfully long time," Diane mused, still running her fingers over the jug.

"If you can think of anything, I would appreciate it if you'd clue me in."

"Certainly. You know, it's almost like there's a touch of magic along with all the energy."

"I thought magic and energy were the same thing," Martin said.

"Well, yes and no. Magic is energy, but it's a unique frequency."

"Okay, you've lost me. No, don't even try to explain it," he told her.

"All right then," she said with a little laugh. "I should get back to my place and I'm sure you've got customers waiting. Give me a call later in the week."

Martin saw her out the door, let Ali know he would be in the shop, and went out to take care of his clients. Several of them had heard about the little bottles he'd had for sale and were disappointed they'd sold out.

"But I'll have some more later in the week," he assured them. "Those were a trial run to see if there was any interest."

Eventually he had a little break and Ali came around to talk to him.

"I don't know what's going on, but there is somebody watching the shop," the genie told him.

"Is he there now?" Martin asked, reaching for his phone.

"I haven't actually seen him, as such. I've felt a presence searching the area, using something like magic."

"Oh, lord. That's all we need on top of everything else," Martin muttered. "Any suggestions?"

"Keep an eye on anybody who comes in. I'll watch out for any more secretive attempts."

"If Diane can feel the energy from that thing, do you suppose other people can, too?" Martin asked.

"I guess so. If they're used to using magic, they could tell something is here. I'll do what I can."

The afternoon was stressful. Martin suspected everyone who came through the door. And what would he do this evening after he locked up? Perhaps he should look up some of his old friends, those who were interested in magic, and see if they could help him set up some protection around his place. So far the police weren't doing too well in that department. Sure, they got to the shop quickly once he'd called, but by that time the burglars were already inside.

It would help if it were smaller. He could hide it someplace besides in this back room or in a closet. Seriously, a closet was the first place anyone would look.

"Ali," he called out as he was locking the front door. "I need to ask you something."

His house mate strolled down the corridor and raised his eyebrows in question.

"You said you can't change the shape or size of the jug. Right?"

"Yep. That's it."

"You also said that if it got broken, you were still bound to it. But since you aren't actually living in it now, would you have to fix it right away?"

"What are you gettin' at?" Ali asked him.

"I want to hide it someplace a little more securely than where it is now. If it were smaller I have several places I could put it. Hell, we could even take up some floor boards and make a space under the floor if we wanted. But as big as it is..."

"You want to hide it under the floor?" Ali asked.

"Well, that would make it more difficult to find, wouldn't it?"

"It would be better than sitting here on this shelf. We could do that."

"I don't have time to dig a hole that big. Could we break it and put the pieces in the hold?"

"Stand back, boss. Where do you want it?"

Slightly confused, Martin thought for a moment. If he could hide it under the floor, where would he put the access?

"How about under the work bench?" he said, just for the sake of argument.

"All right."

Ali seemed to think about it for a few seconds, then he closed his eyes briefly, opened them again and waved his hand.

And suddenly, the jug had disappeared from the work bench as if into thin air.

"Ali, where is the jug?"

"Right where you said you wanted it."

"How do I get to it?"

"If you need it, just ask me. I'll bring it back out."

"But if someone kidnaps you or something..."

"All right. Keep your shirt on."

With another wave of his hand, Ali seemed pleased.

"Take a look under there," he told Martin, gesturing under the bench.

The floor boards seemed a little different from before. Studying them for a moment, he saw a tiny crack between two of them. Taking a knife off the work bench, he pried up on the board and a section of the floor came up, revealing the jug down inside a perfectly dug hiding place.

"Will that do for you?" Ali asked with a wide grin.

"Perfectly. Now, what do you say we have something to eat?"

They fixed dinner in for the evening. Martin had put some chicken on to bake as soon as he closed the shop and there was stuff for salad. He would need to go grocery shopping soon, though. Cooking for two people, even with Ali helping, took more than he was used to.

After dinner, they sat down to watch the news. Thinking back to earlier in the day, he asked Ali if he felt anyone watching the place.

"Not right now. I think maybe they were just getting the lay of the land, kind of seeing the best way in."

"Do I need to strengthen my protective spells?"

"It wouldn't hurt. I don't know how much it will help if you're dealing with a wizard, but it might give us a little warning."

He would definitely call someone the next day. But the next day was Tuesday. Peter should have their little jug ready by then. And that brought new problems of its own.

He could still call one of the other magic students he had known and see if they could give him any advice before they went to pick it up.

But who could he trust? They didn't have any idea who was trying to steal the jug, whether it was only one person or several, or what sort of magic they were dealing with. There were too many variables.

And then there was Diane. They were supposed to go out again, and he wanted to take her out, but her reaction to the jug made him a little bit uneasy. Of course, she worked with energies all day long. He should expect her to sense any energy around the jug.

The energy had to be there due to the binding and the curse. It probably had something to do with Ali living in it for so long, too.

# Chapter 20

Tuesday morning it was cold and drizzling. There probably wouldn't be too many customers today, but Martin would have loads of people in later in the week for cough, cold, and sore throat remedies. Busying himself in the shop, he rearranged shelves, put up a few minimal decorations for the season and tried to keep his mind off all the trouble he'd been having.

Ali was getting some more of the little bottles ready for sale. Martin didn't even want to know where they came from. As long as they sold well, he would be happy. And so far they had been a real hit. He did like Diane's idea of the metallic glitter instead of only the brighter colors. After all, silver and gold were big at Christmas time.

By lunchtime, he'd had a few customers, but the drizzle continued. Not wanting to go out for lunch, he decided to order delivery pizza. Ali had enjoyed it the last time they'd had it, so he got some extra. His flatmate could certainly put it away. Of course, he had been trapped inside a jug for a couple lifetimes.

"Weren't we supposed to go look at our pottery this evening?" Ali asked.

"Yeah. I keep hoping this miserable weather will break, but looking online it looks like we're in for several days of this. If it turns cold, we might even get some snow."

"Snow? Really?" Ali asked.

"Yeah. Why?"

"I've never lived anywhere it snowed before. Might be interesting."

"It's not likely. And if it snows. it probably won't even last all day. It looks pretty while it's falling though."

"Huh. I guess we'll see."

The pizza was a hit, and they did manage to have enough left for later. Deciding he'd had enough of the shop for the day, Martin closed a few minutes early. There were so few customers today, it hardly seemed worth keeping the place open.

While the drizzle had become more of a mist, it was still cold and damp out. Putting the jug in the car, he and Ali drove over to Peter's to look at what he had for them.

"You're a little early," the man said as they knocked on the shop door.

"You know how it is in this weather. I thought we could get here early and get home early."

"I think you're gonna like your jug," Peter told them, cleaning his hands. "It took the glaze really well."

Dodging around all the things he had out on his floor, Peter picked up the small object and brought it to them. Martin could scarcely believe his eyes as he looked it over. And there was a tiny feeling about it, an almost electrical tingle, that somehow felt welcoming.

"How did you get this effect?" he asked.

"I don't know. I've never seen that sort of thing before. I wouldn't even know how to begin to get this combination of effects. Did you make any additions to the clay?" Peter asked.

"Only a tiny amount of dust from an old jug. Maybe an eighth of a teaspoonful. Would that have made any difference?"

"Wouldn't think so. It was already fired, right?"

"Yeah. A long time ago."

"Do you have any more of it?"

"Maybe a little bit. I could probably scrape up that much more. Why?"

As they talked, Martin turned the little jug around in his hands and marveled at it. The overall finish appeared glossy, and where the light hit it, it shimmered. Instead of being a uniform dark brown color, as he'd expected, it was like Peter had taken a little bit of several other colors on a small brush and drawn them down the side of the jug, sort of like when candle wax drips down the side of a candle.

The "drips" were very faint, almost like colorful shadows against the dark brown. In dimmer light he wouldn't have seen them at all. There were hints of forest green, burnt orange, and dark teal running randomly down the sides of the jug.

"If you do, I would love to experiment with it. How did you incorporate it into the clay? You did use the clay I gave you, didn't you?"

"Yes, it was your clay. I just pressed the clay out on the workbench so it wasn't in a ball, sprinkled the dust on top, and kneaded it in, sort of like kneading bread. When I thought it was all mixed through, Ali shaped it for me. I discovered I'm not particularly good at pottery."

"How fine was the dust?"

"Pretty fine. Sort of like the sawdust you get from very fine sandpaper. Or when you file your nails."

"Hm. I can't see where that should give this effect, unless there is some odd sort of mineral in the original clay. Where did you get it?"

"An old jug I had in a back room had a chip in the neck. I wanted to file it smooth instead of leaving it with a sharp edge. For some reason, I chucked it into the clay."

"If you could get me some, I would love to try it for myself. And if it works a second time, I'll get it analyzed and try to duplicate its composition. If I can, you and I need to talk."

"Seriously?"

"Yes. If we can make it work, we might make some money off it," Peter told him.

"Things never work out like that for me," Martin said with a tired laugh. "But if you're serious, I'll see what I can do. What do I owe you for this?"

"Nothing. My pleasure. It cost me nothing extra to fire it, the glaze was inexpensive, and as small as it is it didn't take much anyway. And if we can duplicate this effect, we could both make a bit."

"All right," Martin said. "I'll see if I can get you some in a day or two."

"Splendid. Stay dry."

He and Ali hurried back to the car and were quiet on their way back to the house. Traffic was a mess in this weather and he didn't want to add a fender bender to his current bills.

Once inside and dry, Ali started the oven warming while Martin took a hot shower and put on some warm lounging clothes. By the time he came back out, the whole place smelled of pizza.

"Any idea what happened to that jug?" he finally asked Ali.

"I've been thinkin' on that myself," he answered. "I doubt it's the clay from my jug, but it could be the magic I used to form the clay."

"Really? Wouldn't the heat in the kiln destroy any magic?"

"I don't rightly know," Ali said shaking his head. "I don't see how that tiny bit of dust could give it that result, but magic can do weird stuff."

"True. But if the dust doesn't work, how do we use magic to help Peter? It might be lucrative."

"That's something to ponder," Ali said with a shrug.

Martin thought it over while he ate another slice of pizza. Was there actually any fire in the kiln? Or did Peter use an electric kiln, where there was heat, but no real fire? Would it make a difference?

"Ali, what do you know about magic and fire?"

"Not a whole lot. Why?'

"Fire is supposed to be cleansing. Wouldn't it burn off any magical residue left behind when the clay was heated to such a high temperature? And with the glazing, it is heated twice. Certainly it couldn't be magic."

"I'm not the person to ask," Ali told him. "My magic is completely different to the sort the average human uses, even wizards. We djinn are born with our abilities. They sort of develop as we grow up. Sort of like learnin' to walk. So I don't know how different the effects might be."

Martin thought it over while they cleaned up from dinner. They hadn't had time to see if they'd achieved what they set out to do, but it was after dark, cold, and wet outside. Martin didn't want to to out again, and he doubted Ali did. Maybe they could try the next day.

ALI WAS PUZZLED OVER the effects on their little sculpture. Martin was right about fire and magic, as far as Ali knew. And there shouldn't have been anything in the clay. Or was the effect from the residual magic in the original jug? Diane had noticed it right away when she'd touched it. But again, wouldn't the fire have cleansed it of magic?

Thinking a little more, he wondered if the effect was from the magic being burned out of the clay—if somehow the magic being driven out had affected the glazing effects. With magic involved there was no telling. How hot did those kilns get anyway?"

And what about the jug image they'd made? Had their plan worked? The only way to tell would be to try it. Hopefully Martin hadn't forgotten. He seemed to want Ali free of the jug almost as much as Ali did. Of course, there had been several break-ins. Perhaps once he was free of the jug that would all stop.

He'd taken his time getting together another batch of those little bottles today. Diane had been right about the silver and gold ones. They were particularly pretty and should sell well. Since the holiday colors centered around red and green, he'd done a few more of those than the other colors.

Helping Martin out was the least he could do for the guy. After all, he was feeding him and teaching him about the world as it was today. And that was quite a departure from what he remembered.

Morning would come soon enough, so he followed Martin's example and went to bed.

WITH THE WEATHER A little drier the next day, there were more customers in the store in the morning. And once word got out that they had some more of the shimmery bottles they were inundated until lunchtime. Martin was quite ready to lock the door and flip the sign to closed so they could eat.

"How many more bottles do we have in back?" he asked Ali.

"I put out about half of them this morning, so about that many more."

"At this rate, we'll make rent on the bottles alone. Maybe I should get out of the apothecary business."

"Come on, boss. You know better than that."

"You're right. I do. But they are very popular."

"Are we going to have time to try out the jug thing later?" Ali asked.

"As soon as we sell out of bottles and close the shop for the day," Martin said around a mouthful of sandwich. "It would be nice to know if it works."

"What about the other thing, with Peter?"

"I don't know. I did have a question for him, but I'm not sure how to ask."

"Why can't you just ask him?"

"It has to do with what type of kiln he has. If it is heated electrically, there is no actual fire in the kiln. It might have a different effect on the magic, if that's the reason for the finish on the sculpture."

"I'm sure you'll think of something."

"I guess we could get him a little dust from your jug and take it over. I am a bit interested in the process, so if I ask other questions about how it all works, I suppose asking about the kiln wouldn't be out of place."

"Now you're thinkin'," Ali told him. "I knew you'd get there."

When they returned to the shop there was a queue forming outside. Ali hurried and brought out the bottles and arranged them for display before they opened for business again. By halfway through the afternoon they were completely sold out.

"I hope however you're making these will work a while longer," Martin said.

"We're fine, boss. Don't worry."

They finally reached closing time, locked the door, closed the blinds, turned off the lights, and headed up the stairs.

"I'm beat," Martin said. "How about I take a shower and change clothes. We can grab our mini-jug and see if we can get to that Indian restaurant. It's far enough away to test our theory, and if it works we can have a nice dinner."

"And if it doesn't?"

"I can phone in an order and go pick it up while we re-group and try to figure it out again."

"Sounds good."

Martin was still puzzling over the glaze on the mini-jug. Mini-jug. That was a good name for it. Not that it worked like a real jug, since it wasn't hollow. But it looked pretty much like the original.

What had caused the effect? It had to be something with magic, but where? In the original clay or in the formation of the mini-jug? And how could they duplicate it?

Once he was dressed, he went out, got his coat with the deep pockets, placed the mini-jug inside one of them, and zipped the pocket closed. Taking a deep breath, he stepped through the back door along with Ali, who seemed a little nervous.

"Something bothering you?" he asked.

"What if it doesn't work?" Ali asked bluntly.

"We'll just have to try again. At least you're not inside it anymore."

The first time they'd tried to leave jug behind, they'd scarcely made it to the car. Now safely seated in the vehicle, Martin slowly pulled away from the shop, watching Ali as they drove further and further away.

"Anything wrong?"

"Not so far."

"What's worrying you?" he asked.

"If I get too far away, it's likely to yank me back without any warning. So if I suddenly disappear, I'll be in the jug."

"Won't you feel something first?"

"Maybe. I don't know. But at the moment, the little one seems to be working.

When they made it to the restaurant, had found a table and ordered something to eat, Ali finally began to calm down.

"It's working," he whispered. "I can't believe it. You might be all right, Martin."

"Why thank you, Ali. Now if we can get the rest of it sorted, you'll be a free man, or free djinn."

"I'm almost afraid to hope."

Thursday came around too quickly. Martin had planned to call Diane earlier in the week to see about dinner or something, but between the weather and the mini-jug, he just hadn't taken the time. As he got the lights on in the shop, blinds opened and the door unlocked, her heard Ali in the back room getting together some more the little bottles which were so popular.

They should come up with a name for them, he thought in passing. But his mind kept shifting between calling Diane and wondering what had happened to the glazing on the jug. He had to find time to talk to Peter, too.

Another thing came to mind while he bustled about the shop. He had cast a spell on the mini-jug before it was fired. But once again, the firing should have cleansed it of all magic. Peter was excited about the possibility of discovering a new glazing technique. What if they couldn't reproduce it?

His first customers through the door were some of his regulars, a couple older ladies who used his herbal pain relieving remedies. They claimed they worked as well as the OTC stuff and liked the idea of something more natural.

The next batch of people were hoping he had some more of his bottles for sale. He promised them he would have some the next day. He would have to get together with Ali and Diane and see if they could come up with a clever name for them. A couple things came to mind, but he wasn't sure how well they'd go over with the others.

By lunchtime, he was tired of telling people to come back the next day. Closing for lunch, he went to check on Ali and found him slumped in a corner of the room, with a pile of the little bottles spilling out onto the floor.

"Ali! Are you all right?" he shouted. "What happened?"

"Hm... What? Oh, boss. What's going on?" Ali said as he looked around.

"I don't know. Why are you curled up in the floor? And why are there bottles everywhere"

Looking around, Martin saw Ali had already finished about the same number of jugs has they'd had when they'd started the day before not counting the heap on the floor.

"You've been busy," he said as Ali got up and stretched.

"I guess I overdid it," he explained. "Conjuring stuff up like this takes energy, and I sort of went full out so we'd have enough for tomorrow. I heard everyone comin' in askin' for the things. When I blacked out, I guess I kept conjuring for a bit."

"Yes, they are a hit. Thanks for the idea, and the bottles."

"I think I need some lunch," Ali stated. "And don't worry about the mess. I'll take care of it."

He was probably right. Martin knew from the various energy workers he knew that using energy took a lot out of a person.

"How about a big beef sandwich with some soup?"

"Sounds great. Right at the moment I would eat about anything, though."

Martin ate slowly while he thought about their unique little jug, but Ali wolfed his down as if he were starved. After a satisfied belch, he looked around, found his coffee, and drank it down in two gulps.

"Whew-wee that hit the spot," he said with a grin.

"I thought it might. Maybe you should take a break this afternoon."

"You could be right. It's been a long time since I did much magic. I think I'm out of practice. Time to get back in the game."

"What game would that be?" Martin asked.

"The game of life, at least the life of the djinn. I've been away for too long."

"If we can get you freed from the jug, you can go and check on any family you may have around. You never know. You might have great-grandchildren."

"Wouldn't that be something?"

"Any more thoughts on our mini-jug?"

"Naw. Like you said, any magic should have been cleansed in the fire, even the spell you put on it. I just don't see how it could be magic. But it don't seem right that it's the clay either."

With a sigh, Martin agreed and turned back to the shop. He really had to talk to Diane.

"Well, hello!" he heard when she answered her mobile. "I thought you'd forgotten about me."

He could see the pouting look on her face already. Dinner had better be special.

They arranged to go out on Saturday—he was giving Fridays a miss for a while—and head to the new club he'd heard about. It was supposed to have good food, good music, and decent prices.

"That sounds divine, Martin," she told him. "I may have to buy something to wear."

What had gotten into Diane? She'd never been this effusive before. It had all started with those little bottles. What was Ali doing to them?

Nobody else seemed to be acting weird. He'd had a few people come in a second time to buy more, but they weren't behaving strangely. Something was definitely up with Diane.

During the afternoon he had taken a break and put a beef roast in the oven, with potatoes, carrots, and what-not to have for dinner. It was a good time of year for it. In the summer it was already too warm to add more heat with the oven, but with the chill setting in, he could do two tasks for the price of one.

Trudging up the stairs after work, he heard Ali singing something in a foreign language.

"What's that called?" he asked.

"Oh, I don't know. Just a little tune from a long time ago. Do you like it?"

"It's kind of catchy in a middle eastern sort of way."

"I hope we're about ready to eat. The stuff in the oven is callin' to me," Ali said with a wide grin.

Martin was hungry as well, even though they'd had a decent lunch. It was probably the weather.

While the ate, he asked Ali about the bottles.

"No, sir. I don't add anything to them, magically speakin' of course. You asked me not to, on ethical grounds. Any magic would have to be left over from the process of bringing them into being."

"What's in them?"

"Just a little oil and the glittery stuff. Nothing magical. Why all the questions?"

He told Ali about his conversation with Diane and watched him scratch his head.

"Maybe she just likes you. Did-ja ever think of that?"

"No. It seems a bit sudden. I mean, you remember what she was like when you first met her a few weeks ago? And overnight, once she'd seen the bottles, she's suddenly head over heels? I'm not buying it."

"When you put it that way, I can see your point. Were you seeing her this weekend?"

"Yes. We're going out Saturday night."

"You might want to take along a protective amulet."

"Why?"

"There's been an uncommon amount of interest in my jug," Ali said. "What if our wizard or warlock has used his influence on Diane to see if she can snag it for him?"

"Is that possible?" Stopping to think for a moment, he nodded. "Yeah, it is."

"You've got plenty of time to work with for something that simple. But I wouldn't wait until the last minute, either."

"You're right. I didn't want to get Diane into the middle of this whole thing," he complained.

"I would rather not be in the middle of it either, but I've got no choice," Ali said with a laugh.

"I guess not. Now, what about Peter?"

"I reckon we can get him a little dust from the jug and see if he can make it work. And if it don't, let's see if we can get some more clay from him and experiment a little on our own."

"Experiment how?"

"I can make two different images. Maybe we could try something besides jugs. Anyhow, I make up two of whatever. Then you cast a spell on one of them, but not the other, and have Peter fire them with everything else, and then glaze them, same as he did with the first jug. And we'll see what happens from there."

"Sounds like a plan to me. I'll give him a jingle tomorrow."

Friday was chaos. Everyone who'd heard about the bottles was there as soon as the shop opened. And from the looks of it, they'd brought their neighbors with them as well. Ali had promised to work on a few more during the day. The blue and silver ones seemed to be the most popular, followed by red and gold.

Martin had kept a few back to use for the shop the evening before. He and Ali had put up some fairy lights and then hung the bottles on the strands with little hooks. The light caught the glittery substance inside and made it shimmer marvelously.

By the time he got everyone out of the shop so they could take a lunch break, Martin was worn out, and still had half a day to go. Ali had taken it slowly during the morning, so he didn't get exhausted, but he looked tired, too.

"I don't know about you," Martin told him over lunch, "but I'm not cooking tonight. Should we just order in Indian food again?"

"As long as there's plenty of it. Where did all those people come from today?"

"Not sure, but it looks good in the accounts book."

"Have you talked to Peter yet?"

"I haven't had enough time to make the call," Martin complained. "I'd better get hold of him before we open up the shop again."

Peter was excited to try another firing, so Martin arranged to meet him Saturday morning. That should give them plenty of time to file a little more of the chip away. And he should have enough time for an amulet as well. Ali was quite insistent about it.

"If there's nothing wrong, it won't hurt anything to have it along," he said. "and if it turns up that something is wrong, you'll have some protection along with you. Speaking of which..."

"Leave my love life out of it," Martin warned. "Things have not progressed that far yet, anyway."

"I don't know. She seems awfully eager to me, but it has been a while."

"I don't want to know. All right?"

"You're no fun, boss. You've gotta learn to loosen up a little."

They turned in early, and for the first time in a while, Friday night was quiet. Martin slept like one dead.

# Chapter 21

It had definitely been too long for a variety of things, Ali thought, as he drifted off to sleep. He couldn't believe that conjuring up a few little bottles had taken so much out of him. Of course, he was a couple centuries older and he hadn't had much practice lately.

Now, what about his boss's girlfriend? She did seem to warm up awful quickly. The first time he'd met her, she'd been a bit distant, even to Martin. She was friendly and all, but not what you'd call eager. But if what Martin said about his latest talk with her was true, something had definitely changed.

It couldn't be the bottles. He had checked the last two batches for any residual magic and hadn't put them out until it had all faded away. And he hadn't infused anything into the bottles or their contents. They were simply pretty little bottles full of glittery liquid. They shimmered nicely in the light, but there was no magic involved, except for what it took to make them.

Something was worrying him about Peter using dust from his jug. It had been niggling there at the back of his head for some time, but he couldn't figure out what it was. But suddenly it had come to him.

The reason they had used the dust from his jug and shaped the clay into an image of the jug was to give the law of contagion and the law of sympathy more to work with. If there was enough dust in Peter's new creation, it might have the same effect as the first one they'd done.

Could someone with magical ability trace that dust and conjure with it?

No, surely not. Nobody here knew his name. You had to have someone's real name to conjure with it. And if he and Martin still had the original jug, they should be fine. Still, it wouldn't be a bad idea to ask Martin about it.

SATURDAY MORNING, MARTIN slept in. It had been a rough week and today was going to be busy. First things first. After breakfast. He couldn't face today without something substantial for breakfast.

Ali came out of his room a few minutes after Martin started coffee.

"Mornin' boss. Looks like you slept good last night."

"Yeah. No break-ins, talks with the police, burglars, or anything of the sort."

"I did have a thought last night I wanted to bounce off ya," Ali told him.

"All right," he answered a little hesitantly.

Ali explained his theory about the dust and Martin had to agree. If the dust still held its magic, it would have a connection to the original. Actually, even without the magic, it would have a connection, since they were both made with the same clay. At least there was some of the same clay in each of the jugs.

"Can you sense anything from our mini-jug?" Martin asked.

"I haven't tried."

"After we clean up, why don't you give it a go and see what happens?"

About half an hour later, both men stood in the back room with the two different jugs—the original and the mini.

"Now, can you sense anything from your jug?" Martin asked.

"Yeah, I can sense the magic around it."

Taking the smaller jug into the kitchen, Martin asked him again.

"I just don't know," Ali answered. "I feel something, but I'm not sure if it's something that's actually there, or if I'm imagining it. But it feels a lot like the other jug, only not as strong."

"Hm. How can we test this?" Martin muttered to himself.

"I don't know. If you can think of something, I'm in."

They took some time to get a little dust from the first jug to take over to Peter's house. After they had enough to put into a small bag, they took a drive. Martin once again had the mini-jug in his coat pocket.

"Martin. Ali," Peter greeted them as they stood up out of the car. "Did you bring the goods?"

"What is this? Some sort of drug deal?" Martin teased back. "Yeah, I've got the goods. Hopefully you'll get lucky with it and will get credit for a new glazing technique."

"That would be fantastic. Is this all you used before?" the man asked, peering into the bag."

"I think it's a little more than we had. There should be enough to do something about the same size as the jug."

"I'll give it a try this week and see what happens. Have you two had lunch yet?"

They all rode together to a Chinese place not far from Peter's house. Ali had developed quite a taste for both Chinese and Indian food. As the portions were large, he was in heaven.

They took a leisurely lunch before driving Peter home, and as they were on their way, Martin asked, "Can you sense anything?"

Ali looked at him strangely, tipped his head to one side, and closed his eyes.

"There is a very faint feeling coming from your direction, but unless I concentrate, I can't feel it."

"But it is still there?"

"Yeah."

"If we only knew if it was the fault of the clay, or the fault of the shape, we might be able to make an educated guess about anything Peter makes. Or if it's neither one and part of the spell."

"Yeah. I guess we'll have to wait until he's finished. It should be what, about a week?"

Martin nodded. "Yes. That's about what it took last time. Knowing Peter, he'll find a way to check it out as soon as possible. I wouldn't be surprised if he fires again tomorrow."

"Don't you have a date with Diane tonight?" Ali asked.

"Yes. I'm going over to pick her up at seven. From there we'll drive over to the club and see if it's as nice as I've heard."

"I hope the evenin' turns out good for you. Guy like you should have himself a wife by now."

"We aren't in the Middle Ages anymore, Ali. Some of us wait a while before tying the knot."

"Well, don't wait too long."

Back at the house, Ali seemed pensive as they came through the door.

"What's on your mind, Ali?"

"Is the jug back under the floor?"

"Yes. Remember? We put it back under there after we found the little one worked. Why?"

"I would feel better if you could put some sort of masking spell on it, sort of a precaution. You know, just in case?"

"What's got you so worried, Ali?" Martin asked.

"I couldn't tell ya, but I feel uneasy with you being gone tonight."

"Is it me being gone, or me being with Diane?"

"I couldn't say. You said she's acting a bit odd these days. I don't know. It's probably nothing. Go on and have fun."

Just in case, Martin went ahead and cast a spell over the hiding place, and then strengthened the spell by the doors. Ali was on alert for anything happening and they'd talked over the possibilities. Martin had written down his mobile number in case someone needed to contact him, so everything should be ready.

"All right, Ali. I'm heading out. Are you sure you'll be fine here on your own?"

"I don't know. I should be, but it seems like every time you leave, something happens. I'm beginning to get annoyed."

"And what happens when one of the djinn gets annoyed?" Martin asked, with a little laugh.

"The night could turn exciting."

"Don't do anything rash," Martin cautioned.

"Never rash, boss, but I'll try to keep your place safe for you. Now go on. Git!"

Diane was ready when Martin arrived at her flat, but not quite as excited as she'd been the other day. Who knew? She was friendlier than usual though, which he took as a good sign.

The club was stacked, so Martin was glad he'd called ahead for reservations. Their table wasn't too near the band, so they were still able to talk without shouting. With pre-dinner cocktails in hand, they perused the dinner menu, trying to decide what to sample first.

The drinks were well made, and their meal looked marvelous. The presentation was artful and the first bite convinced Martin that he had a new favorite restaurant for those special occasions.

"What do you think?" he asked Diane.

"This is fantastic," she said around a bite of salmon. "I've been meaning to try this place, but I don't like to come to someplace like this on my own."

"I know what you mean," Martin replied, tasting some of the grilled asparagus. "Same here."

With dinner finished and dessert postponed, they went out onto the dance floor for a few numbers, until Diane excused herself to the Ladies.

"I'll see you back here at the table. Are you ready for dessert yet?"

"Yes, but I haven't decided on it. Give me a few."

Martin ordered some coffee and looked over the dessert menu. The choices were difficult, but he thought something by way of a lemon tart would suit him.

"So, handsome, what are you having for dessert?" he heard as Diane slipped past him to get to her seat.

Holding her chair for her, he wondered what was happening. She'd been friendly before, but now she was more like she'd been a few days ago—just that much too friendly.

"Cocktails kicking in?" he asked with a smile.

"What? Can't a girl be appreciative without being tipsy?"

"Never mind," he told her. "What about dessert?"

"Something chocolate is always good. And chocolate is so sexy, don't you think?"

All right. This was not the Diane he was used to. What in hell was going on?

They ordered dessert and it was every bit as good as the rest of their meal. His lemon tart was just sweet enough to take the edge off, but not overwhelm the custard. Diane seemed quite into her double chocolate and raspberry torte. Martin wasn't a chocolate lover, but it was quite obvious Diane was. Not that Martin didn't like chocolate, but he wouldn't go out of his way for it.

After they'd danced a little more and had more coffee—Diane had had quite enough to drink—they took a short walk to look at the decorations going up around town before getting back in the car to head home.

"Your place is kind of on the way," Diane suggested.

"Did you want to stop by for tea or something before I take you home?" he asked.

"Tea, or maybe a glass of wine," she told him while fluttering her lashes.

Something wasn't right here, for sure. The Diane he knew was not this bold. Somewhere in the back of his mind he wondered about magic, but dismissed it when he felt her hand stroking his thigh.

"Right then," he said. "We'll drop in for a few minutes, have a cup of something to warm us, and then we can get you home and to bed."

Maybe she just couldn't hold her drink. They'd only been out a few times before, and most of those times they'd only had a glass or two of wine with dinner. Perhaps cocktails were too much.

"Let me call my flat and let Ali know we're both coming by."

He listened until the answering machine picked up and told Ali to expect them in about five minutes. He wished he could ask him about Diane. Maybe all she needed was some strong coffee and a good night's sleep.

They finally stopped in front of his shop, with her becoming more amorous by the minute. Under ordinary circumstances he would be pleased. But this was way too much way too fast, especially with everything else going on around him.

The back door opened as they got there and Ali greeted them with a smile.

"I thought you might like some coffee when you got here," he said. "It should be ready by now."

"You read my mind, Ali," Martin told him, wishing he was telepathic.

"Coffee sounds great for starters," Diane told him. "Maybe you have a bottle of sherry hiding someplace, so we could have as a nightcap."

"Hey, boss," Ali called from the kitchen. "Can I see you for just a minute?"

Leaving Diane pouting on the sofa, Martin went in to talk with Ali.

"What's up, Ali?"

"I don't want to alarm you or anything, but that ain't the real Diane in there."

"I kind of thought that might be the case. But if it's not Diane, who is it? And where is Diane?"

"Are you sure you picked her up tonight?" Ali asked.

"Yes. I went over to her flat, picked her up, and we went to the club."

"Was she her usual self when you picked her up?"

Thinking back, she had been fine when he stopped by her flat, and fine right up until she went to the toilet, before they ordered dessert. He told Ali about the sudden change in her behavior.

"Someone is using magic as a glamour, to make themselves look like Diane, and get into your place. We need to do something quick."

"But what about Diane?" he asked nearly in a panic.

"I would guess she is still back at the club somewhere. If they used a spell, it will wear off soon. If they hit her over the head or something, she'll probably be all right in a while. Either way, once we deal with this, you should go back to the club."

Ali mumbled something and snapped his fingers. With a nod of his head, he turned toward the living room and motioned for Martin to follow.

There on the sofa sat "Diane" staring fixedly out the window.

"What do we do now?" Martin asked.

"I'm workin' on it."

After a few seconds, he waved his hand and Diane took in a quick breath, her eyes opening wide.

"Do you want to tell me what's going on?" she demanded.

"No, I rather think you should tell me," Martin replied, holding a walking stick.

"What do you mean?"

"Drop the illusion, whoever you are. You rather overdid it with the impersonation. Who are you really?"

"I don't know what you're talking about. What have you done to me?" the fake Diane demanded.

Picking up one of the books he'd bought several years ago on the subject of magic, he perused the contents and watched the person on his sofa try to break whatever bonds held her.

"Here we go. How to lift a glamour," he said. "This should be about right."

"Oh all right!" the person on the sofa spat.

From one instant to the next, the Diane on the sofa became a man about the same size, with dark hair, grey eyes, and a completely frustrated look on his face.

"Now, how about a name?" Martin asked.

"How about you mind your own business?"

"Since this is my house, this is my business," Martin stated. "Seeing as you're here under false pretenses, I need to call the police. Again. But first I would like a name and your reason for being here."

"Oh, I think you know why I'm here," the man sneered. "As for a name, you can call me Harold for now. That's all the name your getting."

"All right, Harold. So we're all perfectly clear about why you're here, why don't you spell it out for me."

"The jug you brought back from America. I want it. You have it."

"Are you the one who keeps sending people over to steal it?"

"No. That's above my rank in the scheme of things. But bringing it back would have brought me quite a reward."

While talking with the man, Martin had dialed for the police. When they answered, he told them the situation, again, and they told him they would be along soon.

"How about your boss's name? You've been caught out, but you could help your case if you'd let us in on that bit of information."

"It isn't worth the penalty. Do your own research."

Since there seemed not much more to gain, they all sat in silence until the police arrived. Once they were in the flat, Ali released whatever magic he'd used to keep the man there and once again, the police hauled away their intruder.

"Now for Diane," Martin said.

Making a quick call to the club, Martin found out that Diane had been found in the powder room, disoriented, and confused. They had sent her to urgent care. After getting the address from them, he hurried to his his car and drove to see if he could speak with her.

"We went to the club together and when someone broke into my house, I needed to leave, but couldn't find her anywhere," he said. It was close enough to the truth.

"Let me ask her," the nurse told him. Quickly sending someone down the corridor, they were soon back and said it would be fine.

"Diane, what on earth happened to you?" he asked, taking her hand in his.

"I don't know really. I remember we were dancing and were going to get dessert, and then I woke up in the ladies room feeling quite giddy. I had the worst headache ever. And when someone came in and found me, I asked for some paracetamol. I finally remembered you were supposed to be there, too, but I was so dizzy I couldn't go out and find you."

"And then someone sent you here," Martin added.

"Yeah. They still aren't sure what's going on, but I'm beginning to feel better. Martin?"

"Well, something came up at my flat, but I couldn't find you. So I ran back, called the police to take care of the matter, and then called the club. They told me you were here. Any idea when you'll be ready to leave?"

"Why have things suddenly become weird around you?" she asked.

"That's a long story, and certainly not one for tonight. Let's get you ready to go home first and we'll talk about it all later. All right?"

"Yeah. I still don't feel right. That would probably be best."

He stayed with her for the next hour and a half while they ran tests on everything imaginable trying to come up with some reason for the sudden onset of her symptoms. When nothing obvious came to light, the doctor reluctantly signed discharge papers

"You should follow up with your GP in a few days, unless there is a return of your symptoms. In that case, come back here immediately."

With instructions to take something for her headache if necessary, she was helped to the car and Martin slowly drove back to her place.

"Are you sure you'll be all right?" he asked.

"I'll be fine. I'm feeling much better now."

"Is there anyone you can call to come stay with you tonight?" he asked.

"At one in the morning on a Sunday? No. Not really."

"I'll call you in the morning—later this morning—and check on you. Get some sleep, okay?

"I'll do my best. Thanks for coming for me."

"Well, I hated to run out on you, so I thought the least I could do was come to your rescue."

"My knight in shining armor," she teased, finally showing a tiny smile.

"I'll see you tomorrow."

# Chapter 22

What were they going to do about Diane? She would begin to wonder once she was feeling herself again. And then the questions would begin.

"Ali, I guess we should sit down and talk this over," Martin said, grabbing a glass and splashing some Scotch into it.

"Yeah, I reckon we oughta," Bubba agreed.

"This is your life, your history," Martin began. "If you don't want to get Diane any more involved with this, then we won't. But if you think explaining things to her would help, I'll need a little backup."

"I just don't know. I have given it some thought and I like Diane. I don't sense any ill intentions from her, but she might be an asset if we work it right."

"An asset? How?" Martin asked.

"Well, she might have contacts who could help us out with the curse, or at least she's a fresh set of eyes looking at the problem."

"But will she be able to accept my dabbling in magic, and the fact that you're a magical being? A lot of people don't understand about genies and whatnot."

"When did people stop believing in magic?"

"A long time ago, Ali. Back when Science came into its own, people wanted things that were rational and could be explained. And things magical can't be explained, at least not yet."

"Certainly some of it can," Ali countered. "After all, isn't magic just something we don't yet understand? With all the "magical" things you have around you these days, certainly a little more magic would be chucked in with all the rest."

"But our modern magic, like electricity and mobile phones, can be explained with science, hard facts. Your type of magic can't be. It's a tricky subject."

"If you say so. I don't see much difference," Ali huffed.

"I know what you mean."

After a few more Scotchs for Martin and a gin or three for Ali, the two of them went to sleep it all off. The last thing Martin remembered was listening to Ali sing bawdy songs from a time long before the current century.

When Martin woke up Sunday morning, he was sure his headache was going to kill him, as he struggled into the bathroom for some paracetamol. What had he been thinking? And how was Ali? He'd had quite a bit to drink, too. Stumbling into the shower, Martin began to feel better after the pain killers and hot water began to have an effect.

Dressed and as coherent as he was going to be for a while, he wandered into the kitchen to put on some coffee. Pretty soon he heard groaning sounds from Ali's room, and then a string of curses.

"Everything all right in there?"

""What the hell was in that stuff? Yeah, I'll be out in a minute."

Peeking through the door into Ali's room, Martin was surprised by what he saw. The room was a disaster zone, and he was sure most of what he saw had never been in that room before. Beautiful brightly covered streamers were flung around the room haphazardly, and various sorts of jars and bottles were overturned on the floor. The bed looked like a tornado had struck and Ali looked rather under the weather.

"Where did all this come from?" he asked.

"Well, it's like this. I was dreaming, and I'd had a bit too much to drink, so when I reacted to the dreams, I sort of conjured up stuff. I'll get rid of it in a minute. You got anything for a headache?"

Martin had never considered genies and nightmares and their consequences. Who knew a person could do magic in his sleep?

He fixed something fairly light for breakfast. If Ali was in the same shape he was, he wouldn't want anything sitting too heavily in his stomach. Martin had to call Diane this morning. It wasn't all that late yet, and he hadn't planned to call early in the morning. Not after the night she'd had.

"So, Ali, did we actually decide what we were going to tell Diane?"

"I don't rightly remember. I think we were going to play it by ear and see how she felt about the subject of magic. We might ask her what she remembers right before she became unconscious."

"I suppose that would be a good way to start, and then we'll take it from there. Peter was firing some things in his kiln today. I wonder if his attempt will be in with this bunch?"

"I don't know. And I don't know if I hope it works or hope it don't."

"Seriously. If it doesn't, it might make it a little easier on us for now. If it does, Peter will be ecstatic."

"And we still have to find out who is trying to locate the jug. Didn't you say you did psychic investigations, locating people and things?" Ali asked.

"Yes, but I have to have something to work with. I've never seen this person, or if I have, I didn't know they were going to be a problem for me. I need something of theirs or an image of them to focus on. You know, anything at all."

"What do you normally use?" Ali asked.

"Something they owned, like a hairbrush, a set of keys, clothing. Anything that would have a bit of their DNA—that's what we call it these days. Hair, skin, finger hails. That sort of thing."

"And we don't even know the first thing about this guy. Or even if it is a guy. What if it's a woman?"

That stopped Martin short for a minute. He had assumed they were dealing with a man, but anyone could work with magic, if they had a little bit of ability.

"You don't think Diane..." he began.

"No. I don't. I've never sensed the first bit of magic around Diane. She couldn't have that much ability and keep it hidden all the time. At least I don't think she could."

"All right, back to the subject of our mini-jug. I guess we'll have to wait for Peter to do the final firing, after he glazes his bit of clay, to see where we go next with that."

"Yeah. It could be something in the spell you cast," Ali agreed.

"And we still have to figure out the curse."

"What have you found out so far?"

"I believe any kind of magic can undo what your witch did. I think it would help if we knew exactly what the curse said. Do you remember it at all?"

"All right, she ain't my witch. But, yeah, I may have been drunk when I went into the jug, but I was sober as a judge when she laid the curse on me. She made sure of that."

"If we have that, I believe I can use candle magic to undo it. It's what I'm most familiar with. If that doesn't work, I'll look into water or fire magic. One way or another, we're going to get you out from under this thing. And then we won't have to worry about people trying to steal the jug to gain control of you."

"Which would suit me just fine," Ali said.

"All right. Let me make a call and see how Diane is feeling."

She told him she hadn't been up any longer than he and Ali had been and had nibbled at some yogurt for breakfast.

"Do you want to try some lunch later?" Martin asked.

"Maybe. I don't think I'm up to Indian food, but maybe Greek would be good. I haven't had gyros in ages, and I love the tsatsiki sauce."

"How about if I call in an order after a bit, say around one this afternoon and get it delivered? You can come over around the same time, we'll eat, and see if we can figure out what happened last night and just relax."

"I think that is a wonderful plan. I'll take a cab over. I'm still not feeling quite right."

The gyros delivery van was right on time, and Diane was about three minutes behind it. The afternoon had turned blustery, so she was wrapped up against the chilly winds. Taking her coat and getting her settled, Martin and Ali got the food and drinks, and then everyone dug into lunch.

Martin was still trying to figure out how to bring up magic and genies when Diane opened the subject.

"I can't understand what happened last night," she said, frowning and shaking her head. "I was fine until I went to the ladies, and then nothing, until some woman I'd never seen was shaking me awake."

"Do you remember anything at all before that?" Martin asked.

"I remember pushing through the door and remarking about the lack of a queue. You know how it usually is at a club. It seems you have to wait forever.

But last night, there was only one other person in the ladies room when I got there, and she wasn't in one of the stalls."

"What was she doing?"

"Checking her makeup. I didn't really look at her, you know. I just turned toward the stalls. And then I don't remember anything else."

"Hm... what did they say at the Urgent Care?"

"They couldn't understand it. There was nothing they could find which should have caused something like that. It didn't seem like I'd bumped my head or been hit over the head. There was no sign of any drug in my system. I don't have any sort of blood sugar disorder or blood pressure problems. They couldn't find anything."

"What do you know about magic?" Martin asked, deciding to get it over with.

"Magic? You mean like spells and things?"

"Yes. Spells, incantations, magical beings. That sort of thing."

"Not much. I always thought it was mostly sleight of hand."

"Let me tell you a story," Martin began before taking her all the way back to the little town in the American Southeast where he'd first seen the whiskey jug.

"Let me see if I've got this straight," Diane said with a skeptical look. "You're claiming Ali is one of the djinn, an ancient magical creature, who was trapped in your jug?"

"Precisely. Until I bought the jug and pulled the cork. And ever since then I've had break-ins nearly every week. And all of those people have wanted the old jug."

"Why? Who would want the jug enough to steal the thing? I mean, it's interesting and will look good in your shop—if you ever get around to displaying it. But steal the thing?"

Ali spoke up for the first time.

"The one who controls the jug controls me. Martin has been pretty decent, but some others wouldn't be. My people have certain abilities, some of which can be used to do unlawful things. And those sorts of people tend to keep us locked up someplace so we're always available to cater to their every whim."

"Seriously? You two are putting me on. If you're a genie, show me something," Diane insisted.

"What would you like?" Ali asked.

"Make it something reasonable, please," Martin added. "Like, don't ask for a million pounds or anything."

"Spoil sport. All right, how about a black cape with a hood, with some sort of sparkly decorations down the front and around hood? And matching gloves. I need something new for winter."

Ali thought for a moment, getting the image firmly in mind and waved his hand. Instantly a hooded cape with a wide band of what looked like crystal beads in a band down the front and around the hood appeared on the coffee table. A matching set of gloves appeared next to it as well.

Startled, Diane sat back on the sofa and stared at the cape.

"Are you going to try it on?" Martin asked.

"Um.. I'm not sure. Is this some sort of trick?"

"How could it be a trick? We didn't know what you would ask for," Ali answered.

Hesitantly, Diane reached over and ran her fingers over the fabric, testing it between her fingers.

"It feels real enough."

"Why wouldn't it?" Martin asked.

"If it were an illusion, it might disappear as soon as I touched it."

"Try it on. See if it fits."

Slipping the garment on, she fastened the frog type closures before slipping her hands into the gloves.

"These fit like they were tailored for me," she said, frowning.

"They were. I was creating them for you, so of course they would fit," Ali patiently explained.

"All right, let's say you can do this with anything. What does the jug have to do with this again?"

They explained the curse, the fact that he couldn't rid himself of it by breaking the jug, and all the ramifications of it all.

"So what you need is a way to lift the curse?" she asked, chewing her bottom lip.

"Yes. But anyone I know who could do something like that would also be interested in the jug and in Ali. And I don't want to put him at risk."

"How long have you done magic?" she asked, with a soul-searching gaze.

"I hardly ever practice magic," he told her. "I dabbled when I was at university, because it was something to do. Aside from a few protective spells around the shop, I don't practice at all."

"If you've had break-ins, it doesn't seem like they're working real well," she commented.

"I never thought I would have to protect against a practitioner of the arts, either. So far it has worked against the usual sorts."

"Hm... I don't know anything about magic. So what does this have to do with me?"

"Maybe I should get out some wine," Martin said, beginning to feel even more nervous.

"Sounds lovely," Diane said. "I could use a little something after all this. I'm still not completely convinced, but I'm willing to listen."

After a glass of wine to fortify the spirit, Martin explained his theory of what had happened the evening before.

"So you actually thought I was with you?" she exclaimed. "How could you not tell the difference?"

"That was part of the reason I came here instead of taking you straight home. I thought someone had used magic to affect you, so you would steal the jug, or at least find out where it's hidden. I never thought it was a glamour someone had put on."

"A glamour? What's that?"

"It's to make one thing look like something else," Ali explained. "It's an illusion made by casting a spell."

"Oh. What made you think it wasn't me, or that something was wrong?"

Martin explained her behavior after she'd gone to the ladies.

"I can see where that would make you wonder. Even drunk I don't see myself behaving that way."

"Which was my dilemma. Once we got here and Ali recognized what was going on, we confronted the person and they dropped the glamour. Once the police had him in hand, I began to call around to find you."

"It was a man?" she demanded. "A man pretending to be me?"

"Yeah. The illusion was very good, right down to the clothes you were wearing."

"So it must have been someone last night, at the club. You think the woman in the toilet was the one who knocked me out and did all this?"

"I think she played a part in it, yes," Martin replied.

"That bitch! How can I help?"

Martin had never seen this side of Diane before. Eyes blazing a bright blue, she stood and began to pace the room.

"Do you think she was actually that man who pretended to be me? Was she not a woman at all?"

"Maybe. It could have been the same person."

"If I ever get my hands on him, I'm gonna rip his balls off. That is disgusting, hiding out in the ladies. Pervert!"

"Maybe another glass of wine," Martin suggested.

Diane tossed back the wine like it was water.

"I think we need to calm down and figure this out," Martin suggested, rubbing Diane's shoulders.

"I think we need to do some research on curses and spells," Diane said. "Let me check my schedule. If I have a day free, I would be happy to do some research for you. Let's get Ali unbound and catch this bastard."

After a little more wine, Martin took Diane for a drive, reminding Ali to keep an eye on things.

"Do you think you have the hang of the phone yet?" he asked.

"I think so, even if I don't understand it. I pick this bit up, push the 9 button three times, and talk to whatever voice answers."

"Right. The address for the shop is on the pad next to the phone. You've talked to the police several times, so you should be fine if you need to call. Just give me a call first—remember how to do that?"

"I've got it, boss. I'll take care of things. If nothing else, I'll just hold whoever comes for me until you get back."

"That would work as well. I'll be back before too long."

Martin and Diane went for a walk in the park after a short drive. Diane was still angry over the whole affair, but loved the cloak and gloves.

"I can see how this could get out of hand, if Ali was somehow bound to a person's command. Imagine the things they could ask for."

"I have, and I've been tempted a couple times. But I have a good sense of right and wrong, and being selfish with demands would be wrong."

"Of course. You'll have to show me what research you've done, so I don't duplicate it."

"I've barely started on it, what with work, break-ins, and everything else going on."

"Those little bottles you have for sale," Diane started. "Did Ali make those for you?"

"Yes. He wanted to do something to help me out. I suggested some sort of little trinkets and he came up with this idea. So far they've been selling like crazy. He swears there's no magic in them."

"They are adorable. I need to get some for my parents. I know my mother will love them. I might get one in each color."

After finishing the circuit around the park, Martin drove Diane back to her place. She had calmed down, finally, and had checked her schedule. She had most of the afternoon on Monday and a couple mornings later on in the week.

"We should be able to come up with something to try," she told him with a goodbye kiss.

"I hope so. After all these years, Ali deserves a break. I suppose he might have been a threat or annoyance at some point, but he's been decent enough to me."

"I'll call tomorrow and let you know what I've found out."

# Chapter 23

Monday was kind of slow at the apothecary shop, which was good. Martin had too many things on his mind. Ali had made more of his glittery bottles and they were selling well, even as slow as the day was. They had decided to "get new shipments" in only once a week. But they were still trying to come up with a name for the things.

Diane called Monday afternoon and let him know she was working on their problem. Martin couldn't believe how angry she'd become over the whole issue. He'd known she would be upset, but he hadn't realized how much of a temper she had. What seemed to upset her the most was the possibility of a man being in the ladies room getting an eyeful while pretending to be female.

Since their last encounter over the weekend, things had been quiet. Of course, the opposition was probably falling back to regroup and would try again as soon as they had another plan. How could they find the person controlling this whole thing? Without a name or something to work with, what else was possible?

"Hey, boss," he heard as he was daydreaming. "What did you have in mind for dinner?"

He hadn't even thought about dinner. Everything he had was frozen, except for a few vegetables.

"I don't know. I could phone out for Indian or Chinese," he suggested.

"If you'd like, I could get us something Arabic," Ali suggested.

"That would be fine, too. Whatever it was you fixed the last time was delicious."

Martin had stopped worrying about how Ali got the things he did. Ali couldn't explain it to him any more than he could explain mobile phones to Ali. They'd eventually agreed it was all magic and left it that.

Dinner was fantastic, with something like lamb kebabs with rice and flat bread. He might have to see about finding a middle eastern restaurant. Later. Once they had Ali, his jug, and their thief sorted. Maybe Diane would have more luck than he'd had.

POURING OVER INFORMATION on the internet, Diane had come up with several ideas, but her knowledge of magic was rather limited. She had been surprised to learn she would be considered a witch due to her energy healing. Yes, she was sensitive to energies, but nearly anyone could learn energy healing techniques. There was nothing magical about it.

Witch indeed. When she got her hands on the guy impersonating her, he would think witch, and there would be no magic involved.

She'd talked briefly with Martin earlier in the day and found out what he had done up to this point, so they wouldn't duplicate efforts. All in all, it didn't look like it should be too difficult to reverse the spell. It was mainly a matter of coming up with a spell to counter it. Any type of magic should work, if what she'd read was correct.

Martin said he had used candle magic before. It looked pretty straightforward. And since she'd done some creative writing, coming up with a rhyming spell should be a breeze. But what made it work?

Digging deeper into the subject, she lost track of time until her stomach began to make rude noises. Closing all the browser windows she had open, Diane went in to scrounge for something to eat. Any more research could wait.

As she dug into her pasta Alfredo, she thought about Ali. Of course she had heard of genies—the djinn. She'd just never thought they were real. They were sort of a joke or a folk tale used to illustrate a point, not something you would ever actually meet.

He seemed real enough, and if he could create, or find, anything he wanted, it seemed he should be able to undo the curse himself. Unless that was part of the curse. Another question to ask Martin.

And how much did they need to know about the original curse? It would help to know all the parameters, so they could counter all of it instead of only some of it. Would Ali remember what had been said?

Anyway, she had clients coming in the next day during both morning and afternoon. Further digging would have to be put off until the evening at least. But certainly between the three of them they could undo one curse.

ON TUESDAY BUSINESS picked up again, with more people asking about the bottles. They wouldn't have any more in until Friday, and their stock sold out by Tuesday lunch. Martin still didn't understand the fascination with them, but as long as they were selling, he would keep them in stock.

This evening he was going over to Peter's to see what was happening with the latest experiment. Honestly, he didn't know what he hoped to find. Of course Peter wouldn't have had time to glaze it yet, so maybe he would call and save a trip. He didn't like to leave the flat too often these days, especially if he took Ali with him. A phone call would be better.

"Hello, Peter," he said when his friend answered. "I was just calling to see about your latest project."

"The new piece survived the first firing and looks fine. I chose to shape it into a small vase. Once again, it slumped a little bit, but it doesn't look bad. I'm trying to figure out why the addition would make it slump. So far we're two for two. Nothing else in the batch was affected, only the vase."

"That is sort of strange," Martin agreed. "There wasn't that much of the dust in either batch. I guess we'll have to wait for the second fire to see if it has the same effect."

"Yeah. I should be ready to fire the glaze tomorrow. I've done the same color on the vase as I did on the little jug. If it has the same effect this time, I'll have the dust analyzed and see what we can come up with before I try a different color."

"Sounds great. When can we look at it?"

"If I fire tomorrow morning, you could come by any time on Thursday to see the results."

"We'll come by after work on Thursday," Martin said. "Just out of curiosity, what do you use to heat your kiln? I know almost nothing about the process, but after watching you and seeing the results, I'm getting interested. Don't worry. I have no talent in the area," he added.

"I use an electric kiln. It's easy to control and I don't have to worry about fueling it, unless the power goes out. In that case, I have a generator. It beats losing an entire batch of pottery."

"So there is no actual fire?"

"Not any more. They used to use charcoal, but that was ages ago. Why the sudden interest?"

"I guess it was the weird effect on the jug you fired for me. It was only an experiment, but the result seemed pretty random. I hadn't thought much about pottery before, so I suppose it piqued my interest a bit."

"Gotcha. I'll see you on Thursday," Peter told him before they rang off.

Electric. So there was no fire involved. That might explain why the effects of the magic weren't destroyed. Heat alone might not be enough without the actual fire.

Who could he ask?

Wednesday was busy. Of course, everyone wanted one of Aladdin Treasures—which was what they had decided to call the little bottles—and several people had asked if the company who made them did anything else. Martin thought they could talk it over and see what sort of thing they could come up with.

After lunch, Diane dropped by to buy some more throat lozenges.

"Are you ever going to get that checked out?" he asked.

"I was just at Urgent Care. As many tests as they ran, surely anything serious would have been found."

"Did you mention you'd been having throat issues?"

"I do not have throat issues. It's just the change in the weather. Happens every year."

"What are you doing tonight?" Martin asked. Time to get off the subject of sore throats.

"Nothing in particular. Maybe we could all get together. I have a few questions for you and Ali."

"Sure. Do you want to come here, or should we go to your place?"

"How safe do you feel leaving the shop and flat unattended?" Diane asked.

"There is that, of course," he answered wearily. "Why, out of all the things I could have found to bring home, did it have to be that wretched jug?"

"I think Ali is probably just as glad you got it," Diane told him, smiling warmly. "You never know," she said, looking around to make sure no one else was listening, "he could be the reason you originally were drawn to the jug."

"Could be. I guess we'll never know. But I would like to get the thing to where I can display it without worrying about someone coming in and bashing my head in for it."

"That's what I want to talk about tonight. Seven?"

"Seven would be fine. Chinese or Indian? Or Ali makes this wonderful Arabic food."

"Let's try Arabic for a change," Diane said. "I haven't had Arabic food in ages."

"I'll let him know."

At least the rest of the day was busy enough to keep his mind occupied and off his magical problems. Maybe Diane had come up with something that would work.

During a lull in customers, he called to Ali and told him about dinner.

"No, it's not a problem, boss. I'm glad you like it. And I'll have a few more trinkets ready for tomorrow. Since we went with Aladdin's Treasures, I've added a few different shapes to go with the others."

Taking a break from the shop, Martin ducked into the back room to have a look. The work bench sparkled with all the various bottles. Ali had added the traditional Aladdin's lamp, an Arabic coffee pot, and tall slender water pitcher, as well as the perfume-type bottles. All of them were in beautiful cut glass with a nice ribbon around the neck.

"These are great, Ali," he told his flat mate. "I think we'll sell even more of them with the new selection."

"What time did we say for dinner?" Ali asked.

"I told Diane to come over at seven, so around then. She had some things she wanted to talk about with us, and since I hate to leave the place unattended, she said she would come here."

"I sure am sorry, Martin," Ali said in a serious tone. "I like you. You've treated me decently. And you don't deserve all the trouble I've brought you."

"With any luck and a bit of magic, maybe we can fix that."

"We may need more than a little luck,"

THE WONDERFUL AROMA wafting out of Martin's flat was heavenly, as Diane hurried around back to come in the residence entrance. She didn't even care where Ali got his ingredients, if it tasted as good as it smelled.

When Martin opened the door, a warm cloud filled with the scent of herbs and spices seemed to wrap around her and draw her in. Closing her eyes, she breathed in the wondrous aroma until she heard Martin chuckle.

"What are you laughing at?" she teasingly demanded.

"That look of pure delight on your face. I'm sure my face wore a similar expression the first time Ali fixed dinner for me."

"I don't recognize some of those spices," she said, as Martin took her coat.

"Me neither, but they taste wonderful. How about some nice wine before dinner? Ali's getting everything ready for the table."

With a glass of wine, she sat on the sofa in front of the fireplace with Martin and tried to get her thoughts in order. At this rate, it would have to wait until after dinner. She simply couldn't think with her stomach demanding whatever smelled so delightful.

And it was even better than the aroma had promised. They started with flat bread, raw vegetables, and various dips, none of which she could identify. They proceeded to cubed lamb, seasoned and roasted or grilled, with more flat bread and some sort of rice pilaf.

By this time, Diane was about ready to call it quits. Her stomach was happy, her taste buds overwhelmed, and she'd discovered her new favorite food.

"Do y'all want dessert now or in a while?" Ali asked.

"I couldn't eat another bite, Ali," she admitted. "How about we have dessert after we talk over a few things."

"All right. Let me get some coffee and we'll all have a set down and see what we can figure out."

Settling back into the sofa, Diane gathered her thoughts as Martin and Ali waited expectantly.

"Now, from what I've found during my research, we need to know the general gist of the curse and who cast the spell for it. Do we know that?"

"We do," Ali said. "I can tell you exactly what was said when the curse was cast, and I can tell you what the witch called herself."

"Let's write some of this down."

"She was a swamp witch and did all her spells with swamp magic. When she was a young woman, she was quite a looker, so she named herself Belle-Marie. Unfortunately, her life caught up with her and, before she was fifty, she was ugly as sin."

"Belle-Marie. Pretty Mary?"

"Yeah. It would be funny if it weren't sad." Ali said. "Like I said, she was something else when she was younger. But then she let her temper get the better of her and got into black magic. Her looks followed her outlook."

"Now the basis of the curse is that you are bound to the jug and can't get too far away from it. Correct?"

They explained the various ramifications of it to her and Diane made notes.

"Okay. Since we have you and the jug in our possession, we know what the curse does, and who cast it, we should be able to undo it with nearly any kind of magic. But because it has been in place for so long, I would like to try more than one approach."

"What do you mean?" Martin asked.

"You do candle magic. This involves aromatic oils and spices or herbs rubbed into the candle to energize it, then lighting it and burning what you want to happen in the flame. Correct?"

"Roughly, yes."

"All right, so step one is the candle magic," Diane said.

"How are we going to combine different techniques?" Martin asked.

"I'll tell you what I've been thinking. See if you think it'll work. I can use my energy healing techniques to energize water, which is similar to blessing it."

"So it's sort of like holy water?"

"Sort of, but I can decide what effect I want the water to have."

"How does it work?" Martin asked.

"A study was done years ago with water crystals. When people thought pleasant or happy thoughts, the water formed crystals sort of like snowflakes, which were symmetrical and beautiful. Angry or violent thoughts produced asymmetrical shapes. Studies since then have produced the same results. Different thought patterns produce different crystal structure."

"What does that have to do with magic?"

"I'm not sure about magic, but if you energize water to have healing properties, it can hasten the healing process, and so forth."

"All right. What effect will you give this water?"

"I thought I would use cleansing or purifying. What do you think?"

Martin sat and thought quietly for a moment. Ali, scratched his head, with a puzzled look on his face.

"I think purifying would be best. Don't you?" Martin asked. "We're trying to rid him of a curse."

"We can try that and see if it works. If not, we'll try something else."

"Now, that makes two different techniques. Was there something else you wanted to try as well?"

"What would you think of getting some smudging herbs and using those first to smudge around Ali and the jug? That would include herbs and fire."

"I don't see how it could hurt anything," Martin said, nodding his head in agreement. "Like you said, if it doesn't work, we can always try something else."

"Ali, what do you think? We are talking about you."

"I don't know anything about your types of magic. The djinn have their own ways, which don't involve spells and the like. If you think it'll work, I'm game. Let's try it."

"When do we want to do this?" Martin asked.

"How about Friday night? I can get everything we'll need together and see about coming up with words to say for a spell. Martin, why don't you give that some thought, too. I can call you tomorrow night and we can compare notes. Then we can take the two and make one spell out of them."

"I can do that. And thanks so much for giving us a hand," Martin told her.

"Well, I'm about done with people using me to get at Ali. And breaking into your place. It makes going out a little tense, with everyone wondering what's going to happen next."

"Tomorrow right after work, we have to go over to see Peter. He's firing a project for us, which should be ready by then. But after we get back and have something to eat, I'll give you a call. Does that work?"

"That'll work. And I should get home and start getting everything together. Do you have some candles?"

"I'll need a black candle for the spell. I think I have some around. If not, I'll slip out and buy a couple before Friday night. And I have herbs and essential oils to use for the candle as well."

"I have smudging bundles that I use in my studio, to clear any negative energy left behind by clients. Anything else?"

"Just the water. Were you going to use purified water?" Martin asked.

"I was going to buy some distilled water to use. That way there'll be nothing foreign in the water to affect anything. And I thought I would put it into a glass container and set it in the sun before I energized it. A little extra energy shouldn't hurt anything."

"I think we're all set. I'll talk to you tomorrow," Martin said.

When they reached her car, he wrapped his arms around her in a warm hug before kissing her sweetly.

"I truly appreciate what you're doing for us. I had no idea what I was going to unleash when I bought the jug, and I'm sure Ali is about as tired of the situation as he was of the jug."

"I'm about sick of it and I haven't been dealing with it nearly as long as you have. Talk to you tomorrow!"

THURSDAY THEY WERE slammed from the time they opened until lunchtime. Martin was more than ready to flip the closed sign on the door and retreat to his flat for some lunch.

"Where did everyone come from today?" Ali asked. "We didn't even put out any new bottles."

"I know. The sales were about evenly split between sinus remedies, cough and sore throat lozenges, and the last few Aladdin's Treasures."

"Who was this Aladdin guy? Everybody seems to know what's going on but me."

"Sorry. The story of Aladdin is one of the tales from the Arabian Nights. This particular story is about a young boy named Aladdin, who discovers a lamp. When he rubs it, a genie comes out and grants him whatever he wishes for."

"Okay. So do these people know you have one of the djinn helping you?"

"No. Nothing like that. It's just that Aladdin ended up with all these beautiful treasures, thanks to the genie. And the tale is an old one everyone is familiar with. And with the Arabic style of the little bottles, it seemed appropriate."

"You had me worried for a minute there, boss. I would just as soon stay in the background."

"I understand."

"Have you had time to think about the spell at all?"

Ali must be more worried than he let on. He seemed so carefree on the surface that Martin figured he wasn't particularly concerned.

"I have. As soon as we get back from Peter's place, I'll write down what I have and call Diane. Between the three of us, we should be able to come up with something that will work."

# Chapter 24

Thursday turned out to be busy as well. Martin and Ali had sold out of Aladdin's Treasures the day before and Martin was nearly out of throat lozenges again. After lunch, he spent most of the afternoon, in between customers, compounding some more lozenges, and checking his stock on cold remedies.

"I've decided I'd rather not be a shop owner," Ali told him when they closed for the day. "Way too much going on."

"There are days," Martin replied. "All in all it isn't bad. I'm my own boss. If I need to take a day off I can. It's something I like to do and feel good about. But days like today are a little trying. Shall we go to Peter's?"

The new experiment looked great, but it didn't have all the colors the first version had.

"I don't know what the difference is," Peter said. "The first one had several colors which came out in the glaze. This only has one—the green."

"I don't know," Martin said. "Maybe there's something in my shop that makes the difference. Ali and I could try again and see what happened."

"Can you get more of that dust?" Peter asked.

"I'm pretty sure I can," Martin said, glancing at Ali.

"Yeah, we can get some more," Ali assured the others.

"It's still has a unique look," Martin told his friend.

"Yes, it does. If we can fine tune it a little and get some of those other colors, it will be amazing."

Once they were back in the car, Martin glanced at Ali.

"Where are we going to get any more of the dust?"

"I've been thinking on that a bit. I reckon I could try conjuring some up. The clay must have come from somewhere close to where I originally found the jug. So there must be more of it around."

"It's worth a try anyway. After we get your curse lifted. I still have to try writing my spell."

"I guess the green color is from the original curse. Right?" Ali asked.

"I don't know. Either that or it's something with the clay itself."

"Well, how are we going to duplicate the curse? We can use my magic to shape things, and we can use your magic to put a spell on it. But I don't relish the idea of havin' to curse the thing to get a particular color."

"Let's try a few other things first. Peter may just have to be happy with some other colors."

Back at his flat, they dug into the pizza they'd picked up on the way home before Martin sat down to set the spell down on paper. Once he talked to Diane, they'd see how to combine their ideas.

"Okay, Ali. Wish me luck."

*There is a djinn we call Ali*
*Who once was cursed by Belle-Marie.*
*She bound him to a whiskey jug*
*And with a cob it was then plugged.*
*With the witch now dead, his plight is worse.*
*We pray you to reverse the curse.*

He read the rhyme to Ali, who made a face.

"That's a little hokey, ain't it?"

"It doesn't have to be particularly artistic, just cover the facts."

"Let's see what Diane comes up with. Maybe between the two of you, we'll have a shot at it."

Right at seven the phone rang. Answering the call, Martin put it on speaker so Ali could hear what was being said as well.

"Did you come up with anything?" Martin asked.

"Sort of. I'm rubbish at poetry."

"I know the feeling. Want me to go first?"

He read what he'd come up with and waited for her reaction.

"That's similar to what I have. All right. Here goes.

*Ali was cursed by Belle-Marie*

*Bound to a jug most heinously.*
*Ali's plight goes from bad to worse.*
*The witch is dead, but he's still cursed.*
*I seek a spell to let me lift*
*This dreadful curse. It is my gift."*

"I thought you said you were rubbish at poetry. Yours is better than mine," Martin told her.

"Do you think so?"

"Yes. Definitely. Ali, what do you think?"

"I don't know much about spells and such, but either of them ought to work."

"Honestly, I think we should use Diane's rhyme. It's a little shorter I think, it's to the point, and I like the rhyme."

"How about this?" Diane asked.

*"There is a djinn we call Ali*
*Who once was cursed by Belle-Marie.*
*She bound him to a whiskey jug*
*And then the whiskey jug she plugged.*
*Ali's plight goes from bad to worse.*
*The witch is dead, but he's still cursed.*
*I use this spell to let me lift*
*This dreadful curse. It is my gift."*
*The spell is cast. Set Ali free.*
*Hear us now. So mote it be.*

"I like it," Martin said. "It's a little longer than either of the other versions, but the combination works. Thanks, Diane."

"It's my pleasure. I want to help nail this bastard."

Martin hadn't known Diane was quite such a forceful person before. Of course, being knocked out and left in a toilet while someone impersonated her probably had something to do with it.

"Great! Now, do we have everything else we need?"

"I set the water outside earlier today and since it's a full moon tonight, I'll leave it out. Tomorrow I can energize it to clear negative energy and purify. What else?"

"I have a candle, the sage, and the essential oils. I chose myrrh and sandalwood as the oils. I have a nice candle holder to use and a stone mortar to put the burning paper into."

"Anything else?"

"Let's see. You'd said something about smudging, I think," Martin replied.

"Oh! I almost forgot. I'll set those by the door as soon as we finish here. I use it all the time in the studio and even in my flat."

"We should be good then. Have you turned up anything else in your research we should consider?"

"Nothing at all. In actuality, any of the methods should work alone. I think if we combine them we should definitely get rid of the curse. But what about the person trying to steal the jug?"

"One thing at a time. At least if they steal the jug after the curse is lifted, it shouldn't affect Ali. We can deal with the subject of theft later."

After they rang off, Martin watched Ali bend over and bury his face in his hands.

"Hey, what's up?"

"I just don't know. I mean, I've lived with this curse longer than I've been inside the jug. And now I might be free of both of them. I guess I'm afraid it won't work and I'll be stuck with the thing forever."

"You mean this witch kept you around even after the curse? To do her bidding?"

"Yeah, for quite some time. But the last time I went in, something happened to her and I got stuck there."

"If this doesn't work, for some reason, we'll keep trying until something does."

"I do appreciate everything, Martin. And if it all goes to hell, at least you will have tried."

"How about we go out and get something for dessert? Something completely decadent?" Martin suggested.

"How about I fetch us something instead? I know just the thing."

In seconds the whole flat smelled of something similar to baklava, and a large tray holding filled phyllo pastry appeared. Alongside were two other dishes filled with some sort of custard.

"Now what is this called again?" Martin asked digging into the sweet pastry and nuts.

"It's Umm Ali. I've loved the stuff since someone came up with it."

"What's in it?"

"It has coconut, almonds, raisins, sometimes pistachios. And of course the stuff to sweeten it. It's all put together and then baked. A plain custard goes good with it."

"I'll bet ice cream would be wonderful as well," Martin said, reaching out for another bite.

"I hadn't even thought of that. Of course, ice cream is pretty new to me."

"I guess it is. Sometimes I forget you've been out of the loop for a few years."

They finished their dessert and had coffee afterwards. Maybe once this was all done, Ali would stay on for a bit. Was there any reason they couldn't be friends?

Something had been nagging at him, though. At the moment, Ali was bound to the jug and under the command of whoever owned it. Once he was free of the jug, would he go back to being the trickster genies were said to be? Could he trust the guy?

It was late and he had work the next day. Before they settled the whole curse thing, He would sort all that out with Ali.

Friday morning seemed early, as Martin hadn't slept particularly well. When had his life turned into a sitcom? Ali seemed quiet and pensive during breakfast, but he had another batch of Aladdin's Treasures ready to go out onto the shelves.

"So, Ali, what will you do once you're free of the jug?" Martin tossed out.

"I don't know. I suppose I'm waiting to see if it works before I get my heart set on something."

"I can understand that. Let's say it works. What would you do?"

"I guess I would stay around here for a little while, kind of get my feet under me again. Then I might see if I could locate any of the other djinn back home. I should have some family somewhere or some friends. It would be nice to know what they've been doing all this time."

"How long do you guys live, anyhow?" Martin asked.

He knew Ali had been around at least two centuries. How much time did they have on earth?

With the first laugh of the day, Ali said, "We don't live forever, but we live a long time. I don't know for sure what the expected life is of a djinn. I've been around for a long time—besides the two hundred years, more or less, spent in that jug."

"With any luck at all, you won't be spending any more time there," Martin told him. "I would think, once this is finished, you'll be a little more careful about how much you drink and who you drink with."

"You got that right," Ali said. "That's twice now I've been trapped inside some dad-blamed thing like that. Both times it happened because I was too drunk to figure out what I was getting into."

"Most likely a jug of some kind," Martin teased.

"Right. What is it you guys say? Smart-ass?"

"I couldn't resist the temptation," Martin told him.

The morning went by quickly, with quite a few customers. At lunch time, Martin took Ali with him to an Italian place for a change. He liked the fettuccine Parmesan. Ali chose to try the spaghetti with meatballs.

"What do you think?" Martin asked.

"This ain't bad. I could learn to like this pretty quick."

"Once you're free you could go to Italy and taste the real thing," Martin suggested.

"I might hold off on too much traveling just yet. There is too much I don't know."

Their afternoon was frantic, with everyone shopping for the weekend. As the holidays came closer, the weekends would be crazy. Martin normally opened for half a day on Saturday around holiday times. Not only was it good for business, but with so much stress and cold weather, colds and sniffles abounded.

A phone call from Diane was a welcomed break about an hour before closing time.

"I wanted to check on what time we wanted to get started," she said.

"I'll close the store at five. And we need to have something to eat. Unless you want to come over for dinner."

"I don't have any plans at the moment. Can I bring something?"

Checking with Ali, who offered to provide dinner, he asked her to bring some drinks.

"All right, I'll be there about six," she said, with a sparkle in her voice.

"Good. We can have dinner and have a quick talk before we give this a try. See you at six."

Ali had been tidying up around the shop, so he'd heard the conversation.

"Do we need to talk about something?"

"I have a couple things on my mind, but I want to wait until Diane is here, so she can give an opinion."

"All right. Should I go on up and be getting ready for dinner?"

"Sure. If you can get the table set and dinner ready to go, it'll save time later."

Martin had set out everything for tonight's attempt before he left for work. He thought if they did this all in the spare room, they could leave the candle burning without being afraid of anyone knocking it over in the night.

Would it take more than one night to accomplish this? He knew some spells needed more time to work. Since he had no one to ask, they would just have to give it a go and see what happened.

Right at six, Diane knocked at the back door, shopping bags in hand.

"How much did you figure we'd drink tonight?" Martin teased.

"You never know. If we have something to celebrate it could get a little drunk out."

Taking the bags from her, Martin led the way into the kitchen. A marvelous smell came from the oven.

"I don't know what you have in there, Ali, but it certainly smells wonderful," Diane told him, closing her eyes and breathing in the aromas.

"I got it ready a little while ago and put it in the oven to stay warm. It should be fine."

Fine wasn't the word Martin would have used. This put any gourmet food he'd ever had to shame and then some. Succulent pieces of chicken seasoned with an unusual blend of herbs and spices made him want to savor the experience, and yet wolf it down in haste.

With dessert finished—some of Ali's nut-filled pastries—they took coffee into the living room to get their thoughts ready for the spell.

"WHAT DID YOU WANT TO discuss, Martin?" Diane asked.

With an expression somewhere between determination and dread, Martin took one last sip of coffee, set the cup down on the table, and turned to Ali.

"I know you've been the very picture of a polite guest since you got here. But I have doubts about how this will turn out once you're free of the jug," he said.

"What do you mean, boss?" Ali asked.

Diane was confused as well. Why wouldn't Ali be the same person he'd always been?

"Everything I read tells me you guys are tricksters, pranksters. You love to play tricks on people and have a laugh at their expense. Wishes are granted in a way nobody would want, instead of being helpful."

Sinking back into thought for a moment, he continued.

"Right now you're bound to the jug. Since I own the jug, you are bound to me as well, as my servant. According to what you've said, the one who possesses the jug is your master and you are bound to obey him. What happens when this is no longer the case?"

Diane had somehow missed out on a lot of this information, but Martin did bring up an interesting point. If Ali were no longer enslaved to the jug and to Martin, he could do anything he chose.

"Now boss, there's no need to be that way," Ali said, shaking his head. "Haven't I always treated you decent?"

"Yes, but you've been bound to the jug."

"I can see your point. And you're right. We are a bunch of practical jokers a lot of the time. But like I told you. I like you. You've been more than fair to me since you let me out of the jug. Why would I mess that up?"

"I don't know, but I need some assurance before we go through with this. I want no surprises if it works."

"I thought we were friends," Ali said.

"Martin," Diane interrupted, "are you sure Ali would change if he were free? He's always been nice to me."

"We are friends, Ali," Martin said gently. "And yes, he has always treated you well, Diane. I just want to make sure things will continue on this way."

"I will admit that the temptation is there—not to play pranks on you, Martin. Or Diane either. And I will probably have a little fun once I'm free. Let me think for a minute."

Diane could kind of see both sides. After being imprisoned for so long, she would want to have a little fun, too. But Martin had been having enough trouble lately. He would be about fed up with tricks and pranks.

"All right. Martin and Diane, once I'm free, I give you my word, on my honor as a Djinn, that you will have nothing to fear from me or mine, from now through five generations of your descendants. There will be no tricks, no pranks, no harm done to you from now through that time. And if my descendants and I are treated fairly, I see no reason for it not to continue beyond that time. As long as you are friends with Ali, you will have Ali as a friend."

Offering his hand, Ali waited while Martin made up his mind.

"Five generations?" he asked.

"Exactly."

After taking a deep breathe, Martin reached out and shook hands with Ali, and then gave him a big guy hug. Diane shook hands with the two of them and hugged Ali as well.

"Now, can we get started?" Diane asked. "It's no good talking about a thing unless you're going to do it."

"I believe it is time," Martin said, squaring his shoulders.

With a very determined look on his face and purpose in his stride, he led them to the spare room.

MARTIN HAD PREPPED everything earlier in the day, including the candle. Once he'd energized it and used the oil and herbs, he didn't see why it wouldn't work. But first, Diane had a few ideas to add to the spell. Lighting a bundle of sage and sweet-grass, she waited until it was burning well before snuffing it out, leaving it to smolder. She then used a feather to whisk the smoke toward Ali as she moved the bundle around his body from feet to head and back to front. She smudged around the jug as well and then turned the jug so the smoke would go inside.

Once this was finished, she extinguished the bundle completely and picked up a small glass spray bottle filled with water.

"Now this has been energized to remove negative energy and to purify."

Standing back a little, she sprayed a fine mist so every part of Ali had been touched by the water. As she misted, Martin heard her mumbling under her breath, "cleanse and purify, cleanse and purify."

Next it was Martin's turn. Making sure the candle was firmly in the holder, he lit it and made sure it would stay lit, before he took the spell they'd written and looked it over before saying it out loud.

*"There is a djinn we call Ali*
*Who once was cursed by Belle-Marie..."*

Everything he'd read said to say it three times, so he did, leaving a short space between each repetition. It could have been his imagination, but the air in the room seemed to change a little bit with each repetition, almost like it was getting heavier.

"All right, according to what I read, you need to take the paper and light it from the candle," Diane told him.

"That's what I got, too."

They had all agreed that a small bit of something from Ali would help the spell along, so he burned a small piece of Ale's hair with the paper.

The paper and single strand of hair caught up quickly, so he dropped them into the stone mortar resting next to the candle. The orange flame seemed slightly tinged with green and rose in a slender column about twice its original size, with the color flickering in and out as the paper curled and became ashes.

"Anything else?" he asked.

"No. Just let the candle burn itself out. How long will this candle last?" Diane asked.

"They usually last about six hours, so it will be gone by morning."

"Well, that's all we need for now, then," Diane said, which agreed with everything he'd dug up in his research.

"Ali? How are you doing?" Martin asked the djinn who was his friend.

"I don't know, but the air in here is getting a little thick. Do you suppose we can get out of here now?"

Diane had also noticed the change in atmosphere as the spell went on. And burning the paper seemed to make more of a change.

"Yes. I think a drink might be in order," Martin said, leading the way toward the kitchen.

With a chilled bottle of a nice white wine, the three of them sat to contemplate the ceremony they'd just performed.

"DO YOU THINK IT WILL work?" Diane asked, looking like she hoped he had some answers.

"No idea. I don't suppose we'll know until the next time Ali tries to leave the house."

"Yeah," Ali agreed. "I'll know real quick if the curse still holds. I won't make it to the street."

"I think we need to keep a positive attitude," Diane stated firmly. "If we don't believe what we're doing will work, then why would it?"

"Why wouldn't it?" Martin asked, confused. Maybe it was the wine.

"With energy, mindset can mean everything. Negative thoughts can set up blocks so the energy doesn't flow properly. Why don't we all take a moment and focus on a scene of Ali leaving the building and walking down the street, happy and carefree?"

Since Diane seemed certain about the positive attitude thing, Martin and Ali joined in. And the energy all around the room felt a little lighter after even a few seconds.

Once they'd finished the wine and some little desserts Ali made for them, Diane needed to go home.

"I have a client who can only come see me on Saturday morning, so I'll take my leave. Don't forget to bury all the ash and the remainder of the candle tomorrow morning first thing."

Martin walked her to her car and waved as she drove away. He took a moment to look up at the stars, or what he could see of them with the city lights, before returning to the flat.

"Now, Ali, why the long face?"

The djinn sat on the sofa, shoulders rounded forward, and with his face in his hands.

"Too many things to think about," he said unconvincingly.

"All right, now how about the truth?" Martin asked.

Looking up at him with haunted eyes, Ali shook his head.

"I almost wish you'd never found the jug," Ali admitted. "I would still be stuck in the thing, waiting for the day I would pass from this world, with no hope of anything better. Now I'm free of the jug, sort of, hoping against everything that this thing works, so I can have a life again."

"I can see where it would be sort of nerve-wracking," Martin said. "But we can't change the past. We have to go with what we've got. Whether or not this works, and I have a really good feeling about it, I'll help you learn about the world as it is today, find you something to do you feel is worthwhile."

"I guess you're right. But it'll be such a let down..."

"No. It won't," Marin said forcefully. "It's going to be exciting, freeing, and exhilarating."

# Chapter 25

Ali slept fitfully during the night. He wanted to believe the spell would work, but he was afraid to hope. So when he smelled coffee in the morning, he crawled out of bed and made his way to the kitchen. Martin was ready to put bacon and eggs on as Ali poured a cup of the dark, bitter brew.

"Good morning, my friend. How are you this morning?"

"A little rough to be honest," Ali admitted.

"Don't worry. We'll get this sorted one way or another," Martin said, humming a little tune as he turned the bacon.

Once he'd eaten, Ali felt more awake, so he tidied the kitchen before the two of them went in to check on the candle from the night before. It had burned all the way down to nothing, with only a tiny bit of melted wax in the holder and the smallest piece of wick Ali had ever seen.

The paper the spell had been written on had burned to a fine, light ash that looked like powder.

"I say we bury these in the back garden," Martin said, taking the candle holder and mortar from the small table.

Outside in the garden, Ali used his abilities to make a small hole in the soil about one foot square and a foot deep. Using a knife, Martin pried the wax out of the candle holder, along with the piece of wick, and then poured the ashes into the hole as well, using a small tissue to wipe out the residue and tossing it in to join everything else.

Once Ali had filled the hole in, there was nothing to show there had ever been a hole dug in the garden. To mark the spot, Martin moved one of the smaller rocks over it. Since they'd dug fairly close to the rock border, it didn't seem out of place.

"So, what do you say we try it out and see if it worked?" Martin asked.

"I don't know," Ali answered, shaking his head. "Maybe we could do it again tonight just to make sure."

"Come on. Where's your sense of adventure? I could call Diane and get her to meet us someplace for lunch. If it doesn't work, we'll snag the little jug and go anyway. But at least we'll know."

Ali sat and thought about it for a moment, then nodded.

"I reckon you've got a point."

"I know you're probably nervous as hell," Martin said. "But we won't know until we try. Right?"

"I guess. Go ahead and give your gal a call. If nothing else we can have a decent lunch."

"Greek all right?" Martin asked.

"That'd be fine.

MARTIN KNEW ALI WAS afraid the spell hadn't worked, but he'd been feeling happy and light-hearted since he woke up. The atmosphere in the whole flat seemed more cheerful for some reason. And the only reason he could think of was the lifting of the curse. Perhaps the negative energy of it had affected everything around.

And then there was Diane's energized water, which was supposed to remove negative energy. Maybe he'd picked up some negativity from his clients or something and brought it into the flat with him. He would have to talk to Diane about it.

Or maybe he should get some of the smudging herbs and do a monthly clearing of his flat and shop.

Whoa. One step at a time. First they had to make sure Ali was free and then deal with whoever was attempting to steal the jug. Once that was all settled, he could bring the jug out for display and worry about negative energy later.

Diane had two clients in the morning, but would be finished in time for lunch, so they agreed to meet at the Greek Taverna. It was one of Ali's favorite spots, and Martin always enjoyed their offerings.

Ali made up some more of Aladdin's Treasures while they waited, and Martin was more than halfway convinced they sparkled more than the first ones had.

"Naw, there ain't no way for that to happen," Ali told him. "I did them all the same way."

"Let's just see," Martin said.

He'd put a few back on Friday so they wouldn't run out completely. Taking one of the newer ones into the shop, he pulled one of the same color out to compare.

"Well, I'll be dad-gummed," Ali said, scratching his head. "This one does seem brighter. I don't know. I can't explain it."

"I'll bet it has to do with a certain curse being lifted," Martin suggested.

"Now don't start with that again. I'm trying to keep my mind off it."

"I was going to pick out a few to send to my folks for the holidays. I'm glad I waited a little longer. These are the best ones yet."

They puttered around in the shop for a while. Martin had decided to keep the shop closed this weekend, given all the weird things they had going on. But it was soon time to clean up and meet Diane.

Leaving by the back door, he saw Ali hesitate before stepping out.

"Come on. You wouldn't even notice it yet, Ali," he chided.

With a sly grin from being caught out, Ali stepped into the sunshine. Leading the way around the end of the building to the car, Martin waited for Ali to catch up.

"You know, walking more slowly won't make any difference," he said as he leaned against the car.

"Yeah, but it might put off the inevitable," Ali countered.

"Get your ass over here," Martin said with a grin. "I think it's going to be a good day."

If Martin remembered correctly, Ali hadn't made it all the way to the car the last time, so as he approached, Martin kept a close eye on him. Finally standing next to the car, Ali seemed reluctant to actually get into it.

"You've made it farther than you did before," Martin noted.

"Yeah, but I'm not sure how much farther I'll get."

"Bubba, come on," Martin said, using the nickname Ali had used when they first met. "You won't know until you try. Get in the car. Lunch is waiting."

Eyeing the car like it might transform into a dragon or something, Ali approached it, opened the door, and climbed in. Fidgeting nervously, he watched Martin start the car and begin to pull out onto the street.

"Everything all right over there?" Martin asked.

"Seems to be," Ali answered, glancing around nervously.

"Look, we're a full block away from the shop. I'm sure everything is fine. The whole day has been more peaceful and relaxed than I've ever seen it. Relax a little bit."

With a deep breath, Ali closed his eyes and took slow deep breaths, attempting to contain his nervous energy. But his hands were clenched into fists in his lap and his brow furrowed.

Martin shook his head and smiled. As sure as he was that Ali would be fine, he could imagine, at least in part, how the guy must feel. Martin hadn't even lived two hundred years—and had no expectation of doing so—let alone spent two hundred years of an even longer life in a jug. Why Ali wasn't barking mad by this time was the question.

Diane had arrived before them and found a table. Greeting them warmly, she sent a questioning look Martin's way before asking Ali how he felt.

"Kind of strange, if I'm honest," Ali answered. "It's like I'm expecting the other shoe to drop. I feel like my whole world is about to blow up and there's nothing I can do to stop it."

"What could possible go wrong at this point?" Diane asked. "You're free of—well, you know," she said looking around at the other patrons. "If you've made it this far, I think everything we did last night must have worked. Don't you?"

"But if it did, why don't I feel better? Maybe we should go home."

"Ali, does it feel like you're being pulled back?" Martin asked, concerned.

"No, I just don't feel right. Like I'm about to panic," Ali admitted.

"Why don't we have something to eat. As long as there is no compulsion to go home, I think everything is fine. You're just not used to it yet."

The poor guy was pale and his breath ragged. Martin was afraid he might run out the door and try to get home on his own. He could see Ali was trying to remain calm, but was losing the battle.

A girl came over to take their order. Diane was having dolmadakia, while Martin had decided on moussaka.

"Ali, what would you like to try?" Diane asked gently.

"Maybe the souvlaki," he answered, still looking shaky.

When the waitress had left their table, Martin asked, "What has you so upset, Ali? If you're not feeling pulled back, why the concern?"

With a look somewhere between scared and confused, he said, "I can't feel the jug. At all. It's like it doesn't exist. I don't know what to do."

"Isn't that good?" Diane asked.

"It should be, but it scares the hell out of me," Ali told her. "For nearly as long as I can remember, the thing has been there. No matter where I was, I could feel it in the background. And now it's gone."

"And suddenly you're alone in the world, without a place of your own," Martin added quietly.

"Yeah. Because no matter what, I always had someplace to go, someplace to stay. All right, so I had to stay pretty close to the thing, and I could be commanded into it and shut in. But it was always there. It's like I've lost a close friend or family member."

They drank lemonade while they waited for their food and talked about what they were going to do during the next week. Ali was in a state still, but trying to get used to the idea.

Once their food was presented, and Ali had something in his stomach, he began to look better and seemed to relax a little.

"We still have to figure out something for Peter," Martin said, hoping to draw him out a little more.

"Yeah. What are we going to do there?" Ali asked.

"That all depends. Were you planning to stay around here a little longer? Or were you going to go out exploring?"

The look of panic on Ali's face startled his two friends.

"Do you mind if I stay on a while?" he asked.

"Not at all. Glad to have you."

"Thank you, Martin. You're a good man and a good friend. I'll think on the problem and see what I can come up with. Of course, a lot of things may have changed since last night. Look at Aladdin's Treasures."

Martin had to explain to Diane what they'd discovered earlier.

"So somehow the magic affected the way the clay and glaze fired?" she asked sipping more lemonade.

"Yeah. We're trying to see if there is any way to duplicate the effects. If it requires Ali and me to use magic in the shaping of the forms, we'll have to figure something out. I don't know about the dust from the jug."

"Did the curse affect the jug?" she asked.

"We don't know. But I don't want to grind up the whole jug so Peter can make pottery either," Martin said.

"True. Are you going to be able to display it now?"

"I don't know. We still don't know who is responsible for the break-ins. And we don't know if they will sense the change now that Ali is released from it."

"So you're just going to wait and see if they try to break-in again?" Diane asked.

"Any other suggestions?"

"Well, no. Not at the moment. Maybe it would be better to display it and draw them out. You could notify the police first and see if they can keep a closer eye on your shop."

"It's something to think about. Maybe we'll wait a few days and let Ali settle in first."

"Yeah, this is going to take some getting used to," Ali told them, still fidgeting nervously.

"Why don't we get back to the flat and take it easy for the rest of the day?" Martin suggested.

"I'd like to come by later and have a look at your new shipment of Treasures," Diane said.

"Sure! I'll chill some wine and we can have cheese and crackers, too," he said. "I'm sure Ali wouldn't mind the company either."

"No, come on over. But you kids need to take some time alone. If I can get a handle on this whole thing, and we can get this other stuff sorted out with the jug, I can watch the place while you go out on the town. And you won't have anything to worry about and spoil your evening."

"You haven't spoiled anything, Ali," Diane said giving him a hug. "I actually think all of this has brought us a little closer."

That look said a lot about where her mind was. Maybe they could find Ali a place of his own in the not too distant future.

ALI WAS PRETTY UNSETTLED for a few days. Something which had been with him for such a very long time was now gone. And while he was glad it was gone, it left a strange empty feeling, like something was missing.

"I'm sure you'll find something else to take its place," Martin told him. "We'll have to find you a hobby or something. Maybe making trinkets to sell in the shop."

"That is kind of fun," Ali admitted.

He had been surprised at how many people wanted the Aladdin's Treasures for their holiday. He had thought the market would be saturated by now, but people kept coming in. Some of them came in more than once, just for the trinkets.

"Maybe we should sit down and figure out what to make up next," Martin suggested. "Maybe we could come up with something a little different for New Year's. And then there's Valentine's Day in a couple months. We'll split the profits on anything you provide. That way you'll have enough to do whatever you want to do with your time."

Ali had been contemplating his future. He knew nothing about this world, which was so foreign to the one he'd left behind. Of course, it wouldn't cost him much to do a little traveling, since he could whisk himself anywhere he wanted to go. He wasn't sure Martin understood what being one of the djinn was all about.

For now he was happy where he was. He could help out his savior, learn something about the world, and maybe coax along the romance between Martin and Diane. They would make a nice couple, if either one of them would take the first step. Maybe just a little nudge here and there...

Ali had brought in some more pottery dust and they'd handed some of it off to Peter in exchange for some clay. He and Martin thought they could put together a couple things and they could all fire at the same time and judge the results.

Peter's figures would have no magic involved, except for Ali bringing the dust across. His would be shaped using his magic. Martin was going to form something simple and then cast a spell of some sort on it to test the theory. The last one Ali would form and Martin would say a spell over. Maybe one of them would work.

Now, what about their thief? How could they go about catching him?

Or was it a her?

WITH ONLY TWO MORE weeks before Christmas, Martin was busy. The winter had turned colder than normal, so he'd had a lot of customers in for his herbal medicines and remedies, as well as people buying Aladdin's Treasures. The things sold as fast as Ali could make them, so they'd slowed their shipments, claiming holiday shipping delays.

He had talked with Ali about a special New Year's edition of the Treasures and they were coming up with ideas for them. While he'd been happy before he'd inadvertently brought Ali into his life, he was glad he was around. The guy had quite the sense of humor and had helped out around the flat and the shop since he'd arrived, giving Martin more time for compounding remedies without having to sacrifice tidiness around the flat.

He was a hit with Diane, too, especially now that she understood how he'd come to be here. And her help with lifting the curse had been invaluable. Maybe once Ali got a little more independent he could ease things along a little with Diane. She seemed to like him, and he was quite attracted to her, but he didn't want to move too quickly and spoil things.

Maybe once they got this thief out of their hair they could see how things developed. They still had no idea who was responsible, though Martin was certain it had to do with Ali and his jug. Still, there had been no attempt for over a week. Did they sense something different? Or were they deciding on a new tactic? It was too much to hope that they'd given up on the idea.

Oh well. Christmas was almost here. Time to celebrate, not worry about what might happen in the future.

# Chapter 26

With Christmas rapidly approaching, Diane was trying to make sure she had all her gifts ready. Her family lived a pretty fair distance, so she had planned to visit them after New Years. Her parents were going to visit her brother and his family up in Scotland for Christmas anyway, which would be nice. But she had clients right up until Christmas Eve, and then starting again two days after Christmas.

Yes, she could have scheduled more time off, but when people needed healing, how could she say no, especially with the weather turning so cold and nasty? Between the stress of the holiday and the weather, this was one of her busier times of year.

Now, what could she get for Martin? Or Ali. True, she and Martin had become closer during the past few weeks, but what sort of signal did she want to send? She wanted to give him something personal, not overly romantic, but it had to be something more than just friends. They had passed just friends, hadn't they? She wasn't quite sure.

And Ali... What did you get for someone who could conjure up anything he wanted? Something handmade perhaps. She liked to bake and had a couple specialties. While he could have anything he wanted, he had to know about it first. Maybe her mother's recipe for chocolate torte with raspberry creme...

FRIDAY NIGHT, MARTIN and Diane were going out to have dinner again. He had reservations at one of the nicer restaurants in town, and their seasonal menu began this week. Christmas Eve was the following Friday evening and he wasn't sure what Diane was doing for the holiday. He had begged off going home, and Ali had nothing planned, so maybe the three of them could get together and do something nice.

Martin's week flew by, and he was glad he'd done his shopping online this year. With everything else going on in his life, he didn't need the headache of all the crowds on top of it. He had explained to his family why he wasn't coming up this year, and they understood, even if they were disappointed. He and Ali had put together gifts for them, including some of Aladdin's Treasures, which he was sure his mother would adore.

As Friday approached, he phoned to confirm their reservations for dinner. You could never rely on a reservation, unless you confirmed it at least once before your visit. He'd been embarrassed a couple times when he'd forgotten to make that call, and it wasn't happening again. And especially not tonight.

He was closing a little early on Friday. The weather was bad, his stock on everything was getting low, and he was simply out of the mood to deal with anyone else. Just as he was flipping the sign, he saw an older woman hurrying toward his shop, waving frantically for him to stop.

"I'm sorry. Can I help you?" he asked.

"Please tell me you have at least one more of those little Aladdin's Treasures," she said, trying to catch her breath. "And some of your cough lozenges. This winter air is killing me. Are you usually closed this early?"

"No, I'm taking a little bit of time off tonight," he explained as he got her some of the lozenges. "Now, let me see if I have any more of the trinkets in the back room. Was there a particular color you wanted?"

"I simply adore the blue and silver ones, but any color would work for tonight. I have a friend visiting from out of town and I didn't have a gift for her."

"Let me take a look."

On his way to the store room, he called for Ali to join him.

"I don't think we have any more of your trinkets, but there is a lady out front who is desperate for a couple. Could we find a couple more in the next minute or so?" he asked, knowing Ali obtained them by some arcane means. "She prefers blue and silver."

"Sure boss. Let me take a look and see what we've got," he called as Martin went back out.

"My assistant is looking to see if some of those got pushed to the back of a shelf. With any luck he'll find one or two for you."

They chatted for a moment, until Ali strolled into the shop.

"I think these will do the trick," he said as he handed the small items to Martin.

"What do you think?" he asked the lady in question.

"Oh! These are marvelous. I think they're even prettier than the other ones I bought a while back. I don't know where you get these, but I hope you'll have some next year, too."

Martin had convinced himself he was imagining things, but his customer had noticed the difference in the Treasures also.

"We'll have to see about next year. So much can change. Have fun with your friend," he told the woman as he saw her out the door.

Damn. He hadn't managed to actually close early after all, but it made for good customer relations.

"Weren't you and Diane going out tonight?" Ali asked.

"Yeah, if I can get ready. I hoped to have a little extra time, but now I'm running behind."

A quick call to Diane confirmed that she was on schedule, so they would still arrive at the restaurant on time. After a quick shower, he threw on his clothes before pulling on his overcoat to keep out the winter chill, which had set in for the season. A woolen scarf around his neck finished the look, so with a wave to Ali, Martin hurried to pick up Diane.

ONE THING DIANE LOVED about winter was jumpers. She loved jumpers in all forms—cardigans, pull-overs, anything knitted. Even knit dresses. If it was in any manner knit, she loved it. Tonight she had chosen a cowl neck jumper in a blue which closely matched her eyes and paired it with a charcoal grey ankle length skirt. With a hooded winter cloak in a rich tweed, it should look stunning.

While they weren't actually dating, she was excited about dinner. The restaurant Martin had chosen was one of the finest in town and was sure to be filled to capacity tonight, as it was every evening on the weekend. There was room for dancing and usually with live music of some sort.

Maybe Martin would suggest moving their relationship forward a little tonight. They had seen a lot of each other lately, and seemed to get on well enough. If not, at least it shouldn't be goodbye.

She had finally decided on gifts for both Martin and Ali, so her shopping was all sorted. She knew her mother and sister were going to love the Aladdin's Treasures, along with the other things she found. Maybe she could help with ideas for the other holidays this coming year.

When Martin arrived, he seemed impressed with her outfit. He washed up nicely, too. With their reservations confirmed, they were seated within a few minutes of arriving at the restaurant.

"What do you like here?" she asked, hoping for some indication of any price limitations.

"I don't know. I haven't had anything here I don't care for. Perhaps I'll go with the porterhouse steak. My appetite has been craving steak for days." Looking up at her, he added, "Order whatever you like. It's holiday season."

She decided on the salmon, which was as good as it sounded, and as they lingered over dinner, she thought she saw a spark of something new in Martin's eyes.

"Shall we check out the ensemble?" he asked, indicating the dance floor.

"Sounds like a good way to work off some of dinner," she replied lightly.

He was heaven to dance with. He'd obviously had a few lessons somewhere along the way, and he was at about her level of proficiency. Disappointment set in when he suggested taking a break for something to drink. Diane hadn't realized how comfortable he was to be around. And she'd had no idea how delightful it would feel to be in his arms.

As they sipped on coffee, they talked about the upcoming holidays, families, and expectations.

"Yes, I'd always been interested in herbal remedies, but my parents wanted me to do something more "useful" with my life."

"More useful than giving people an alternative in their health care?" Diane asked.

"You know how parents can be. I should have gone into traditional pharmacology, if I had to do something in the field. But herbal studies? Not too keen."

"My folks still aren't sure about my energy healing. Massage they can sort of get their head around, but energy is another subject altogether. I'm sure they think I'm a witch and dabbling in the dark arts," she said with a laugh.

"I want to thank you again for your help in getting things sorted with Ali," Martin told her earnestly. "This is such a busy time at the shop, I was struggling with the research."

"I'm glad I could help. I've enjoyed spending more time with you."

"It has been nice, hasn't it?" he answered. "Maybe we should do more of it."

"Hm... I wouldn't have any objections."

"It'll probably have to be after the holidays, though, except for Christmas Eve. You were coming over to celebrate with us, weren't you?" Martin asked.

"Of course! Are there any carolers singing down your way?"

"Usually, and they're not bad. At least they can carry a tune."

"We'll have to make sure and listen. What can I bring?"

"Whatever you like. I was going to pick up some wine and cheese to nibble by the fire. Ali said he would whip something up—and who knows what he'll come up with."

"I'll bake something," Diane suggested.

"Home baked goods? That's a definite yes," he said with a smile.

After another spin on the dance floor, they collected their warm coats for the trip home. It was a little later than Diane planned for, but she wouldn't have changed anything. At least she had no early clients in the morning.

The two of them hurried up the walkway to her door, trying to keep the cold at bay.

"Good night, Martin," she told him. "I had a lovely evening."

Wondering whether a kiss might be in the offing, she leaned a little closer and tilted her face up to his. She needn't have been worried, and the sizzle took her by surprise. From the expression on his face, he must have felt the same way.

"I'll give you a ring tomorrow," tucking a lock of hair behind her ear.

"Good night, Martin. Sweet dreams."

HE DOUBTED HIS DREAMS would be considered sweet, but he would undoubtedly enjoy them. The effect of her kiss had caught him unawares. Though she was an attractive woman, he hadn't been strongly attracted to her until recently, and had certainly had none of the thoughts about her spiraling around in his head at the moment.

This could get tricky.

Back at his flat, Ali met him at the door.

"Anything wrong?" he asked.

"No, everything's fine. No intruders, no thieves. Just peace and quiet for a change. Did you have a good time?"

"I need a drink," Martin said, grabbing the bottle of Scotch.

"That good a time, was it?" Ali said with a laugh. "I could do with some good news. Feel free to leave out the juicier bits."

"No nothing like that," Martin began before tossing back the Scotch and filling Ali in on the details.

"She is a mighty fine woman. You could do worse," Ali told him.

"It's way too early to be thinking along those lines."

"I don't know. You run an apothecary, she does massage and healing. The two of you could throw in together, save a little money, have a little fun..."

"Enough already. We'll be seeing each other again, probably more often, and see what comes of it."

"A little magic wouldn't hurt," Ali suggested.

"There's been too much magic around here already," Martin told him. "And we still have to figure something out for Peter."

# Chapter 27

He and Ali got together over the weekend to make their clay figures. Since Martin was rubbish at pottery, he'd gone with something simple—a shallow bowl, he'd finally been able to smooth out and straighten a bit so it wasn't lopsided. Ali, of course, had done something decorative—a clay replica of an Arabic style coffee pitcher.

For the one they worked on together, Ali formed a pretty vase. Once they were all dry, Martin would say a spell over two of them and see what happened. Peter was going to fire on Monday and then glaze on Wednesday. With any luck, they could see the results on Christmas Eve.

The first part of the week was slow. They'd taken their pottery attempts over to Peter on Sunday, and though he knew they wouldn't be ready yet, Martin was impatient. Ali tried to keep him distracted, but it wasn't working.

"I know, Ali. But if this doesn't work, we'll have to come up with something else to try. Why does it take so long?"

"Some things you can't hurry," his friend explained once again. "Why don't you think about Diane instead? Have you got her something for the holiday?"

"I got her a little something I think she'll like," Martin said, not sounding at all sure.

"So what's wrong with it?"

"I'm not sure if it's the right sort of thing for someone I'm dating. I mean, when I bought it we were just friends. Not even close friends. But things have changed in that department."

"Yeah, I'd say," Ali chuckled. "What did you have in mind?"

"I don't know. And that's the problem. I know she's likes to stay healthy, so I hate to buy chocolates or anything like that. Jewelry might give the wrong impression, like I'm trying to rush things along. I could probably buy a scarf or a scarf and gloves set."

"You can do better than that. How about something decorative for her place? Something completely frivolous that would look nice on her table?"

"Where am I going to find something like that at this late date?" Martin complained.

"If you could have anything you wanted, what would it be?" the djinn asked.

"I would love to see one of your Aladdin's Treasures as a full sized thing, only completely functional as a pitcher. You know, the ones you call water pitchers."

"Nothing more?"

"No. Why?"

With a snap of his fingers, Ali pointed at the cut crystal pitcher sitting on the coffee table, standing about a foot tall and accented in gold.

"Something like that?" the djinn asked.

"What the hell? Are you sure?" Martin asked.

"After all you've done for me, without asking anything in return, I'm positive. If you'd like to have this for the love of your life, it is yours."

"No, I couldn't. I can't pay you for this," Martin insisted.

"It didn't cost me anything," Ali stated, examining his fingernails.

"Really? You would let me give this to Diane?"

"Of course, ya numbskull. Why else would I conjure the thing up?"

After fussing around all day Monday and most of Tuesday, the call from Peter was welcomed. The first firing had gone well, and all of the pieces with the new dust in them had slumped slightly, as had the first ones he'd fired for them. He would begin glazing soon, and with luck would fire the glaze on Wednesday.

"So we could have a look at them as early as Thursday?" Martin asked.

"Should be able to, yes," Peter assured him. "Then if we need to tinker with them some more, we'll look at them after the new year has begun. Too many holidays and plans for the next couple weeks."

"We're good so far then?" Ali asked.

"Yes. At this point, everything is going just as it should. He'll have them ready on Thursday, unless something happens between now and then."

"Did you ever get any of those smudging things from Diane?" Ali asked.

"Actually, I did. I haven't used them yet, but I did buy some. Not sure where I put them, though."

"Want me to take a look around?"

"Sure. Something wrong?"

"Just an uneasy kind of feeling. Not like the other day, after you lifted the curse. I'm getting used to that now. This is something different, like something is slightly out of kilter. I thought maybe smudging might help."

"Look around. I think I bought them after work one night, so they may be in the flat. Look in the kitchen somewhere," he told Ali.

"Have you noticed anything unusual, or anyone who seemed off somehow?" the djinn asked.

Thinking back, there had been a couple times during the past few days when he'd felt like someone was watching him.

"Yeah, that's kind of the feeling I've got. But right now we don't have any customers. Do you remember when you got that feeling?"

Casting his mind back, he'd had the feeling off and on since the middle of the previous week, but hadn't paid much attention to it. What with everything else going on in his life, he wasn't surprised at it, so he dismissed it. But there had been this man who'd come into the shop...

"Which man?" Ali asked.

"He was just this guy, middle-aged, kind of stoop-shouldered. Something about him didn't ring quite right, but I couldn't place what it was. I'd never seen him in the shop before."

"But that's when you started having this feeling?"

"I think so. He came in again yesterday, late in the morning. All he bought was a packet of throat lozenges. Said hardly a word, just paid for them and left."

"Did he show any interest in Aladdin's Treasures?" Ali asked.

"I don't think he even went over to that area of the shop. He just came to the counter and asked for the lozenges."

"Can you think about it now and figure out what didn't feel right about him? Was it the way he was dressed, the way he moved? Anything that stood out?"

What had it been? The man hadn't been rude. He'd paid in cash. There was nothing notable about him. He was dressed about like anyone else who came into the apothecary, probably middle-class, bundled up against the winter.

His eyes... While he was very quiet, sort of shuffling across the floor, his eyes were very sharp and clear, darting around to take in everything around the shop. And when their eyes met, there was an edge to his glance for just a half second before he dropped his eyes to the counter top.

"You know, that could be our guy. You say he shuffled as he walked. Did it seem natural?"

"At the time I didn't make much of it, but now, it did seem odd. His feet scuffed the floor as he walked, but the rest of him moved too freely to match. I should have watched him as he walked away, but the shop was a little busy at the time. Should we call the police?"

"And tell them what. That we feel weird?" Ali asked rolling his eyes.

"Yeah, they'd get a real laugh. Go find that bundle of sage. It might help, if there is any negative or unhealthy energy in here. Is there anything he could have done here as kind of a magical surveillance kind of thing?"

"Did he touch you?"

"No. He didn't."

"Did he linger in any one spot anywhere before he come up to pay for his goods?"

"Not that I remember, not the first time. Yesterday I know he didn't. He came through the door, at a shuffle, stomped his feet on the mat, and came straight over to me."

"Was he mumbling or anything?" Ali asked.

"Mumbling? I don't know. I was busy."

"Let me go look for the sage. You might want to strengthen your protective spells around the place tonight, and maybe say a spell to rid the shop of any negative energy or curses he might have placed when he got here."

"Do you think he was looking for the jug?"

"He could have been. If all the magic surrounding it has been released, and he can't sense it anymore, he may have come looking for it. Since it isn't on display in the shop, he might take another crack at breaking in."

"But he normally does that when I'm gone." Martin said.

"Like tomorrow after work when we go see Peter." Ali added.

"Yeah. What do you think we should do?"

"We could set a trap." Ali suggested.

"What sort of trap? We will get into trouble if the guy gets hurt breaking in."

"You're kiddin'," Ali stated. After seeing Martin's look, he added, "Okay, you're not kiddin'. I can set something up to where he can get in but can't get back out."

"We could try that. What if he tries to break out through the windows?"

"He won't get out. If I rig the place, he'll be here until we let him go, or the cops come get him."

"All right. Let's plan on that. Sage."

"Sage."

Ali finally found the smudging herbs in the canned goods pantry. Why he'd stuck it in there Martin had no idea. After they closed up for the day, he smudged the place thoroughly before they went upstairs to the flat.

"How about some kebabs for dinner, Martin?" Ali asked. "I know you don't feel like cooking and I hate to leave the place any more than necessary."

"That would be fantastic, Ali. I still have spells to cast tonight."

Diane called shortly after dinner and they talked about the weird man who'd come into the shop. He told her about the precautions they were taking.

"I think I left the energized water over there, too," she said.

"Okay?"

"I mean, you could use it to mist down the counter top, the door handle, door mat, anything you know he touched and dispel any negative energy he brought in with him. Did he pay in bills or coins?"

"Well, the total came to £3.10. I think he gave me a five pound note. Why?"

"If you haven't already taken it to the bank, mist the notes as well for good measure. If he's using magic, there will be an energy there. It should help."

After talking with Diane, he and Bubba found the spray bottle Diane had forgotten and sprayed a fine mist of water all around the shop. Opening the cash drawer, Martin pulled out all the notes, fanned them out on the counter, and lightly misted those as well.

Next he set Ali to smudging the place while he got a candle, wrote a quick spell, and got all of that in motion. By the time he had the spells said, the words burnt in the flame, and crumbling to ash, Ali was finished with the sage and the shop was fairly aromatic.

"That should do the trick," Ali said. "And if it don't, there ain't no helpin' it."

"I believe you are correct," Martin said, nodding. "We can pay close attention to our customers tomorrow, and if that guy shows up, we'll... do something. Not sure what."

"Yeah. So far we can't prove he's done anything wrong."

"Let's sleep on it and see what we can come up with."

Thursday was cloudy and drizzly out, but business was still brisk. Of course, with Christmas only two days away, everyone was out doing last minute shopping, and stopping by for herbal remedies and supplements to help against winter ills. Though Martin and Ali watched for their possible thief, they saw nobody who seemed out of the ordinary. No one bore any resemblance to the man Martin remembered.

A last rush of customers delayed closing the shop. Before they left to go look at the pottery, Martin checked all the spells around the place. He had taken care of the candle remains early in the morning before work, so the spell should have done its work.

Ali stopped before stepping out the door and snapped his fingers, but Martin didn't see anything change.

"Ali? How is that supposed to stop anyone?" he asked.

"Invisible web. They break in, walk down the corridor, and pull what is pretty much a giant spider web down around them. They'll be here waiting for us when we get home."

"How will that work if we call the police?"

"I snap my fingers and the web disappears. No injuries, nothing to say anything at all happened to him. It looks like we came home and caught him in the act of burglarizing the place."

"Gotcha. Let's get going."

The drive took a little longer than usual with the streets heavy with traffic, and a puzzle awaited them at Peter's place.

"All right you two. What are you doing to me?" Peter asked.

"Nothing. Why?"

"Come look at your pieces."

This time, the ones created with no magic, only the dust from the jug, had the same type of faint color streaks down the side, only in a deep transparent wine red color, instead of the green.

Ali's project that he'd formed with his magic and the dust had two colors—the wine and a gold color.

The one Martin had hand-thrown with the dust produced the same wine color and a dark midnight blue from the spell he'd cast.

"All right. What's going on?" Martin mused, knowing full well what had caused the various colors.

"What about the last one?" Ali asked.

"Now that one is interesting," Peter told them. "Take a look."

Removing a towel which had been covering it, Peter revealed the last item. There was, of course, the wine red, Ali's gold, and Martin's blue. But also, over the whole of the jug, there was a faint silvery sheen, almost as if an ultra-fine mist had settled on the outside of the jug and dried to a faint shimmering silver.

It wasn't like a coating or a spray finish, as it was only actually noticeable when the light shone on it at an angle, or if it was turned in the light. Running his fingers over the surface, Martin felt no difference where the stripes of color flowed down the sides of the jug, and no pebbly feeling from the silver sheen. Somehow, combining his spell with Ali's magic had brought about the startling effect.

All of the items had the same type finish as the first jug they'd brought in as well.

"Well, I'll be a monkey's uncle," Ali declared.

"And I'll be the monkey," Peter added. "Any ideas?"

"Maybe, but I think we'd better wait until after the holidays. Got anything to drink?"

Martin figured one drink wouldn't hurt anything and he definitely needed something. How were they going to explain this to Peter? If he told him it was magic, the man would laugh in his face and tell him to get real.

"All right, you two," Peter said as they turned to go. "Happy Christmas, and try to stay out of trouble."

"Right. Happy Christmas."

# Chapter 28

Martin was almost disappointed when there had been no surprises waiting for them when they got back . Ali removed his web, Martin checked on all his spells, and they decided on an early night. The next day could get hectic.

For those last minute panic shoppers, Martin elected to stay open half a day on Christmas Eve. All in all, they had done well during the holiday so far, and Aladdin's Treasures had been one of the major contributors to their bank account. There were still a few left, but by the time they closed for the holiday, they had sold out and had to turn a few people away.

After he and Ali had lunch, he gave Diane a quick call to confirm what time she would be over in the evening. She'd had no clients and had spent the morning baking goodies for them. Martin had sort of been spoiled lately with Ali's desserts, and he'd never tasted anything Diane had made. But she seemed confident, so maybe they'd be all right.

Martin took the afternoon to clean his flat. Seriously, the place needed a good hoovering. He could ask Ali to do one of his quick cleans, but that seemed a lot like cheating. And who knew where it all went?

Later in the afternoon, he sat and watched a little something on the telly before he got out the cheese and biscuits, some crisps, and a small tray of finger foods he'd bought at the local grocery. The wine was chilling nicely and should be just about right when Diane got there.

Seven o'clock came. And went. By seven-thirty, Martin was worried. He'd tried Diane's mobile several times, but got no answer. She seldom used her landline, but he tried it as well, with the same results.

"I'm not sure what to do," he told Ali. "It's too early to file for missing persons. I could phone all the hospitals and see if she was in a car crash or something."

"Can you get into her flat?" Ali asked.

"No. She may have a spare key somewhere, but hasn't shared that with me."

"Would you like to get into her flat?" Ali asked him.

"Why? Can you get us in? We could at least see if she's there and maybe injured or something."

"Does a bear... Never mind."

Ali had been to her flat once or twice with him, before everything went weird, but how was he going to get them in?

"Hang on, son. Let's see what we can see."

The world around him blurred for a moment, and he was sure his stomach flipped over a couple times in the next few seconds, but when it all settled down, they were standing in Diane's living room.

"I don't even want to know how you did that," Martin stated. "Let's look around and see what we can find out."

They didn't have to look far. Posted on the refrigerator door was a full-sized sheet of paper, huge letters printed on it with felt-tipped marker.

"Want the girl? Bring me the jug."

"That's wonderful. How am I supposed to bring him the jug when I don't know where he is?"

"Won't she most likely be wherever he is?" Ali asked.

"Yes..."

"So if you found her, you should find him. Right?"

"You're absolutely right, Ali. And since we're in her flat, there is plenty here I can use with my psychic ability, with a little bit of luck."

"Hey, boss, not too fast," Ali said as Martin turned toward the bathroom. "We need a plan first. We can't just show up and hope to get Diane back. First we need the jug. Then we need the location. And I'm thinkin' that if you can convince the law you know where she is, we could use some of those boys as well. And I think there's a message here on the note, something done with magic. Maybe we can find a way to read it."

"Yeah. You're right. Let's think about this," Martin said trying to calm down. "Let me grab her hair brush and this note, and then let's go back to our flat."

Suiting actions to words, Martin went into the bathroom and came back with a hairbrush containing some of Diane's hair. In the kitchen, he found a large storage bag that would hold the paper they'd found on the refrigerator door. Nodding to Ali, Martin gritted his teeth against the unsettling sensations of being transported by magic, while he hoped and prayed nothing would happen to Diane.

Settling down on the sofa, he and Ali laid out what they would need to do. The kidnapper obviously thought Ali was still bound to the jug, so they should have a few seconds before realization struck for Ali to restrain the guy. But they would have to have the jug with them for the exchange.

They had to locate Diane, who they assumed was somewhere close to her kidnapper. Either way, they had to find her to rescue her, kidnapper or not. With some of her hair, Martin should be able to find her. If not, maybe Ali could do something so they could read the invisible message on the bottom of the note.

And of course, they would have to notify the authorities and get this guy taken care of.

Great way to spend Christmas Eve.

"Ali, do you want to have a go at that message first, or shall I try to do a locate?"

"Why don't we do both? It'll save time if one or the other doesn't work."

Ali picked up the bag containing the paper and began to make various gestures to try to bring out the remainder of the message.

Martin sat with a little strand of Diane's hair wound around his finger, closed his eyes, and tried to calm his mind. This was easier when he was working for someone else, when he had no personal stake in the outcome. Trying to relax down to the proper mental state took so long, he was about to believe he couldn't get there, until that familiar floating feeling began to come over him.

He seemed to see everything from Diane's point of view, beginning with seeing a gloved hand in front of her face, right before the darkness closed in.

The next few seconds were confused, as if she were coming out of a drugged state. How long had she been gone?

"Don't worry," a man's voice told her. "You won't come to any harm as long as your boyfriend does the right thing."

"Who are you?" she asked.

"That's none of your concern."

There was no face to go with the voice, so the man was either behind her or somewhere in a dark part of the room. As a matter of fact, there was very little to be seen where she was, and very little light. Perhaps he'd cast an invisibility spell so she couldn't see him.

"Where are we? What do you want?" Diane asked in a shaky voice.

"He knows what I want, and with his little helper, he should be able to find me."

"Little helper?"

"You talk too much."

Apparently Diane hadn't been conscious when she arrived wherever she was, so he wasn't getting much this way. Opening his eyes, he found a city map and grabbed a pendulum. Maybe dowsing would help. Forming his question, he began moving the pendulum slowly over the map in a grid pattern, waiting for a response. Using her flat as the center point, he worked his way further out from it.

At first there was a slight tug about a mile to the east of her place. Moving more slowly, he got a definite "yes" at one particular spot on the map. Opening his laptop, he brought up a map of the area and zoomed in to see what was there.

"It's a neighborhood, just houses," he muttered under his breath. "So our guy must live there and took her back to his place."

"Are we talking basement? Shed? What kind of thing are we looking for?" Ali asked.

"As dark as it is, I'm thinking basement. Any luck with that message?"

"I think if we heat it up, we'll be able to read it," Ali told him. "But we'll have to take it out of the bag."

Martin thought it over. The police would be annoyed if he tampered with evidence, but if he didn't this might all be in vain.

"Let's do it. I'll light a candle."

Since he had the candle lit anyway, he wrote a quick spell to reveal what was hidden, burned it in the flame, and then used the candle flame to gently warm the paper. And sure enough, the message began to appear. The address was a car park near the address Martin had found dowsing.

"Do you suppose he'll bring Diane with him?" Ali asked. "Or will he leave her behind and deliver her later?"

"I don't know," Martin told him, chewing his thumb nail. "Why would he think I would hand over the jug without proof Diane is all right?"

"Arrogance?"

"Probably. But I think it's time to call the cops. Let's get the jug out and get ready to leave. Say, can you make yourself invisible?"

"Yeah. Why?"

"He's going to think you're in the jug, isn't he? So if I show up with a jug to trade for Diane, and you're invisible, you should be able to do something to distract him if need be, or go find Diane, before the cops show up."

"All right. I gotcha. Why don't you give them a call while I get the jug out. Is the stopper still in it?"

"I think so," Martin said. "I guess that would be a good idea as well. Are you sure there is no longer any connection between you and the jug?"

"Pretty sure. But if you'd like, we can run a candle flame over the jug, and maybe turn it over to let the flame up into the jug, in case there's any residual magic hangin' around."

"Let me make a call and we'll do that."

DIANE WASN'T SURE WHAT had happened. She'd run out to the grocery for only a few minutes, come back into her house, and then...nothing. Not until she woke up here, wherever that was. It was dark and smelled musty, like an old basement.

What was most worrying was her hands bound behind her, and her ankles tied as well. Who would do such a thing? She wasn't sure whether to call out and see if anyone was near, or just hope someone found her soon. If she called out, she might alert whoever had kidnapped her to the fact that she was once again awake.

She sat for what seemed like hours, as still as she could be, but eventually she had to shift. Her bum was aching from sitting on the hard floor.

"Oh, so you're awake finally," she heard a man's voice say. "Don't worry. You won't come to any harm as long as your boyfriend does the right thing."

"Who are you?" she asked.

"That's none of your concern."

Diane tried to find out a little more, but he cut off any further conversation. Apparently this had to do with the break-ins at Martin's shop. What could he have that anyone would want so badly? An old jug? That was ridiculous.

But if this person had left Martin instructions, perhaps he would be here soon and she would be free.

Or perhaps this guy would kill them both to keep them from talking.

Surely Martin would alert the authorities, wouldn't he? What time was it anyway? She was supposed to go over to his flat for Christmas Eve. How would he feel when she didn't show up?

The threat of a gag kept her from asking any more questions. All she could hope for now was that Martin would be able to do something to help.

So far, she hadn't seen the man's face. As dark as the place was, he could be nearly anywhere and she would never know. As far as she could tell, she was propped up in a corner, so she should have a good view of the entire room, but she could see nothing but the odd bit of paper trash and rubble.

"Don't worry," said the voice. "It shouldn't be long now. They've been to your flat to check on you."

How could he possibly know this? Did he have someone watching her flat? She hadn't heard a phone. Of course, he could have the sound muted. And if they'd sent an SMS, she wouldn't have heard anything.

After another eternity of sitting and waiting, with dread settling in closely around her, she heard movement across the room.

"It's time I went to meet your friend," the voice said. "I do hope you can be patient a little longer."

Diane saw no need to answer this, so she closed her eyes and leaned her head back against the wall. She heard a door open and then close, a key turn in the lock, and footsteps that sounded like someone climbing stairs.

Martin would be here soon, wouldn't he?

THE POLICE HADN'T WANTED to come out. They were already busy with drunk party-goers, domestic incidents, and traffic snarls.

"I'm telling you, my girlfriend has been kidnapped. I have a ransom note," he shouted into the phone.

Eventually someone agreed to drop by as soon as he could get free. In the meantime, sit tight and let the police do their job.

"Sod this," Martin muttered.

"I beg your pardon?" the cop on the other end of the line said.

"I will be at this address," he told the man, reading off the address on the note. "If you're on the way, come to this address. It's where they said to meet them. I'll have the ransom with me, but I would prefer it if you came by and arrested whoever it is, rather than hand it over."

"Now don't do anything rash," the man said calmly.

"Bloody hell!" Martin shouted. "I can't just sit here knowing Diane is in danger when I can do something about it. Either get off your ass and meet me near there, or leave me alone so I can bring Diane home."

"I don't believe you've thought this through thoroughly," the officer told him.

"I've done all the thinking I need to do. If you're coming, meet me here," he said, giving the man an address about a block away from the parking lot.

"I'll see what I can do," he was told. "Do me a favor and wait five minutes before you leave your flat."

"Okay. Five minutes, but not a second more," Martin said hotly.

"Do you know who this is?"

"Not a clue. I assume he's somehow linked to the break-ins at my shop and flat, but I don't have any idea who he is."

Martin couldn't sit still and began pacing the floor, keeping an eye on his watch.

"Calm down, boss," Ali told him. "Everything's gonna be fine. Between you, me, and the cops, she'll be all right."

"But what if she's not? It'll be my fault for getting her involved in this mess."

"Don't see how. You ain't done nothin' wrong. Did you hire someone to kidnap her?"

"Don't be stupid."

"Well, there you are then. Not your fault."

While they waited for the five minutes to elapse, they rethought their plans for when they were at the location.

"I'll stay out of sight unless I need to do something. Otherwise, you won't see me until the shooting is over."

"With any luck, there won't be any shooting."

As soon as the slowest five minutes in the history of the universe had passed, Martin and Ali, jug in hand, hurried to the car and drove toward the rendezvous spot. Martin tried not to speed. All he needed was to get stopped for a traffic violation on the way.

As they pulled up to the address he'd given the officer, another car pulled up behind him. Two men stepped out of the vehicle and came up toward the front doors of his car.

"Mr. Pritchard?" one of them asked, once he rolled down his window.

They didn't look like cops initially. In plain clothes, they could have been anyone, except for the warrant cards they showed him.

"I'm Martin Pritchard, yes," he told them.

"Good evening. I'm DI Jones, and this is DS Warren. We're waiting for an armed response team, just in case. It shouldn't be much longer."

A tense few minutes passed, with little conversation between them. He'd given them all he had on the phone, so there wasn't much else to say.

Eventually—all right, it had probably been less than five minutes—another car pulled up. These guys were in uniform and carried weapons. After a brief conversation, the armed officers slipped into the darkness.

"Are you ready, Mr. Pritchard?" DI Jones asked.

"Quite."

"Go to your meeting. Forget we're here. We'll be watching and step in once we have something to work with."

Walking to the back of the car, Martin opened the boot and pulled out the jug.

"This is the ransom?" the man asked, dubiously.

"It's what the man wants. Don't ask me why, but someone has been after this since I brought it back from the US."

With a brief look at Ali, Martin got into the car and slowly drove to the car park. Once out of sight of the police, Martin turned to Ali.

"If you're going to do the invisible thing, I guess you should do it now."

"I don't much like anyone else seeing this, but what the hell?"

And disappeared.

Martin couldn't even sense the djinn next to him, so it wasn't only visual. All he could hope was that whoever he was meeting wouldn't sense him either.

Closing in on the parking lot, Martin stopped just outside the lit area and scanned for anyone else around. As he waited, a vehicle pulled into the parking lot, into the shadows at the back, on the side opposite from his position. With any luck, the cops would be in place.

Taking a deep breath and hefting the heavy jug, Martin began to walk toward the other vehicle. He stopped for a minutes, put it down, and switched hands before starting off again. As he got closer to the vehicle, a figure slipped out of the driver's side and moved a short distance from the car, leaving the door open.

Closing the distance between them to about ten yards, Martin stopped, still holding the jug firmly.

"I see you've brought it then," the man said confidently. "Just set it down and walk away."

Martin had never seen this man before that he could recall. He wasn't the man they'd seen in the shop. In fact, he couldn't remember him ever coming to the shop. Nothing about him seemed familiar.

"I want to see Diane first," Martin said firmly. "I need to know she's all right."

"Put the jug down and walk away. Once I've determined everything is as it should be, I'll call you with where to find her."

What should he do? What would the police have him do? For all he knew there was another person involved who could harm Diane if he didn't do what he was told. Setting the jug on the ground, he backed away from it for about another ten yards.

"No, go back to your car and get in, then throw your keys toward me," the man told him.

Still backing away, Martin reached his car, opened the door, and flung the keys about halfway to the other man. As the man watched, he got into the car and closed the door. Where were the cops? Why were they waiting so long to do something?

And where was Ali? There should be something he could do. Of course, that would rather give away his identity to anyone else around, so maybe that's why he was holding back.

After a few seconds, the man approached the jug. As if he wasn't sure what to do, he rested his chin in his hand and stood examining it for a moment or two. Why didn't he just take the jug and leave? What was he waiting for?

As the tension mounted, Martin's heart began to pound. He had to find Diane, but couldn't leave. And where was Ali? He hoped he had some sort of plan, because Martin was now helpless.

Very carefully, the man reached for the jug. Dropping down onto one knee, he worked the stopper out of the neck of the jug and jumped back quickly. And nothing happened, of course. Ali wasn't in the jug.

"Genie of the jug, I summon you," the man intoned dramatically.

Still, nothing happened. As Ali was no longer bound to the jug, he had no compulsion to obey, summoned or not

Angrily, the man restated his demand, and then a third time through clenched teeth. Shouting across the car park, he demanded to know what Martin had done.

"I don't know what you mean," Martin told him. "I bought the jug in America and brought it home. I haven't done anything except wash it."

"If you want to see your girlfriend again, you'll tell me how to summon the genie," the man shouted.

"I don't know," Martin said, truthfully. He'd never summoned Ali and had no idea how one would go about it. "What genie are you talking about?"

Snatching the jug off the ground, the man stormed back to his car and put the jug inside.

"I now possess this jug. You are beholden to me and you will obey!" he insisted.

"Look, man, I just want Diane. You have the jug. That's what you said you wanted."

"No! I wanted the jug with the genie inside," he snarled. "And you knew that. Maybe you have to relinquish ownership of the thing before the genie will obey me."

"Where is Diane?" Martin asked.

"Give me the genie!"

"How can I give you something I don't have?" Martin asked him. "All I have is the jug. Besides, who believes in genies?"

"If you want to see your girlfriend again…" the mans began.

A voice spoke up from the trees near the car park and Martin whirled around.

"Martin? Martin! I've been so scared," Diane said, running to him.

About the same time, all sorts of lights went on and officers surrounded the man on the other side of the car park. Once the situation was under control, DI Jones came over to him.

"How did you find Diane?" he asked.

"We didn't. Your friend did. He said you were psychic and helped people find things. Apparently after you called us you did whatever it is you do and located a possible location for her."

"Well, yes. But after I called you, I followed your instructions."

"Ali here told us the address and in investigating, we found his accomplice. When Diane heard the commotion, she began to call for help. Once we got here with her, the rest was a piece of cake."

Diane hadn't loosened her hold on him yet.

"Diane, come on. I need to talk to the officers. You can stay right here, but you're making talking difficult."

Her tear-streaked face stared up at him, and she moved the arm from around his throat and wrapped it around his waist.

"What happens now?" Martin asked.

"We'll take him downtown and charge him. And we'll need to talk to the three of you as well. Hell of a Christmas Eve."

"Yeah. I bet the cat ate all the cheese," Martin said, wondering why that had been his first thought. It might have been a good thing however, as Diane started to giggle.

"If I can find my keys, can we meet you at the station?"

"That's fine. With any luck at all, it won't take long to get your statements. Of course, we'll need to ask you more later, most likely. But that can wait until after Christmas."

"Thanks Officer," Martin told him. "And happy Christmas."

"Happy Christmas to you as well."

# Chapter 29

It was very late by the time they got back to Martin's flat. And Martin had been right. Joker had eaten most of the cheese, some of the biscuits, and munched his way through half a bag of crisps. Of course, Martin hadn't been home at his feeding time, and the cheese would have been a little funky after sitting out for hours, but still, a few snacks would have been great.

Seeming to know Diane needed some comfort, Joker curled up in her lap almost as soon as she sat down on the sofa, purring like a fool. She had calmed down some on the way back from the police station, but tonight had shaken them all.

"Hey, boss," Ali called. "Should I whip something up to eat? We never did get our party going."

"Go right ahead. I'm too keyed up to sleep anyway."

A few minutes later, Ali had cleaned the serving dishes of their detritus and filled them with assorted cheese cubes and two different sorts of the biscuits to go with them. The wine was still chilling in the fridge, so Martin opened the first bottle and poured them each a glass.

"Here's to friends and their safe return," he toasted.

"And here's to heroes," Diane added.

"Well, I'm not sure I'm a hero, but a guy has to rescue the maiden in distress, hasn't he?" Martin answered, sipping wine to keep from blurting out something ridiculous.

"And how about a toast to Ali, for his help and friendship through this ordeal."

"Aw, shucks boss. I couldn't do much without getting you in trouble with the law," the djinn told him.

"I think justice would have been better served if we could have stuffed him in the jug for a while. Of course, not being one of your people, he couldn't have gotten back out," Martin mused.

"Where is the jug?" Diane asked.

"They took it as evidence. I'll get it back after the trial," Martin said sadly.

"What if he escapes?" Ali asked. "He is a wizard of some sort."

"I guess we'll figure it out if it becomes necessary. How about some more wine?" pouring some more into Diane's glass. "This isn't how I'd intended to spend Christmas Eve. Sorry about all the trouble."

"It's all right, Martin," she told him. "At least they got the guy. None of this was your fault."

As late as they'd returned, and as early in the morning as it was when they finally decided to go to bed, Diane stayed over in the guest room. Martin would have called her a cab, but she was understandably afraid to be alone in her flat. They had missed the caroling and all of the city's festivities because of a greedy man who wanted a captive genie at his beck and call.

The sound of Joker carrying on woke Martin later in the morning. He had closed his bedroom door when he'd gone to bed, and assumed Diane had done the same. And even though the monster cat was stuffed with cheese the evening before, it was well past time for him to eat this morning.

"Just a minute, cat," he grumbled, as he struggled into a robe and tried to get to the kitchen, with Joker wrapped around his ankles.

Nobody else was out yet, not that he was surprised. He hoped Diane had been able to sleep after her ordeal. As quietly as he could with Joker howling, he fed the beast and started some coffee. Waiting for it to finish, he thought he heard a noise down in the shop.

Creeping down the stairs, with an empty wine bottle in hand, he followed the sounds to his workshop. Swinging the door open quietly, he let out an oath at what he saw.

"Ali, how long have you been up?" he asked.

"Well, ya know, I couldn't sleep after all the excitement, and we don't really need much sleep anyway. So I thought I'd get started on New Years."

Lined up along the bench where Aladdin's Treasures had been was a new set of trinkets—clinking champagne flutes, champagne bottles, and Happy New Year with the year underneath. All of them were in the same cut glass as Aladdin's Treasures had been, and all shimmered, their different colors twinkling in the light.

"I know we talked about some of this a week or so back, so I thought I'd run up a few and see what you thought," Ali said.

Even in his un-caffeinated state, Martin was impressed.

"I think these will be marvelous, Ali. Thank you."

"Well, I do feel I owe you for getting me out of that jug. And I've had a couple thoughts about that, too."

"Really? What?"

"Let's leave it for now. It's your holiday today after all."

Once Diane was up and about, they opened their gifts and called family and friends. Diane adored Martin's gift, which made both him and Ali happy. Of course the evening's events had been in the paper, so the phones seldom stopped ringing.

"No, Mom. I'm fine. Martin and Ali came to my rescue and brought me home. Yes, I'm with him now. I'm sure, Mom. Look, we were going to have dinner soon. I'll talk to you later."

Diane shook her head and grinned up at Martin.

"Mothers. She's worried sick, according to her. But the good news is she told me to hang on to you. She figures anyone who would risk life and limb to help me is worth keeping."

"Is that so?" he asked with a grin. " Do I have a say in the matter?"

"Depends on what you have to say," she returned.

"Let's just say I won't put up a struggle, shall we?"

"Happy Christmas, Martin."

"Happy Christmas."

# Chapter 30

Ali absolutely refused to take the money Martin tried to give him.

"But Ali, we earned this with your Aladdin's Treasures. Half of the profits should be yours."

"Boss, how many times do I gotta explain it? I don't need it. I'm one of the djinn. I can have anything I want whenever I want it. Besides, you were kind enough to help me out when you could have been like everyone else."

"Still, a little money wouldn't hurt," Martin insisted.

"Take it and go buy your girl something special if you want. Or put it in your safe. Or set in on fire."

"I'll put it in the safe. If you change your mind, let me know."

"All right, boss. You do that."

"When were you going on your holiday?" Martin asked.

"I don't know. We still have to get a schedule sorted with Peter. Ther's the trial comin' up. And I've got to see you and the girl hitched."

"Now, Ali, I've told you. We're taking things slowly. No need to rush."

"You ain't gettin' any younger, you know," Ali told him. "And you ain't gonna live as long as I have, so you might want to build a fire under it."

"I'll think about it," Martin finally said, to get off the subject.

Martin and Diane had been dating seriously since Christmas. With the holidays behind them, things had slowed down in the shop and he had a little more leisure time. And with no more problems with break-ins, his mind was a little easier when he went out in the evening.

They were still waiting for the trial, so Ali couldn't take off until after that. They had come up with a new line of Aladdin's Treasures for St. Valentine's Day, which were selling every bit as well as the very first trinkets Ali had fashioned.

As far as Peter was concerned, they had sat down over some Scotch and filled him in on the pottery. At first, he thought they were joking, but after Ali showed him a few things he could do, at least he began to believe in magic.

The first firing they did with all of them working together came out beautifully. Peter fashioned all the pieces, as he was the artist. Ali used his abilities on the whole batch to make them ever so slightly larger than the originals, which fused his magic into them.

As Peter watched, Martin lit a candle and said a spell over the items getting ready to be fired. Not having a particular interest aside from the color changes, he simply asked that they bring joy and peace to those who bought them.

As they'd expected, there was the slightest slump in all of them after firing. It was so slight, that if they hadn't seen them beforehand, they wouldn't have known the difference. Peter had been about to tear out his hair waiting for the kiln to cool sufficiently to open it up and peek inside.

Once he'd glazed the items and fired them, they were all anxious. What if it didn't work? After all, the spells had been different. Ali hadn't actually fashioned any of the pieces. What if changing the magic changed the effect?

They needn't have worried. Yes, there was a change in the colors, but in a good way. Somehow, the colors were more subtle, but had more effect. The silvery shimmer over the whole of the batch was fainter, but still there. Peter thought he liked it better, because it allowed the decorations on the pots to show through a little more, while they still bore the odd sheen.

And they sold like they were made of gold.

Once the sales were over, they all sat down again. While the items were brilliant, they decided to limit their production. Most of the time, Peter would sell items he'd done himself, with the occasional pot thrown in with a little of the dust added to it.

But around holidays or special events, they would all get together and produce a batch or two of the special pots. In between times, Ali and Martin would practice with different spells, to see what difference it made in the final product. So far, they'd found a spell which produced a golden shimmer, one that produced a coppery tone, and the original one with the silver.

Sometimes the different spells produced different colors of blue as well, though Ali's gold stayed the same. But they were still experimenting. Who knew what they might come up with.

And then Martin had a thought.

Diane did energy work. And magic was a type of energy, wasn't it? What if he could convince Diane to try her hand at infusing energy into the pieces? But that was for a later time. Right now, they were trying to get their lives back together after her ordeal.

DIANE WAS SURPRISED at how close she and Martin had become in such a short time. She'd known him for about a year and a half, and though they'd gone out every now and again, it had never been serious before. She'd always thought he was a nice guy, but hadn't thought of him as more than a friend until recently.

She couldn't believe he had come to her rescue after she'd been kidnapped. And he'd been so very caring and sweet ever since, her knight in shining armor, that she couldn't help but feel drawn to him. Was it simply because he'd rescued her? Or was it something else? Did she want it to be something else?

He was intelligent, charming, good looking, and fun to be around. She'd never dated much, but since Christmas the two of them spent several evenings together each week. Not romantically, but more just hanging out, having fun and relaxing. He never pushed for more. But part of her was ready for more.

He and Ali had taken on a project with a mutual friend, Peter. The man did beautiful pottery, but the pieces the three of them worked on together were particularly stunning. It had to do with Ali and his genie magic, Martin and his magical spells, and the interaction between them all.

Martin had asked her about her energy work, and whether she would try an experiment with them and she'd agreed. Why not? If magic used a particular form of energy, maybe healing energy would have an effect on the outcome as well.

After thinking about it, she had agreed to get together with them and put together a plan. And tonight would be the first attempt at something new and exciting, with a little bit of luck.

"Ready for the grand experiment?" Martin asked after they'd had a cup of tea to take off the winter chill.

"I suppose I'm as ready as I'll be. I'm not exactly sure what I'm doing, but let's give it a shot."

Back in Martin's workshop she saw several pieces of pottery drying on the work bench. Looking back at Martin, she threw him a questioning look.

"All right, I know this seems a little weird. Ali shaped all the pieces, adding a little of the dust he conjured up in the clay beforehand. Once he'd formed all of these, I cast a small spell over them. Now what we do with Peter is a little different, but this should give us something to go on."

"So what do I do?" she asked.

"I guess you try to use your healing energy to infuse happiness or health, or something like that into the clay. Then once it dries and is fired, and all that stuff, we'll see what difference it makes."

"Well, I have five different frequencies I use. I think I'll start with the most basic and work up. All right?"

"Sounds good. And if you just want to try one for now and use it for the whole batch, that's fine, too. Or you can use a different one for each piece. It's up to you."

Pondering the question, Diane chose to just use one symbol for now, to see if it worked. If it did, they could fool around with the others at a later date.

Drawing the symbol out in the air and asking for direction to begin the session, she quieted her mind and let the energy flow into her, out through her hands, and hopefully, out to the pottery. Not knowing exactly what else to do, she envisioned the energy imbuing the clay with joy. As with her healing, she paid attention to the flow of energy and kept her focus until the flow began to slow down.

Drawing the symbol once more, and asking for the session to end, she turned back toward the other two.

"What do you think?" she asked.

"I could feel energy in the air," Martin told her. "Part of it must have affected the clay."

"You call it energy," Ali stated. "I call it magic. But whatever you call it, I could feel it, too."

"Do you think it'll turn out all right?"

"Only one way to find out. And it'll take about a week."

Diane couldn't believe how nervous she was during the next few days. The guys had taken the pottery over to Peter's on Tuesday and it was set to be fired on Wednesday. Sometime after that it would be glazed and then fired, probably around Saturday. So it wouldn't be until Sunday or Monday before they could see what happened, if anything.

And it was only Thursday so far. The next evening, and she, Martin, and Ali were getting together at her place. She should be thinking about wine and nibbles, not pots. She was going over to Martin's flat after work to visit for a little while. Maybe that would take her mind off pottery and glazing.

"I know how you feel," Martin told her, his arm around her shoulders as they sipped wine on his sofa. "The first time we intentionally tried to use magic on the pottery I was jittery all week."

"How many times have you done this?" she asked.

"Only a few times, but the results are repeatable. Every time we work together it comes out the same. We still haven't figured out the silvery sheen over the whole piece."

"What sort of spell do you say when you work with it?" she asked.

"I normally ask for happiness and peace," he told her. "Then proceed as usual with the spell."

"It could be because you are asking for two separate things. Peace and happiness. In energy healing, you can use two different symbols together for a slightly different effect."

"Really? So maybe if I asked for peace alone, we would only have either the dark blue or the silvery sheen? And the other one would produce the other effect?"

"I don't know. You may need to use the two of the together to get one of the effects. Like, peace gives you the blue, happiness might give you another color, but together you get the blue and the sheen."

"Hm..." Martin thought for a moment. "I guess we'll have to give it a try and see what happens. And you need to try another one of your symbols."

"We don't know what the first one did yet," she told him.

"True, but we don't actually have to wait, do we? We could go do something tonight, and give it to Peter when we go look at the others."

"Why not? Even if it does nothing, it's kind of fun. Do you have any more clay?"

BETWEEN THE THREE OF them, they shaped six new items. Of course, Ali's were done with the snap of a finger. Diane did a little better than Martin did, but it still took a while.

"Okay, now what do we do?" Diane asked. "Do you wait until they're ready to go over to the kiln? Or do you go ahead and do your magic with them now?"

"The last ones we waited until they'd cured," Martin told her. "I don't know why we would need to, though. Ali? Any thoughts on the subject?"

"Not really. I don't reckon it'd matter either way."

"We could go ahead and do it tonight, or we could do it tomorrow night. I know we were going to go over to your place, but we could always change plans, if you like."

"That might be fun," Diane told him.

"Let's plan on it then. Maybe a little champagne will help my rhyming skills for the spell."

"Come on. Your rhymes aren't bad," Diane protested.

"We'll see you tomorrow evening," Martin told her as he walked her out to the cab.

Back in the workshop, he and Ali looked over the new pieces.

"What do you think?" Martin asked. "Will there be another weird effect?"

"I think so. I mean, I felt the magic while she was doing whatever it is she does with the first one. I know," he said as Martin opened his mouth to complain. "It isn't magic. It's energy. But where I come from it amounts to the same thing."

"Where exactly do you come from?" Martin asked. It was something they'd never discussed.

With a long, sad face, Ali shook his head.

"It seems the place no longer exists. At least not as I knew it."

"Ali, I'm sorry. I didn't mean to upset you."

"It's all right. After this much time I didn't expect it to be the same. But you know how it is. You always think you can go home."

"Are you sure it isn't there?" Martin asked. "Maybe it just has another name now."

"Oh, I'm sure the land is still there, but I can't find the oasis where I lived. It was only small, and the climate has changed a lot since I lived there. I guess the spring that fed it dried up."

There didn't seem to be much to say, so Martin reached over and clapped his friend on the back.

"You're always welcome here, man," he told him.

"I appreciate that. Didn't we have something to drink around here?" Ali asked. "I could sure do with something a little stronger than that wine."

"How about some single malt?"

"That'll do."

DIANE WASN'T SURE WHAT to expect when she arrived. Their experimental pieces should have cured most of the way, and she and Martin planned to do the energy infusion tonight. What if it didn't work? Or what if it turned out to add something really ugly?

No, it shouldn't do that. From what she understood, anything coming from joy, happiness, or peace should bring out something beautiful. She had read of the experiments with thoughts directed at water. Loving, peaceful thoughts caused it to produce beautiful and symmetrical crystals, while mean, vicious thoughts turned out misshapen, ugly crystals. Hopefully it would work the same way with the clay.

Ali had dinner ready for them. She didn't know where he'd found his recipe ideas, but his food was amazing. Lamb kebabs with flat bread and a lovely salad went down a treat with the wine Martin had.

After one last glass of wine, they went in to see what they could do with the pottery. She had chosen to use the same symbol again instead of getting too crazy until they found out if it had any effect at all. She also wasn't sure how much overlap there would be if she used different symbols on different pieces.

"Ready?" Martin asked.

"I think so. Who goes first?"

"Does it matter?" Martin asked Ali.

"I don't know. I've never seen it done before, so your guess is as good as mine."

Mulling it over for a moment, Martin chose to do his spell first.

"That's the way we did the other one, so we might as well continue the trend for now. Here goes nothing."

Lighting a candle, he placed it in a pretty brass holder on the workbench holding the pottery. With a simple spell asking for happiness and joy for all who were touched by the pieces, he lit the slip of paper in the candle flame and put it in a bowl to finish burning.

They watched until it was ashes, and then he turned to her.

"All right. Your turn."

Thinking through everything carefully, she mentally drew the symbol on the palm of each hand, and then using her finger, she drew the symbol in the air over the pottery. Turning her palms to the pottery, she asked for the blessing of peace and joy to be placed on the pottery and shared with all those who admired it.

The energy surged in her palms and she jumped at the sensation. Her palms began to itch and the feeling continued on for a short time before it began to dissipate. After about five minutes, it faded altogether.

Drawing the symbol to close the session, she took a deep breath and turned to the two guys.

"Wow," was all she could say for a moment.

"What happened?" Martin asked.

She told him about what she'd felt, though she couldn't explain it.

"Is that the same thing you asked for when you did the first one?"

"Yes. I wonder if it has to do with the number of pieces?"

"Could be. I guess we'll figure it out as we go along."

"I just hope it actually does something," she admitted.

"Come on," Martin exclaimed. "I have champagne chilling."

Ali turned in right after midnight, but Diane and Martin stayed up a little longer. They began talking about New Year's resolutions, and with one thing and another, ended up having a bit of a snog which very nearly ended in bed. It was quite early in the morning when Martin called a cab for her.

Who knew he could kiss like a champion? Maybe it was the champagne. Whatever it was, she needed to do some serious thinking about one Martin Pritchard.

# Chapter 31

The experiments went well. Diane had been nervous for some reason, but adding her energy added a faint translucent blue-violet hint among the other colors.

"Well, that is a lovely color," Martin told her, and Peter agreed. "We'll have to try again and see what happens with the other symbols you use."

"Definitely," Peter told her. "If we can get this all so it's repeatable, we can begin to select the effect we want and do different batches. We can choose the color to match the final shade of the glazing. And we can either add the sheen from Martin's work, or leave it out, depending on what we're hoping to achieve."

Peter had experimented with different colors of glaze, and the effects remained unchanged.

"I suppose it depends on how well they sell," Diane mused.

"So far, everyone who's seen the new effect has loved it and asked when they'll be for sale."

"Haven't you sold the other ones?" Ali asked.

"I sold the first ones we made, just to get an idea of the demand, and they did wonderfully. I'd kind of like to wait on the rest, until we are sure we have repeatable results."

"It looks like it's definitely repeatable," Martin said. "We had a couple more things to try, but I don't see why you couldn't begin thinking about selling them."

"Pricing is part of the issue. It's a new effect I haven't seen before. And we'll have a limited quantity. But I don't want to price them out of reach."

"I'm sure you'll get it sorted," Martin told him as they got ready to leave.

"You guys take care, and bring me some more samples."

All three of them were excited about the outcome of their pottery trial, so they decided to go out for Indian instead of cooking in. Ali had definitely gotten behind curry, claiming it reminded him of some of his mother's cooking.

"I thought you were Arabic," Diane said.

"Well, I am, or was. But even back them there was trade between places, and my mother loved to swap recipes anytime she could. I don't know, maybe some of her food came to her by way of India, or whatever it was called back then."

It was difficult not to jabber on about the pottery, but with Peter trying to keep it under wraps for the time being, they shifted their attention back to Christmas Eve.

"I was scared to death," Diane admitted.

"Of course you were," Martin told her. "Any idea how he got in?"

"No. I always lock my door. Every single time. I close the door, lock it, and then try it to make sure. When I was growing up we had a break-in once, and ever since I've been paranoid about locking doors."

"Well, he is a wizard of some sort," Ali suggested. "Some of those guys have a way with locks and such."

"I'm going to be worried until I know that guy is put away. Any idea when the trial is?"

"Not for another couple months. You know how long things take to get through the system," Martin told her.

With a sigh, she went back to her chicken masala, her thoughts turning back to her relationship with Martin.

She'd never seen him as the strong, determined type before all this began, but since her ordeal, he had been a rock. Maybe what she'd always seen as passivity was simply trying to be polite to customers he would rather throw out the door. Really, the way some people treated shopkeepers was criminal.

She had never seen him work out, but his muscles were as hard as flint and the few times they'd had to jog down the street to catch a cab, he hadn't been at all out of breath, unlike her. And she actually did try to work out at least every other day.

"Penny for your thoughts," she heard.

Looking up into those beautiful grey eyes he had, she smiled and shook her head.

"What makes you think they're only worth a penny?"

"Oh, so you're going to play it that way, are you?" he teased back. "Maybe I'll have to up the ante."

"What did you have in mind?"

"Now that would be telling," he told her, with a devilish grin.

Reaching over, Diane brushed a stray lock of brown hair away from his forehead, suddenly wanting to run her fingers through his hair. She managed to stop herself, but only just.

"Well, you get no thoughts until you make an acceptable offer," she said in a mock stern tone.

His suggestion, when he leaned close and whispered it in her ear, made her blush and giggle. Ali laughed out loud.

"I don't know what he said," Ali told them, "but I know when to say good night."

"Oh, we have to get home first," Martin told him. "Then maybe you could make yourself scarce for a while."

"Can do boss."

THINGS HAD CERTAINLY warmed up with Diane, Martin thought as they drove back to his place. And New Year's Eve had nearly got out of hand. But he had a bottle of wine they could open before they got cozy on the sofa in front of the fire. He'd never thought of pursuing Diane until recently, though they'd been friends for a while. But she certainly seemed to warm up to him during the past few weeks.

How far did he want this to go? Ali had made a few good points the other day about the two of them. They had fun together and their professions were complementary. With this new sideline going with Peter, they might have a little extra income soon. Which was another thing they needed to think about.

Ali had decided to stay with him for now. He'd had no luck finding any remnant of his family or friends yet. And the area had changed so much with all that had been going on in the Middle East, there's no telling what had happened to his oasis. Maybe they could buy him someplace of his own if things turned more serious.

Ali was still deep in thought when they got back to the flat. After Diane had arrived and sat down with Joker on the sofa, he said goodnight and left the two of them alone.

The cat had really taken to Diane, too. Whenever she came over, Joker was in her lap the minute she sat down. And if the cat liked her, who was Martin to disagree?

Back in the kitchen, he opened some more wine. Enough pondering on the future, especially when he had a lovely lady waiting for him in the living room. And hopefully she was waiting for the kiss he'd promised her for her thoughts. With any luck, it would be more than one.

THE TIME FOR MR. RHYS'—THEIR wizard—trial finally came around, and they all had to give testimony. Mr. Rhys' solicitor was very aggressive, so the ordeal was nerve-wracking. In the end, Mr. Rhys was found guilty of aiding and abetting, breaking and entering, and kidnapping, and sentenced to several years in prison.

"Well, that should be finished," Diane said. "I feel like a weight has been lifted from my shoulders."

"Yes. Now maybe you can sleep better, knowing he's locked away."

"Maybe you could come tuck me in," she suggested with a sly look.

"Come on, kids. Give a guy a break," Ali complained, though he was grinning widely at the time.

They'd almost made it to Martin's car when he got a call on his mobile.

"Hello," he answered.

"DI Jones here. Is this Martin Pritchard?"

"Yes, it is."

"Is Miss Sinclair with you?"

Beginning to be concerned, Martin said, "Yes. Is something wrong?"

"Where are you parked?"

He gave the man their location and said they would certainly wait there for him. When he arrived, he jumped out of his car and hurried to meet them.

"Mr. Rhys has escaped custody," DI Jones informed them. "I need for you to go down to the station, so we can discuss security measures for the two of you."

"How did he escape?" Martin demanded.

"That's a good question. I have someone going over the security footage now. But we can talk at the station."

Diane began to shiver, as tears welled up in her eyes. Ali began to curse in some unknown language, and Martin was stunned. They had just seen the man being escorted from the court.

Putting his arm around Diane, he got her into the car, all the while trying to calm her.

"But Martin, what are we going to do? If he could kidnap me once, he could do it again."

"That's why the police want us to go to the station. We'll see what they have in mind and do whatever it takes to keep safe until they catch him again."

What he wasn't going to tell her was that he was as upset as she was. The man was intent on having Ali as his personal slave and thought Martin had somehow cheated him out of what he wanted. Which was true in a way. He had, after all, lifted the curse and freed the djinn.

Could Mr. Rhys come up with a way to recapture Ali and put him back in the jug?

"Ali, tell me there is no way he can do anything to bind you to the jug again."

"Unless I get drunk around him or one of his associates under some fairly specific circumstances, I would have to say he could not."

"What sort of circumstances?" Martin asked.

"He has to have my name. My real, full name. And I'm not handing that out," Ali stated.

"Even if he had something of yours? Like hair or nail clippings? Some of your clothing?"

"He could probably find me with some of that stuff, but without a name he couldn't bind me to anything or summon me."

"As long as you're sure," Martin told him, not completely convinced.

"But we could find him," Ali suggested. "Or set another trap for him."

"What do you mean?"

"He is human, not djinn. If I had him in sight, I might be able to give him a taste of his own medicine, so to speak."

"Tell me more."

"After we talk to the police."

"BUT WE CAN'T CLOSE down our businesses for an indefinite period of time," Diane told DI Jones once again. "I suppose we could move into a hotel for a while, but that's going to get expensive. Who's paying the bill for it all?"

"It would be the easiest way to keep you safe," he explained once again. "If we had you all in one place until we recapture the guy, there would be less chance of him getting to you. We wouldn't need as many officers to do the job, either."

"Look, I'm not saying it isn't a good idea," Martin told them, as Diane sat with her head in her hands. "But we still have to make a living. People depend on my products. I have regular customers who will have to find another place to buy alternative care. Diane has regular clients who come to her for massage and energy work. This could be a big setback for both of us."

"Would you at least consider taking a few days off?" DI Jones asked.

"How many days?" Diane responded.

"No more than a week. If we find him before that, you would be free to open up at your convenience."

"And if you haven't found him?" Martin demanded. "What then?"

"We'll talk again. I never did understand what it was he wanted from you."

"Who knows?" Diane answered. "The man is insane, thinking there was some sort of genie in the jug. I mean, seriously?"

"Can you give us a few minutes in private to discuss this?" Martin suggested.

"Of course. There will be an officer outside the door. Let him know when you've come to a decision."

Watching DI Jones slip out the door, Diane turned to Martin, feeling the tears begin again.

"Come here sweetheart," he told her, taking her into his arms. "We'll figure this out. I think we should seriously consider what they're suggesting. I could afford one week off. When was the last time you took a vacation?"

"It has been a while. I hate leaving my clients in the lurch like that. I wouldn't mind a vacation, but I would normally give them a bit of warning before just locking up."

"I know what you mean. But they might find him in the next day or two, and then we could go back to business as usual."

Worrying a thumbnail, which she'd already bitten down to nothing, Diane thought it all over once again. It wasn't fair. They had done nothing wrong.

With a sigh, she shook her head.

"As much as I hate to do it, you're right. It would be safer, easier for them, and with any luck, it won't be for long."

After another hug from Martin, she sat down at the table while he went to let them know they were ready with their decision.

They were taken out through an employee only door and hustled into an unmarked car. After driving around for what seemed forever, their driver pulled into a parking structure behind a moderately sized hotel. Bypassing the front desk, they were met by a man in plain clothes who had room keys for them and gave them the names under which they were registered.

Martin and Ali would share a room, while Diane had a room of her own next door to them, with a door connecting the two.

"It would be best if you ordered up from room service," one of the officers told them. "You can all get together if you'd like, in one room, but we would prefer it if you didn't go down to the lobby or the dining room."

"How do we know the room service people are all right?" Diane asked.

"There will be an officer with anyone who comes up. Always check the peep hole on the door before you open it. If you don't see at least two people, one with official ID, call security immediately."

"And what will security do?" Martin asked.

"We'll have one of our men with security at all times, in case there's trouble."

"Fine. I guess that's all we need to know," Diane said feeling weary.

"Also, don't use your cell phones to make any calls. Meals and incidentals will be billed to the room. Don't use your credit cards."

"Anything else?"

"Try not to worry," the man added before he left them on their own.

# Chapter 32

"All right. We know the guy escaped using magic, somehow," Martin stated, as the three of them sat in one room. "Any idea what kind?"

"Without seein' it happen, there are too many possibilities," Ali told them.

"Any ideas on what we can do to locate and disable this guy?"

"Well, we have his name. That's a start. Do we have anything that might have something of his on it?"

Thinking back over events, Martin couldn't think of anything.

"Without a way to locate him, we're sort of up the creek here," Ali told them. "Which only leaves waiting for him to come for us."

"I don't like that option at all," Diane stated flatly.

"Nor do I," Martin agreed.

"I don't much like it," Ali said, "but it would be the easiest way right now. Unless you can think of a way to find him."

Something had been puzzling Martin for a long time, but he'd never mentioned it to Ali. This seemed like as good a time as any.

"Ali, you play the dumb hick part really well. But it is all an act, isn't it? And occasionally, you slip up. You're far too bright to be as ignorant as you like to pretend."

Ali looked at him for a long moment, before his face broke out in a wide grin.

"Sometimes playing dumb can be an advantage to a guy," he admitted.

"How so?"

"It's kinda like that old story about the little boy and the coins," Ali stated, as if they should know what he meant.

"What story?" Diane asked, intrigued.

"Aw shucks. Everyone thought the little guy was a bit light in the brains department. One day a family friend and some of his buddies were standing around and the boy asked for some money."

"So? Kids do that all the time."

"The man offered him his choice of a dime or a nickel. After pondering it for a minute, the little boy chose the nickel, making the others laugh."

"What was the joke?" Diane asked.

"The nickel is about twice the size of a dime, but only worth half as much. So the little guy only got five cents instead of ten."

"What happened?" Martin prompted.

"Out of sight of the others, a kinder gentleman told the boy he should have chosen the other coin, assuming he'd only picked the nickel because it was larger."

"That would have been my thought," Martin said with a nod.

"Yeah, but the little boy was a little smarter than they all thought. He told the gentleman this way he got five cents. But if he chose the dime, they would quit playing him for a fool and he wouldn't get anything at all."

"Pretty clever of him," Diane told him. "So you're playing like the little boy?"

"It can make life easier and get you more information sometimes," Ali said. "I've been at it so long, it's natural to fall into character."

At Martin's look, he added, "I've not been trying to deceive you or anything, boss. Nothin' like that. But if people think you have an idiot for an assistant, they'll let down their guard."

"At least you answered my question," Martin told him. "From the time we've spent together, I would assume you and I are of about equal intelligence. You probably have the advantage in years lived."

"Maybe. But remember, while I've lived quite a while, I've missed everything of this era. All the new inventions, what's happenin' in the world, what places are called these days. Do we have a problem, Martin?"

"No, Ali. No problem. I've just been curious. You're all right."

"Now, about our criminal wizard. What are we going to do?"

They discussed ideas for more than an hour and then called room service for some lunch. It wasn't anything nearly as good as what Ali would have made for them, but it was probably safer for the time being.

"Can this guy track us by sensing any magic we use?" Diane asked.

"Possibly, but he would have to be near us when we used it in order to spot it," Martin said. Ali agreed.

"How much magic would it take?"

"No telling. And we have no idea where he is. He shouldn't have been able to follow us. Should he, Ali?"

"I don't know. If he has an invisibility spell and saw what vehicle we got into, he might have been able to put a magical tracer on us. Or if he had something of Diane's still in his possession, he could use something like your ability to find things to locate us through Diane."

"Do we know if he took anything of hers from her apartment?" Martin asked.

"If he can get into the apartment, which apparently he can, he could take something anytime he wants and then use a locating spell."

"What do we do if he up and appears in the room with us?" Diane asked.

"I doubt he could pull that off," Ali stated. "That takes either considerable psychic ability or a powerful spell, or both. I'm not sure he's that strong."

"But what if he is?"

"We'll do whatever it takes," Ali said. "Where is that jug, anyhow?"

"I think it's still in the police evidence room," Martin answered. "Why?"

"It would be easier if we had it here. Do you think they'd notice if it went missing?"

"Ali, what are you planning?" Martin asked, with a sly look.

"I've about had it with wizards, witches, and other practitioners of the dark arts."

"But there is no residual magic left in the jug," Diane told him.

"Correct. But if he showed up here, I might could work a little magic of my own and give him a taste of his own medicine."

Martin thought about it for a minute, and then asked, "Does it have to be the same jug?"

A sudden flash of understanding showed on Ali's face.

"No. I don't suppose it does. One jug is pretty much the same as another, unless one has a curse on it."

Almost immediately, a dark brown jug which looked like a duplicate of the one in police evidence appeared in front of them, complete with corn cob stopper.

"Very nice, Ali," Diane said with a grin. "What's the plan from here?"

"Now we find a way to let him know where we are," Ali stated. "But I suggest we have something to eat first and get some rest. It could be a long night."

THE PROBLEM WASN'T so much letting the guy find them, as what to do with him once they did. Ali turned the problem over and over in his head as they ate the mediocre meal room service brought up.

"If we have to order in, I wish it could be from the Greek or Indian place," he complained. "Or let me fix something tasty. This guy is putting a crimp in my eating style."

They had all discussed the problem until they were sick of the subject. The main problem was what to do with him once he was in the jug.

"I just don't know," Martin told him. "If we leave him in there, he'll die of starvation before too long. But if we turn him over to the police, he'll just escape again and we'll be right back where we started."

"That's just it," Diane told them. "Isn't there some way to like put him in stasis or something? Suspended animation?"

"I didn't know you were a science fiction fan," Martin teased.

"I don't know. There has to be something we can do. It's a shame Ali hasn't located any of his relatives yet. Maybe one of them could take him and the jug and put him to work somewhere out of the way."

"I've still got a few feelers out for any djinn around the area. Of course, they're kinda hard to track down. Over they years they've sort of tried to blend in with the regular human population and not make a scene."

"Understandable, but not helpful," Martin muttered. "How will they reach you if there is anyone?"

"There are a couple possibilities, but I doubt they'll be any help any time soon," Ali admitted.

"Why can't we come up with a spell that would keep him from harming us?" Diane asked.

"I don't think I've got enough knowledge for something that complex," Martin told her. "And we'd be working against whatever abilities he has at the same time."

"Only if he's conscious," she countered.

"So what do you plan to do? Hit him over the head with a table lamp?" Martin said with a laugh.

"Why not? I'm beginning to get irritated."

"Now hold on, you two. Once we get him here, I have to get him into the jug, but nothing says we can't put him out first."

"I'll get the lamp," Diane offered.

"Now, not so fast," Ali cautioned. "There's no need to hit him over the head."

"But I want to," she answered hotly.

"I think it would be better to hear what Ali has to say," Martin suggested.

"Fine," Diane said, rolling her eyes and putting the lamp back on the bedside table.

"I was thinkin' more of like what I did at your place, Martin, when those guys broke in. You know, just hold him frozen in place until I could get him in the jug."

"Will that keep him from using magic?"

"It will if I change it just a little and put him to sleep instead," Ali told them. "And we can leave him that way, in the jug, until we figure out a spell to use, or something else to do to him."

"Ali," Martin asked, "could we rework that spell Belle-Marie put on you, binding you to the jug?"

"I don't know. Since he isn't djinn, there's no way he could put himself in the jug. I can put him in it, but I don't think that particular spell will work."

"Can we adapt it?" Diane asked. "Something like he can't use magic for personal gain or something? Prevent him from enslaving others to do his bidding? And make him bound to the owner of the jug?"

"And then give the jug to some antique shop dealer to forget in a corner someplace," Martin added.

"Maybe. But we'd have to have it ready to go as soon as we got him here. And we need to figure what kind of magic to use."

"Hm... I'm not sure about candle magic in a hotel," Martin mused. At Ali's questioning look, he pointed to the ceiling. "Smoke detectors."

"What about water magic?" Diane asked. "There's water all over the place here."

"I don't know too much about water magic," Martin complained. "Do you feel comfortable enough to make it work?"

While they were all musing on the subject, the phone in the room rang.

"Did they say anything about the phones?" Diane asked as it rang again.

"No, but why would anyone from the police call? They'd just come up, wouldn't they?"

"I don't know. Why would anyone else call us?"

"To make sure where we were?" Ali suggested. "Maybe our magician friend is trying to locate us."

"So what do we do?" Diane asked as the annoying thing continued to make noise.

"We're not ready to deal with him yet, but if this is him, he may decide to risk it and come here anyway."

As they dithered, the answering service picked up to take a message, taking the decision out of their hands. Apparently the person left no message, so they decided to call room service again and talk to the officer who came up with them.

"No, there shouldn't be any calls coming in for you, from law enforcement or from the hotel. It was either a wrong number or someone hoping to find you. Don't answer if they call again and I'll see if we can get a trace on the number."

Once they were alone again, they went back to planning.

"I'm thinkin' we're not gonna have much time to figure this out," Ali admitted. "So if you've got something to try, let's get it ready."

Martin had been quietly thinking for a few minutes, and shook his head.

"I don't think we need to do anything too quickly. All we have to do is incapacitate the guy, put him in the jug, and put the stopper in. As long as he's asleep, or unconscious, we can take our time to deal with him, can't we?"

"You might have somethin' there, boss," Ali admitted. "Anything you'd like to add?

MARTIN HAD BEEN THINKING furiously about their situation, and it seemed they were getting a little ahead of themselves. As long as the guy couldn't use his magic, they would be fine.

"For now, let's just get him asleep and in the jug. Then we can wait out the rest of our time here, get back to the flat, and then deal with this idiot."

"Even if it takes us a few days, he should be all right in the jug. We can come up with some sort of spell to keep him out of our hair and get back to life as usual," Diane added.

"Precisely. But the first thing is to get him in the jug."

"Is there any way to set up some sort of alarm so we know he's in the vicinity, before he's actually here?" Diane asked. "I don't like the idea of being at his mercy even for a few seconds."

"Maybe. Ali? What do you think?"

"I might could put something together, to either let us know he was trying to come in or to trap him before he could use his magic."

"Like your spiderweb thing?" Martin asked.

"Somethin' like that, yeah."

"Will it trap anyone else?" Diane asked. "I don't want to catch any of the room service people or any of the officers. That could be difficult to explain."

"I should be able to make it work only in the presence of magical ability," Ali told them, "excluding us, of course."

"I think we should set up something before we go to sleep," Martin said. "I had planned on us standing watch anyway, but I don't want to take any chances with this guy."

"We have a slight advantage, anyway," Diane said. "He still thinks Ali is bound to the jug. While he's trying to make that work, we should be able to get him under control."

"And he still doesn't have Ali's name," Martin added. "So he can't cast another spell to bind him."

"How do we want to go about this?" Diane asked.

"Ali and I will take turns keeping watch. You try to get some sleep," Martin told her.

"Why can't I stand watch?" she demanded.

"No reason, I guess," he admitted. "Or you can stand watch with one of us."

# Chapter 33

Ali insisted he would be fine, so Diane stood watch with Martin, both of them dozing off and on and neither of them sleeping well. When they all met in the morning, it was clear they needed to do something different. Ali hadn't slept any better than they had, and there is nothing quite like a grumpy genie in the morning.

"Shall we go ahead and order up something to eat?" Martin asked. "I know I could use some coffee."

Checking the door before opening, everything was fine, so they thanked the officer and room service attendant and ate in silence.

"This is only our second day in here, and I'm already stir crazy," Diane told them. "How long were we going to be here?"

"They were talking about no longer than a week," Martin told her, shaking his head. "But I agree. What we need is a distraction."

"What kind of distraction?" Ali asked, still grumpy.

"I don't know. A game of cards? Monopoly? Or maybe we could see if they have a movie channel on the telly."

"Maybe movies," Diane suggested. "Something funny. I know I could do with a good laugh."

"I'd like to get something better set up for our wizard," Ali told them. "Any suggestions?"

Martin had given it some thought during the night, which was one of the reasons he didn't sleep well. What they needed was a way to lure him into a trap.

"They told us not to use our mobile phones or anything like that," Diane said. "And we all discussed using any sort of magic. I think if we tried either one or both of those, we might have a shot at it."

"The police will be monitoring us for mobile usage, but they can't keep track of magic. Ali? What do you think?"

"I don't understand these phones, but it's your modern kind of magic, so I suppose there would be a way for them to know if you're using it. We could try using a little magic and see what happened."

"But first, let's get a better trap set," Martin told them. "What we need is a way to trigger the trap automatically."

"How do you mean?" Diane asked, confused.

"When he touches the jug, the spell to shrink him down to size and put him in the jug is automatically triggered. We don't need to do anything."

"How would we know if it worked?" Diane asked.

"I could put some sort of alert on it, so we'd see if it had been set off," Ali said, with a grin. "I like the way you think, boss."

"Can you also put some sort of spell on the jug so he can't use his magic to get out?" Diane asked.

"If I rig the trap right, he'll be asleep, but I could add a layer to the spell as a backup, I guess," Ali told her.

"How long will it take to do all this?" Martin asked.

"Not too long. I'll take the jug in the other room and get it set. We can use any magic we want to use in there, to lure him to that room while we stay in here."

"If he doesn't find us near the jug, won't he be suspicious?" Diane asked.

"I don't know, but as long as we all stick together, we should be fine. We just have to get him to touch the jug."

"And if you've put a spell on it, it won't seem unusual in any way. There will be the feel of magic around it."

"Of course, we're still stuck in here for a week," Martin complained. "Even if we trap our thief, we're still here until they determine they're not going to catch him and let us go."

"We also don't know how long it will take for him to find us," Ali said. "So I suggest y'all get comfortable while I get to work. You should order up some popcorn if you're gonna watch movies."

Grabbing the jug off the floor, Ali strode into the adjoining room, muttering to himself. With a look over at Diane, Martin shook his head and laughed.

"I thought having a week off to do nothing would be a lark."

"Maybe if we could get out of the room and do something fun it would be, but this is more like being imprisoned."

"And we're not the criminals," Martin added. "I think Ali has the right idea. How about some popcorn?"

The two of them ate popcorn and watched movies until after lunchtime. Ali had been in and out a few times, still muttering. Finally, Martin decided to ask.

"Well, boss, this isn't the sort of spell I would normally use for anything. I don't want anything to go wrong and leave us up the creek, if ya know what I mean. So I'm going slow and running everything through my mind before I give it the final shape."

"I'm sorry to put you to so much trouble, Ali."

"It's my fault, in a way," the djinn told him.

"No, it isn't," Martin insisted. "Getting stuck in the jug might have been your fault, but everything that has happened since I let you out is from someone else. You've done nothing but help me out in the shop and my flat, including fixing dinners and making trinkets to sell."

"But if I hadn't been in the jug to begin with, you'd be free to get on with your life, instead of stuck in this place with me."

"On a completely different subject," Diane interrupted, "have you had any luck locating any of your people?"

"I did get a query from one of my marks, but nothing definite yet."

"One of your marks? I wondered how you were going to contact anyone. It didn't seem likely you'd put an ad in the paper looking for any of the djinn."

"No. We have a way of leaving a magical signature or locator, so anyone wanting to get in touch has an address, sort of."

"Kind of like the travelers or hobos leaving chalk marks on buildings?"

"I don't know much about travelers, but I guess it would be sort of the same."

"When will you know anything definite?" Martin asked.

"Who knows? That was a couple weeks ago, before all this came to a head."

"Ready to join us in some movies?" Diane asked.

"Not yet. I should be about ready to give this the final spin," Ali told them.

"We'll order more popcorn," Martin assured him.

ALI HAD BEEN WONDERING about the other djinn for several days now. The query had come from his mark at the Indian restaurant, so the guy must be fairly local. But all he'd asked was how long Ali had been in London, and then nothing, even though he'd answered back shortly after the query had come in.

Back to the damned jug. He thought he had the spell down to knock the guy out, shrink him in size, and pull him into the jug. He'd already placed the spell to prevent him using magic from inside the jug. Now all he needed was the trigger. If it was too sensitive, they risked one of them being sucked into the jug if they got too close. If it wasn't sensitive enough, the wizard might sense something wrong before it triggered, and then they'd have to try again, if they had the chance.

Could they be certain he would touch the jug? Back before the man was arrested, he had grabbed the jug and yanked out the stopper. If Ali could be sure he would do the same thing this time, it would be easy to set everything up. There was no way the guy could know Ali was no longer bound to the jug. Certainly he would try once again to summon him.

No matter what they did, they were stuck here until the authorities let them go.

Weren't they?

Once they had the guy captured, nothing said they had to stay in the room. Officially they did, but maybe they could sneak out and not let anyone know. He was sure he could set up some sort of alert on the room and whisk them all back before anyone could miss them.

With that bright note to bolster him, he got busy on the jug again. By this point, he was heartily tired of jugs in general and hoped he'd never see another one, especially from the inside.

DIANE HAD FOUND A COMEDY, which should have been hysterical, but Martin couldn't keep his mind off their predicament. What if Ali got it wrong and they missed their target? What would the guy do? He was a wizard after all.

What if he didn't sense their use of magic until they were finally able to go home? How long would they need to keep everything prepared, just in case?

Finally Ali dragged into the room, looking tired and pale.

"Are you all right?" Diane asked him.

"A little tired. Maybe I should eat something."

Another call to room service brought sandwich plates up and Ali dug in with gusto.

"It's as near to perfect as I know how to get it, boss," Ali said between bites. "If this don't catch him, I don't know what to do."

"Don't worry. We can only do so much. And it's not your fault," Martin added when Ali began to shake his head and opened his mouth.

"Yeah, I know. But I still feel responsible."

"We'll worry about all that once we're free of this guy. If you still feel you owe me, we'll work out a deal. All right?"

"I suppose you're right. Let's get this guy. I'm tired of all this waitin' around."

They ate for a few minutes without speaking, until Diane asked, "What have you been up to these days, before all this happened, I mean? I know you worked with Martin, but you must have had some time to yourself."

With a sheepish grin, Ali shrugged his shoulders and answered, "Oh, you know. This and that."

"This and that what?" she asked.

"You remember tellin' me about that guy Aladdin, Martin?" the djinn asked.

"Yes. Why?"

"I thought I'd find out what it was all about. The guy really got it wrong with Ali Baba and the thieves."

"Got it wrong? How? It's just a story."

"Well... Maybe it is and maybe it ain't."

"What do you mean?" Martin asked. "I thought it was one of the stories from the Thousand and One Nights."

"Not in the original, no. It was added in later."

"And you know this, how?" Diane asked.

"I read the original when I was much younger. It was a collection of stories from long ago, by different people, all set into a framework when they were put together. Ali Baba wasn't in the original."

"How did they get it wrong? If it's only a story, what difference does it make?"

"It's based on a real story, only with a completely different take on the facts."

"So give. What was the real story?"

"In the first place, Ali Baba wasn't a thief. He was only helping those girls get free."

"What girls?" Diane asked, confused. "There are no girls in Ali Baba."

"Let me tell the real story. The local sheikh wanted to build up his harem, so he would ride through the streets looking for pretty girls. When he found one he wanted, he would have her picked up and taken to his palace."

"Couldn't the families do something?"

"He was the sheikh. This wasn't like the way you folks run things now. Anyway, he also feared magic and had his palace and courtyard warded against all kinds of magic."

"Even against the djinn?" Martin asked.

"Especially against the djinn, which is what made it impossible for a couple of these girls to escape. They were djinn, but couldn't use their magic on the grounds. And since they were never allowed out, they were stuck there."

"How does Ali Baba fit into this?" Diane asked him.

"One of the girls was his sister, and another his cousin. Both families knew they couldn't barge in there and grab the girls back, so they devised a plan. Ali's cousin had a brother who sold olives, wine, and olive oil to the town and palace. Sometimes Ali helped him, if the order was particularly large. After his delivery to the palace, this cousin was allowed to camp out near the gate until the morning. One night when the sheikh was having a big party, Ali went along to help his cousin with the delivery. Once there, he hid

217

until after dark. The jugs of wine for the party had been doctored, so before long the sheikh and his guests began to get sleepy."

"How is this going to help anything?" Martin asked. "He still can't use his magic."

"They had managed to get a message to the girls to be ready. When the sheikh was asleep, he crept in, opened the door—the eunuch in charge was drunk and asleep too—and led the girls out to the wagon."

"So he just drove out?"

"Pretty much. The two girls had brought along several more, so they hid them inside the oil and wine jugs, covered over with a blanket. The guard gave it a quick look and let them pass."

"So they just waltzed away?" Diane asked.

"Well, as soon as they were off the grounds, Ali Baba thought it would be safe to use his magic to take them home, but someone saw them and reported back to the sheikh."

"What could he do at that point?"

"Eventually he found out Ali Baba's name and tried to hunt him down. Once the family learned of his plans, they moved away to someplace safer and started over."

"And the girls?"

"After they were reunited with their families, they were fine, if rather shaken. Ali's sister married a powerful djinn a few years later, and as far as I know they were happy."

"How did the story get so twisted, if your version of it is true?" Martin asked him.

"Would you be tellin' anyone the real story if you were the sheikh? How two djinn snuck in and stole half the women out of your harem? No. You'd make it a whole gang. Like forty thieves maybe. And of course, the thieves would be foiled. Am I lyin?"

Diane thought about it for a minute, and then shook his head. "No, you're right. I wouldn't want that story to get out. If a guy can't even keep his women safe, what about the rest of his people?"

After a moment, she asked, "How about the other stories? Are any of them based on an actual event? Or are they what they claim?"

"I wouldn't know about the rest of them. Some of them could be based in reality. Others... Who knows?" Ali answered. "I only know about Ali Baba."

"How exactly, do you know about him?" Diane asked.

"Let's just say he was someone I knew a long time ago and leave it at that."

"A FRIEND?" MARTIN ASKED, sitting up and leaning forward. "How old are you, Ali?"

"Old enough, I reckon."

"Yeah. What other secrets do you have, I wonder?"

"Wouldn't be secrets if I told them, would they?" Ali answered with a chuckle.

Before they could continue, there was a knock on the door. The detective was looking down at his feet, waiting for them to answer when Martin looked through the peep hole.

"Detective. Any news?" he asked as he let the man into the room.

"Nothing yet. Do you have everything you need?"

"Except for something to do," Diane answered.

'Come on. It's only been what, two days?" the man said. "With any luck it won't be too much longer."

"What do we do after a week if you haven't found him? Just go home and pretend everything is fine?" Martin asked, trying to keep the irritation out of his voice.

"As you know, we are doing everything we can. We have people watching your business and residence, and that of Ms.Sinclair."

"And what about my cat, Joker? Is someone looking out for him?"

"That hairball is just fine. He's boarding with a local establishment until you can all go home."

"I suppose having him here would complicate things," Martin muttered.

"Rather. And we can't let him run around the neighborhood on his own. So he's boarding."

"Poor Joker," Diane added. "He's such a sweet cat."

"You might want to tell that to the attendants where he's staying. They seem to think he's a demon from hell."

"Why? What did he do?"

"Apparently he doesn't like his accommodations," the detective said dryly. "He tries to bite or scratch anyone who comes near and yowls all day and night.

If there's nothing you need, I'll leave you to it," the detective said.

"We're about as fine as we can be," Martin told him. "Just find this guy so we can all get on with business."

"Yes, sir. We're on it."

As the detective closed the door behind him, Diane grumbled, "Yeah, they're on it for sure. How soon can we try to set the trap?"

Both of them looked at Ali, who shifted on his feet and looked at the floor.

"Well, I suppose if we're gonna do it, we should get on with it. How about starting tomorrow morning, when we're all rested and able to think clearly?"

With all of them in agreement, the discussed how they were going to go about attracting the attention of this wizard.

"Since he can sense djinn magic, I suggest we have Ali do some things to make this incarceration a little more bearable. Maybe it'll draw him out."

"What sort of things?" Diane asked.

"It's a shame we're not beginning until tomorrow. I could do with a decent meal," Martin complained. "I mean, room service is fine, but it doesn't compare."

"What else can you do?" Diane asked Ali.

"There are always stories to be told," he answered. "Djinn style, of course, with magical images to go with them."

"Magical images?"

"Yeah. Kind of like TV, only... I don't know how to explain it."

"We'll try it tomorrow."

"Maybe we'll get lucky. Surely he has associates or apprentices watching for any indication of where we might be," Martin suggested.

"I would think so," Diane agreed. "The city is too big for him to do it all on his own."

"Not with a location spell," Ali answered. "If we weren't shielded, I'm sure he would have been able to find us by now."

"We're shielded?" she asked.

"Of course," Ali explained. "Especially with me working on the jug with my magic. We don't want him here until we're ready for him. In all the confusion, I guess I forgot to mention it," Ali said.

"And I forgot all about it," Martin added. "I'm glad one of us is thinking."

"Don't worry, boss. I'll take care of you. At least, I'll do my best."

"Why don't we order up something to eat and get a good night's sleep? Tomorrow could get busy."

# Chapter 34

Ali slept fitfully during the night. If he'd only had himself to worry about, he'd have been fine. But others were in danger, friends were at risk from a wizard of unknown power. He'd never built anything quite like the trap he'd set for this wizard and his nerves were beginning to get the better of him.

What if the wizard didn't come himself, but sent an apprentice or some flunky instead? They'd catch the wrong guy and show their hand. How could he have lived as long as he had, given how dense he was? And now his only friends in this time and place might be killed because of him.

Ali hadn't heard back from the djinn who'd contacted him, but then again, how could he? The rooms were shielded. For all he knew the guy had tried reaching him hundreds of times. He might even think Ali had died. First thing, after breakfast, he'd try to get in touch. His fellow djinn might have some ideas about this wizard, or be willing to help them somehow.

Drifting off into chaotic dreams of mad sorcerers and strange magic, Ali got what sleep he could.

"Ali," he heard in the distance. "Ali? Is everything all right?"

It was Martin.

"Yeah, boss. Something wrong?" Ali asked as he stumbled out of bed.

"You were about to turn the bed over, mumbling something about wizards and sorcerers."

"Yeah, I had bad dreams all night. I'll sure be glad when this is over."

"So what's the plan today? Shall I order up breakfast? Or do you want to whip up something a little better?"

"Have you ever had ful medames?" Ali asked. It was a traditional Egyptian breakfast food of mashed fava beans with tomatoes, onions, and fried or poached eggs.

"I don't believe I have."

"Give me a minute to finish waking up and we'll have something nice. And it should be hot, not lukewarm like the stuff from room service."

"That would certainly be a welcomed change," Martin grumbled. "Let me go see if Diane is awake yet.

Ali stretched, did some deep breathing, and washed his face. It was definitely show time. He heard Diane talking with Martin and laughing at something humorous, so she must be awake. At least they were trying to keep their spirits up. Perhaps they didn't understand the risks they were taking.

"All right, Ali. I think we're ready. I'm as awake as I'm going to be," Martin said.

Ali couldn't remember the last time he'd had ful medames. He preferred them with a poached egg nestled on top, surrounded with chopped fresh tomatoes, and topped with a sprinkle of green onions. Just thinking about them made his mouth water.

"Here we go. I'm letting the shielding down. Keep your eyes open, Martin."

With a quick gesture, a full breakfast of ful medames, crisp toast, and orange juice sat on the small table, the food still piping hot and the juice chilled to perfection.

"That smells heavenly, Ali," Diane told him. "The eggs are perfectly poached. I wish you could teach me how to do that. I might eat breakfast more often."

Suddenly another object appeared next to Martin—a heavy cudgel of some kind.

"What's this for?" Martin asked.

"Backup," Ali told him. "If we can't get him into the jug, we can at least knock him cold."

"I like it," Martin said. "Come on. Dig in. Today may be busy."

"Don't mind if I do," Ali said, dropping down on one of the wooden chairs. "What do you think?"

They must have liked it, as fast as it disappeared. With another wave of his hand, the dishes disappeared, leaving only the scent of the delicious meal they'd eaten.

"Now, with that done, I'm going to try to contact that other djinn. I hadn't thought about it, but even if he's tried to reach me, he probably couldn't get through the shielding."

"Go right ahead. I have my club. Just warn me if he's going to appear. I'm a little jumpy and would hate to cosh the wrong guy."

Entering the other room and closing the door, Ali reached for the other djinn. It didn't take long for the mental connection to form. And Ali had guessed correctly. The fellow had tried to reach him, but couldn't get through the shielding.

"Why are you in hiding?" the guy asked.

"It's a long story, but let's cut it down and just say there's a wizard trying to get hold of me and has threatened friends of mine. The local authorities had him in custody, but he escaped. So we're someplace they feel we'll be safe and are keeping an eye out for him."

"I take it there's a little more to the story."

"Yeah. I was bound to a jug when he first located me and thinks he'd like to have a captive genie at his beck and call."

"And you're trying to avoid this. I see. Need some help?"

"Now that you mention it, a little help might be nice."

"Let's talk. Shall I come to you or do you want to come to me?"

"Why don't you come to me, meet my friends, and we'll all figure out the best way to get the job done."

"Be there in a moment. Leave your shielding down, if you don't mind."

"You're good. Come ahead."

A few seconds later, Hassan appeared.

"You must be Ali," he said with a smile. Tall and dark, like most of the djinn Ali had known, he seemed a friendly sort.

"And you are Hassan. Pleased to meet you," Ali told him.

"There's something I don't understand. You said you had been bound to a jug. Are you now free?"

"Yeah, that's part of the long story I told you about. My friends in the other room helped me with the jug predicament, which is why I don't want anything to happen to them."

"Got it. What's the plan so far?"

"Why don't you meet the folks first? Then we can talk and come up with something we can all agree on. And maybe have some lunch after a while."

Pulling the door open, Ali cleared his throat and announced, "Martin, Diane, I have someone here I'd like you to meet."

The surprised looks on their faces was priceless. Martin stood up and stumbled, Diane shrank back into the sofa, and both of them looked like they'd rather try to hide.

"Ali? Who is this?"

"This is my friend, the one I told you about. Hassan, meet Martin and Diane."

"You are the ones who helped Ali with his trouble?" Hassan asked.

"Well, yes. I didn't know he was in the jug when I bought it, but once I'd let him out, I didn't want him to spend the rest of his life stuck with the thing. So Diane and I got together and released him. And he could go free now, but he's trying to help us out with a wizard problem."

"Ah, yes. Wizards," Hassan sighed. "Always trying to lord it over others. We need to teach this one a lesson. I'm in, Ali. What have you got so far?"

They ordered up coffee, and then discussed the situation for Hassan's benefit until lunchtime.

"What would you like?" Ali asked.

"How about some of those kebabs you've made for us before," Martin suggested. "They should sustain us through the afternoon."

"Maybe we should order something up from room service," Diane suggested. "They might begin to wonder if we don't eat."

"Hm... How about some chef salads from room service to go with the kebabs?" Martin offered.

"Sounds like a good idea," Diane said with a laugh. "You'll do anything for those kebabs, won't you?"

"What can I say? I love the things."

The salads were up about fifteen minutes later, and Ali brought in some kebabs once the attendants had gone. As they ate, they tossed around ideas.

"That jug in the other room is the one you have booby trapped?" Hassan asked.

"Yup. The original is with the police as evidence. This one should snare and imprison our wizard when he shows up though."

"If he shows up. Have you considered that he might send someone else to steal it for him?"

"Yeah, I have," Ali admitted. Martin and Diane suddenly looked worried.

"I hadn't even thought about that," Martin told them. "What should we do?"

Hassan shrugged. "If we catch an apprentice, we turn him over to the police and then reset the trap. Eventually the man will come himself to find out what's happening."

"Or we take the apprentice someplace else and let him find his own way back home." Ali suggested.

"That works, too," Hassan agreed with a mischievous grin.

"And if we catch the wizard?" Diane asked. "Do we simply vanish the jug back to Martin's shop and hide it away somewhere, like someone did to Ali?"

"Oh, I have a better plan than that," Hassan chuckled. Turning to Ali, he asked, "Did you ever hear of a djinn named Romina Sahira?"

"Romi the witch? Everyone's heard of her. Actually, I think I'm distantly related to her. Why?"

"We may be related, my friend. Romi was my great-grandmother. My grandmother, her daughter, grew up and married an Irish sorcerer."

"Sounds like a very volatile pairing," Ali suggested.

"It could have been, but they got along famously, from all accounts. Among their children, they gave birth to my mother, who inherited their combined talents."

"I'll bet she's a humdinger when she gets mad," Ali said with a laugh.

"Rather. The thing is, Umi likes her little playthings, if you catch my drift."

"I think you and I are going to be great friends, related or not," Ali told the man, throwing his arm around his shoulders. "Let's go check our trap and make sure it's ready."

As the two djinn turned toward the other room, Martin looked at Diane, looking slightly confused.

"Did I just miss something?"

"I'm not sure, but I think the wizard might be sorry he messed with the djinn."

HASSAN HUNG OUT WITH them for the rest of the day, and then took off to go make some arrangements. But something had been bothering Martin.

"How do we know who we've trapped?" Martin asked. "Do we have to have someone watching the jug constantly?"

"I suppose that would be best," Ali admitted. "Up until today, I hadn't really given it much thought. I figured the only person who'd show up would be the wizard, but then I got to thinking about it and began wondering."

"Do you trust this guy, Hassan?" Martin asked.

"I do. We had a long talk in the other room and I'm sure he is who he claims. And like most djinn, he hates wizards and sorcerers, so he's happy to help."

"What is his plan, exactly?" Diane asked.

"Oh, now, don't you worry about a thing. We've got it covered," Ali told her with a devilish look. "I remember the stories of Romi, and if her granddaughter has anywhere near her abilities, that wizard is going to wish he'd never been born."

"Don't all the djinn have the same powers?" Martin asked.

"Well, the same kind abilities, kind of, but not necessarily as much power, if you understand. Or, like in normal humans, some of you are better with mechanical things, some can write books, others are chefs. And then there is the difference in the limits of those abilities. Or like strength training. Martin, you or I either one can pick up five or ten pounds. Diane, too. But someone who works out for strength could, say, lift a hundred pounds with no problem."

"Or the difference between the power at the outlet in your house and the power in an adapter for your mobile," Diane suggested.

"I don't know about that," Ali admitted. "As far as I'm concerned it's all magic. But I would imagine it might be like that."

"So this Romi, what's-her-name..." Martin began.

"Romina Sahira. Means Romina the witch."

"She must have been something else, the way you guys talk about her."

"She had a lot of ability and a great deal of power to go with it. For one djinn to call another one a witch, well, let's just say she was extraordinary."

"And somehow her granddaughter is going to help us out?"

"Yeah. That's the plan."

"Where is this granddaughter?" Diane asked. "Is she here in London?"

"You'd have to ask Hassan, but I think she's in another country. It doesn't matter. She'll keep him too busy to worry about you."

Hassan slipped back in the next morning. The night had been quiet, with Martin and Ali taking turns watching the jug in the other room.

"You guys look worn out. Go take a nap. I'll watch the jug for you. What does this wizard look like, anyway?"

Since it had been in the news, Martin was able to come up with an image of the guy in question. so Hassan could identify him if he turned up.

"Got it. If we get him, I'll let you know before I take off with the jug," Hassan told them. "Go get some rest."

Martin's dreams were filled with flying wizards throwing lightning bolts, strange djinn disappearing and reappearing to create confusion while the police tried to capture the wizards. When he woke, he wasn't sure he'd rested at all.

"Martin, at the very worst, he'll take the jug and run with it. Since Ali isn't bound to it any more, there shouldn't be a problem."

With a sigh, they explained about him kidnapping Diane.

"That settles it. I need to talk to Umi," Hassan said. "Back in a minute."

Turning on his heel, he went into the room with the jug and slammed the door.

"He's a bit aggravated," Martin mused.

"Yeah, we djinn don't like it when people mess with our family. I know you and Diane aren't family yet, but she's special to you. And you just don't fool with another man's woman."

A little while later, Hassan came back into the main room.

"That's all settled now. Umi's ready for us, whenever we have the wizard."

"Do I want to know?" Diane asked.

"I doubt it," Hassan said. "Umi is not happy with our wizard, and when Umi isn't happy, well, it's best to stay out of her reach."

They waited all that day and night, but nothing. Martin and Diane were getting tense and starting to get on each other's nerves.

"Folks, why don't you take a breather? Fighting isn't going to help. We need to get this guy before the authorities decide to cut you loose and send you home."

"Haven't we used enough magic to attract his attention?" Diane asked.

"We could step up our game. How about some evening movies?" Ali asked. "I could show you some of the real Arabian Nights."

Setting up a watch schedule for the jug, Ali and Hassan got together to plan their evening entertainment. Dinner was lamb and rice, courtesy of Ali. Hassan brought them Turkish coffee and Turkish Delight. Once they'd eaten and cleaned up the mess, Hassan went to guard the jug while Ali told his tale.

It was almost like watching something holographic, with the dreamlike scenes playing out in mid-air in front of them. As Ali spun the tale, the figures formed and shifted to illustrate the story. It was a truly magical performance.

When he had finished, Martin and Diane gave him a standing applause.

"I had no idea such a thing was possible," Diane exclaimed.

"We djinn have been doing it for thousands of years. It's part of our storytelling heritage."

"And how big of a show would that have made for anyone watching for magic?" Martin asked.

"It should have gotten his attention," Ali said. "I expect him to show up during the night, whenever he decides to try for the jug. Wizards seem to like nighttime for their activities."

"Will you and Hassan be on guard?" Diane asked.

"Yeah, neither of us needs much sleep and we can cloak so we can't be seen, but he'll still sense us in the room, so he'll think I'm in the jug."

"Won't he be suspicious if he doesn't see anyone watching it?"

"One of us can always nudge him toward it," Hassan called from the doorway. "Just one quick push to get him close enough, and in he goes."

"All this waiting is getting to me," Diane admitted. "I think I'll try to get some sleep. Call me if anything happens."

Martin chose to stay up a little longer. How had he wound up in this situation? All he'd wanted was an interesting looking old jug for his shop, not all the drama it had brought with it.

Of course, he was happy to have met Ali. They guy was quite a character, especially since he'd been out of the world for so long. Perhaps, once this was wrapped up, Hassan could take him around and catch him up to date more easily than Martin could. At least Ali had found some of his own people finally.

Would Ali want to hang around once they had the wizard out of the way? After all, Martin was just your average Englishman. Now that Ali had Hassan, why would he need Martin?

He tried to go to sleep, but couldn't manage, so around one in the morning, he got up, grabbed a snack, and wished he had some coffee. About the time he opened the door to the other room, the show started.

Suddenly the hallway door to the other room flew open as if a great wind swept down the corridor. The noise woke Diane, who stumbled over to where Martin stood in the doorway between the two rooms.

Seeing the two of them, the wizard laughed.

"So you thought you could hide from me? Now, give me the jug and the djinn," he demanded.

"The jug is right there," Martin stammered, pointing to where the jug stood on the coffee table.

The man stalked over toward the jug, not quite close enough to trigger it, and asked, "And is the djinn inside?"

"He must be. I don't see him anywhere in this room, or in the other one. And the stopper is in the neck, so..."

"I'll take the vessel, and you will tell me his name and how to summon him," the wizard told them.

"I don't know his name."

"Then how do you summon him?" the wizard demanded.

"I don't. He does what he wants, when he wants," Martin said with a shrug.

"You fool. You have one of the most powerful beings you could possible command and you don't use it?"

"I have everything I need," Martin answered, wondering where Ali and Hassan were. Perhaps they were waiting for him to get a little closer.

"How could such an imbecile happen on something like this? I assure you, I have better plans for this djinn, once you tell me how to summon him."

Wheeling back toward the jug, the wizard took another step and then seemed to trip. Reaching for the coffee table to break his fall, he came within range of the spell. As Martin and Diane watched, the cork popped out of the jug, the wizard sort of elongated and shrank, and was sucked into the jug. It reminded Martin of water going down a drain.

As soon as all of him was in the jug, the cork slipped back into place and both Ali and Hassan appeared.

"You guys had me worried for a minute there," Martin told them.

"Yes. Me too," Diane added. "What took you so long?"

"I had to make sure he was close enough for the push to work. He would have known a djinn was in the room otherwise, and might have had a way to bring us out into the open."

"All right. And now, what do we do with him?"

"We? Nothing. Hassan will take possession of the jug and take it to his mom, who has all kinds of plans for him."

"Where exactly is your mother?" Diane asked.

"She and my father are in Turkey. After Gran died, Mom and Dad moved back to the old country and finally ended up near Istanbul. A lot of the family moved there a century or so ago."

"And Ali? What are you going to do?" Martin asked.

"Right now, I'm going to bed. We'll all talk in the morning."

"Will that thing be all right in there overnight?" Diane asked.

"Oh, I'm taking it to Mom right now," Hassan said with a wicked grin. "I'll be back around lunch time here. You aren't rid of me yet."

ALI HAD BEEN WONDERING what to do after they had things taken care of. He wouldn't mind visiting with some of his own people for a while, and Hassan assured him he would be welcomed. But he owed Martin and liked the guy. It was kind of fun helping him in the shop, making seasonal trinkets to sell, and there was the pottery to consider.

He went to sleep still mulling it all over.

The next morning everyone slept late. Martin was the first of them to wake, and only because of a knock at the door. Ali wandered in to see what was going on.

The detective had come by to check on them once again. Their week was almost up and they'd seen no sign of the escaped man.

"I know how worrying it will be for you, Mr. Pritchard, but we're sending you home tomorrow if nothing happens. We haven't been able to locate him anywhere, and he hasn't come here. I'm sure you understand our position."

"Yeah, I do. And frankly I feel like I'm the one in prison at the moment."

Diane nodded her head, yawning. "Cabin fever has definitely set in," she told the man.

"I can see you just got up. I'll get out of your way and get back to work. I just wanted to bring you up to date."

Now that they were all awake, Martin ordered coffee from room service, to keep everyone's curiosity at bay. Ali conjured up a good breakfast for them and they ate silently, each thinking about what the future held for them.

"I don't know about you," Martin said, "but I'm for a nap. Last night's events didn't help me sleep at all."

"I think I'll do the same," Diane told them. "I hope I never meet another wizard."

"Y'all go on," Ali told them. "I'll tidy up and try to sort out what's going on with Hassan.

Sitting back on the sofa, Ali let his mind run back over the events since he escaped his jug. Though hectic, life here in London had been fun. It wouldn't hurt to hang around for a while. Hassan lived in London, also, and ran a shop selling imported Turkish goods. According to him, there were quite a few djinn around the area. Ali could stay, work with Martin, and still have friends of his own. It seemed like the best solution all around.

WHEN MARTIN WOKE, HE heard voices in the other room. Hassan must be back. Rubbing the sleep from his eyes, he strolled over to the door and knocked.

"Come on in, Martin," he heard Ali say. Opening the door, he saw the two djinn were having some lunch and it smelled fantastic.

"Hope we didn't wake you," Hassan told him.

"No, I think I finally got some rest. Diane is still out. This has been pretty hard for her."

"We've been discussing options," Ali said. "Once you two are up and awake, we can all sit down and figure out where we go from here."

"Sounds good. I need coffee," Martin said, turning toward the phone.

Suddenly, coffee and snacks appeared on the table in front of him, enough for both him and Diane, who had sat up on the edge of the bed, looking delightful, if somewhat muzzy still.

"Thank you, whoever..."

"My treat," Hassan said. "You've been of great service to a family member. Our family is in your debt."

"Oh, no. Really."

"It is our way," Hassan explained. "Ali has already made you a promise. The rest of the family concur. If you are ever in need, contact Ali. Someone among us should be able to take care of your trouble."

"How kind of you," Diane said. "But right now, that coffee is awfully inviting."

The four of them chatted while Martin and Diane ate, and once everything was cleared away, the talk turned serious.

"Ali, now that you have friends and relatives here in London, what are your plans?" Martin asked. "You've been a great help in the shop, but I don't want you to feel obliged to stay. I'm sure you have things you'd rather do."

"Well, boss, I've been giving that some thought. It seems I have a few more relatives in Turkey. I'd kind of like to go visit, let them know I'm still around and all."

"I understand. Keep in touch once in a while. I'll miss you."

"So will I," Diane said with tears beginning to trickle down her cheeks.

"Oh, now, don't do that," Ali scolded. "Let me finish. Unless you're tryin' to get rid of me, I thought I'd take a couple weeks off, go with Hassan to

Turkey, and then come back to London with him. I like working in the shop, making up items to sell, and we still have our pottery to figure out."

"Are you serious?" Martin asked.

"Yeah. I've still got a lot to learn about the world as it is today and London seems like a good place to do that."

"And I want to see this pottery," Hassan told them. "Imagine magic influencing the glaze. That could bring you quite a bit of money, as long as you keep the secret of how it's done."

"We're still figuring it all out, but I'd be glad to show you some of the pieces we've already done. They're fetching a good price."

"If you get to where you have enough, I might be interested in selling them in my shop," Hassan said.

"Where is your shop? I'd like to visit it," Diane said.

"Here's my card," he told her, handing her his business card. "I'd be honored."

BACK HOME THE NEXT day, they waited for Hassan to get there. Ali was a little nervous about leaving the only place he'd known in this current age, but still anxious to meet some of his people again and find out what had happened while he was in the jug.

Around eleven, just before lunch, Hassan knocked on Martin's door.

"Come on in," Martin told him. "Ready to leave? Ali has a case of nerves."

"No need for that, my friend. Everyone is excited at finding you still alive."

Turning toward Martin, Ali stammered a bit before saying, "If you need anything while I'm gone, just call me. I'll come back and take care of it."

"How am I supposed to call you, Ali? You don't have a phone. And Turkey is quite a distance to just pop back from."

"Not the way we travel," Hassan said with a grin.

"There is that, of course, but still, how do I call you?"

"Call my name out three times, with the intention of me hearing you. And I'll hear you and come back."

"But I don't know your name. Just Ali."

Ali, bit his lit, gave him a crooked grin and shook his head.

"You ain't gonna like this, boss."

"What am I not gonna like?"

"First, I won't give you my full name. That is never happenin' again, after the jug."

"I simply need a way to get in touch, Ali. I have no intention of conjuring with your name."

"You know when we first met and I told you to call me Bubba?"

"Yes..."

"Well, that's sort of the Louisiana way of saying a part of my name. Down South, they sort of use it as a nickname for guys anyway, so I decided to use it when I wound up there."

"All right. I'm not with you."

"Bubba is my second name. Ali is the first."

"So how do I call you?" Martin asked.

"Oh for cryin' out loud," Hassan said. "Just tell him already."

"My friends call me Ali-baba."

"You're kidding. No, you're not. You son of a gun." Martin exclaimed as the two djinn stepped out the door, waved, and disappeared, with a hint of laughter left behind.

# The End

# About the Author

Sultonna Nadine is the pen name for Mellie Miller. She writes stand alone books which are not part of Mellie's book series. She has one previous novel published--Master of the Fleet.

Read more at https://sultonnanadine.com.

# About the Publisher

Published author of two series, Mellie Miller publishes her series books under who own name,. As Sultonna Nadine, she publishes stand alone books.

The series:

Gambler's Folly

Esperance

Stand alones as Sultonna Nadine:

Master of the Fleet

Moonlight and Shadows

Whiskey Jug Genie

Read more at https://melliemiller.com.

9 798223 931225